EMERALD FIRE

Book 3 of The Jewel Series

by

HALLEE BRIDGEMAN

Published by

Olivia Kimbrell Press™

Olivia Kimbrell Press ™

COPYRIGHT NOTICE

PUBLISHED BY: Olivia Kimbrell Press™*, P.O. Box 470, Fort Knox, KY 40121-0470.

The *Olivia Kimbrell Press™* colophon and open book logo are trademarks of Olivia Kimbrell Press™.

Olivia Kimbrell Press™ is a publisher offering true to life, meaningful fiction from a Christian worldview intended to uplift the heart and engage the mind.

Some scripture quotations from the King James Version of the Holy Bible.

Some scripture quotations from the New King James Version of the Holy Bible, Copyright © 1979, 1980, 1982 by Thomas-Nelson, Inc. Used by permission. All rights reserved.

Original cover art by Amanda Gail Smith (www.amandagailstudios.com).

Library Cataloging Data

Names: Bridgeman, Hallee (Hallee Bridgeman) 1972-

Title: Emerald Fire; The Jewel Series book 3 / Hallee Bridgeman

    286 p. 5 in. × 8 in. (12.70 cm × 20.32 cm)

Description: Olivia Kimbrell Press™ digital eBook edition | Olivia Kimbrell Press™ Trade paperback edition | Kentucky: Olivia Kimbrell Press™, 2012.

Summary: A terrifying past imprisoned Maxine Bartlett all her adult life, shackling her with fear anytime a man even touched her.

Identifiers: ePCN: 2017900483 | ISBN-13: 978-1-68190-050-6 (trade) | 978-1-68190-051-3 (POD) | 978-1-68190-076-6 (hardcover) | 978-1-68190-052-0 (ebk.)

1. Christian romance fiction 2. man-woman relationships 3. suspenseful love stories 4. sisters family saga 5. sisterhood relationships 6. redemption faith grace 7. marriage holy matrimony

PS3568.B7534 E447 2012 [Fic.] 813.6 (DDC 23)

EMERALD FIRE

Book 3 of The Jewel Series

by

HALLEE BRIDGEMAN

Emerald Fire was a finalist as **Inspirational Novel of the Year** for the 2012 RONE Award.

ᗪEDICATION

For my Grandmother.

Grandma, you have always been my biggest fan.

Thank you!

A special thank you to Sara who was always ready to answer my endless stream of legal procedural questions.

Also, special thanks to Hanna and Amanda who were always ready to answer my endless stream of medical questions. I am blessed beyond measure to have you ladies in my life.

TABLE OF CONTENTS

$\mathscr{P}$ROLOGUE

That afternoon, **Maxine Bartlett** had watched two policemen drag her sister, Robin, kicking and screaming, away. Maxine could remember with perfect clarity Robin's blood soaked clothes, the blood on her hands, the ferocious look on her face, her blonde curls damp with sweat born of fury, one shoe kicked off in her struggle with the police. They'd separated the girls, bundling Robin into the back of a police car and Maxine into the back of an ambulance. For the first time in her fourteen year long life, Maxine no longer had Robin beside her. She felt completely alone.

And absolutely terrified.

Maxine clutched the broken strap of her backpack tightly while she stared down at the hole in the toe of her sneakers. She let her straight black hair dangle down in front of her face while she kept her head bowed, effectively shielding her from the outside world. Despite her many questions, no one would tell her anything.

The visit to the county hospital in the heart of Boston

had humiliated her. A rushed female doctor poked and prodded and scraped and assured that "this won't hurt a bit" right before hurting Maxine quite a bit. The whole while, a female nurse with bored and somewhat distracted eyes and an absent touch chaperoned the ordeal, snapping occasional Polariods each time the doctor requested one. Someone brought her some new underwear and a pair of scrubs that hung loosely on her long skinny body. The clean scrubs looked starkly bright against Maxine's darker skin and straight black hair.

Five long hours later, a harried social worker arrived and collected Maxine. She introduced herself politely and Maxine instantly forgot the woman's name.

So here she stood—her fourth foster home in just under two years. She could hear other kids playing somewhere out of sight. She wondered, briefly, if anyone her age lived here. She took time to wonder, yet again, where Robin was and what was happening with her—or to her.

She zoned in on the conversation the nameless social worker was having with foster mother number four, catching the last part of the sentence. "… watch her closely for any kind of symptoms, since she refused any prophylactic measures. She has two sisters, and is looking for information on them. I'll see what I can find out."

Maxine flinched and shifted away as the foster mother tried to lay a hand on her shoulder. She felt heat flush her cheeks when she realized what she'd done and tried to relax. The woman didn't reach out again. Fine by Maxine.

"… any other injuries? Does she have stitches or anything that will require special care?"

"Just bruises. No broken bones or open wounds, thank goodness. I'd say she's lucky except, of course, he hurt her in other ways…"

Maxine wished she could drown out their voices. She missed her music, her earphones. She wondered if her Walkman made it into her backpack or if it got left behind. She'd investigate what got packed later.

"Do I need to worry about the other children?" foster mother number four asked.

The social worker flipped through the file in her hand. Maxine knew it was all about her and felt the flush on her cheeks spread to her ears and down her neck. "There's no telling, honestly. Her mother died violently, her sister obviously displays violent tendencies, her last home environment was less than ideal…"

Maxine lowered her head and let the curtain of hair encase her in solitude once more. She kept her head bowed and tried to make her hair completely hide her strong Native American features.

She let her thoughts drift away again, not wanting to hear them talk about her anymore. She imagined herself on the docks listening to the sound of the water slap against the side of the boats harbored there. In her imagination, seagulls squawked overhead, flying against the bright blue sky. She could smell fish and wet wood and salt water and felt the bright spring sun shining down on her black hair.

Her second grade class had gone to a seaport museum once. Maxine fell in love with the docks then and used those few hours she spent there years ago as her refuge—her solace against the horrible outside world.

In her mind's eye, she imagined that her sisters Robin

and Sarah stood on either side of her, each holding her hands, as they looked out over the expanse of the sea. The breeze blew Sarah's little curls against her pale cheek. Maxine wondered if Sarah was still really tiny or if finding a good foster home had helped her put on some weight. Almost two years had gone by since that fateful night, and she'd looked like a six year old instead of a nine year old. None of them had ever really eaten well, and Sarah's body just couldn't handle the lack of nutrition.

Robin stood strong and tall against the wind, a force to be reckoned with at the ripe old age of seventeen. She acted as Maxine and Sarah's protector, their defender, and their caregiver. Without her, Maxine didn't know what would have happened to them.

All of a sudden, Robin's face started to lose detail. Then she faded away altogether. Where was Robin? What would happen to her, now? Would Robin vanish just as Sarah had vanished from her life?

If she could find the right song, if she could figure out the right music to pump into her ears, it would make all the bad thoughts go away. She wanted her earphones. She wanted the bad thoughts to go away.

Their mother had used a lot of drugs, which really meant she had used a lot of men to get drugs. When she tired of them or they tired of her, she'd move on to the next man, dragging her daughters along in tow. Robin knew of the dangers, through experiences she would not talk about, and taught her sisters how to hide in closets, how to be quiet as mice, how to go unnoticed in a room filled with used syringes and empty gin bottles, smelling so much like old copper and cheap pine cleaner.

Robin would put her arms around her sisters in the

dark and sing under her breath, sometimes. She didn't like music so much, but it soothed her younger siblings. What did Robin used to sing when things got really bad? She couldn't remember.

The sisters survived it. Their mother didn't. While the sisters hid in the closet and their mother argued with the man who would be the last in a long line of boyfriends, an unseen killer burst into the apartment and murdered them both. When the police came, they took Sarah to a good home and took Robin and Maxine to the first of several foster homes. The two older sisters clung to each other and vowed to get Sarah back one day so that they could stay together and face the world as one.

Now they were all separated. Maxine didn't know what to do without Robin there to guide her, so she clung to Robin's hand on that imaginary dock. She breathed in the scent of the ocean. They continued to talk very loudly about exactly what had happened to her just as if she weren't standing right there next to them. She tried to hum really loudly to drown out the noise of what's-her-name the social worker and newest foster mother four million miles away from the place in her thoughts.

"Maxine?"

Startled, Maxine returned to the little house in the suburbs of Boston and realized that the social worker had departed. Maxine stood alone in the foyer with new—newest—foster mother. She brushed her hair out of her eyes and blinked. "Yes?"

"Maxine, I'm Juliette. Do you like to be called Maxine?"

Maxine shook her head.

"Well, I have to call you something. What do you like to be called, sweetie?" Juliette asked.

"Max. Or Maxi." The words came out slowly, as if she had to form them out of a sticky dough and let the dough rise first.

"Max it is, then. You can call me Juliette or Jules. My husband, Steven, will be home from work soon. You'll meet him then."

Maxine nodded and tried to swallow around the fist of fear that had closed on her throat. What would Steven be like?

"Max, Steve is a very good man. He was named for the disciple, Stephen, in the Bible. Do you know that story?" Maxine shook her head. "Well, that's okay. I'll tell you the story later if you like. Or maybe he can tell you."

Maxine could feel her lip quivering and she tried to make it stop. She didn't want to show any weakness or uncertainty. She couldn't afford it. She had to remain strong until she could find Robin. She made herself a promise that she could endure anything that happened until she found Robin again.

"There are four other children here. Three girls and a boy. I expect you will get along fine with my girls. But you know, little boys are different. He's going to be sad that you aren't a boy. When we got the call this morning, he was hopeful." Juliette smiled, but Maxine was still thinking about the husband, Steve, Stephen, from the Bible, who was due home any second. "They're in the play room, for now. I thought maybe you'd like to help out for a little while instead of meeting them just yet."

Maxine tried to keep her face composed, and forced a

whisper out. "Help you do what?"

"I have a studio in the garage. I'm cleaning out some of my old paintings so I'll have room to store my new ones. Why don't you give me a hand and we'll talk and get to know each other better."

The idea of paintings caught Maxine's attention. She loved paintings and loved to draw. She felt the fingers of apprehension loosen their grip around her gut and shifted her backpack to her other hand. "Sure."

Juliette smiled and gestured grandly. "This way to the garage," she said. "We'll keep the scrubs on you for now, because there are some dusty corners in there. I have my husband stopping at the store on his way home to get you some decent clothes. Just enough until you and I can go to the store tomorrow morning. As soon as he gets here, you can go take a long bath and stay in the tub just as long as you want. Just for tonight, it's okay."

Maxine slowly nodded her understanding.

Jules put a hand on Maxine's shoulder and searched her eyes. "You wash every single inch and scrub really good. And when you get out of the tub, you put on your fresh new clothes, and then I am going to give you a manicure and a pedicure. Do you know what that is?"

Maxine guessed she was just keeping her away from the other kids because of her "less than ideal" previous home, but she was okay with that. She wasn't quite ready to face other kids without Robin by her side, anyway.

"You want to do my nails?"

Juliette smiled. "The girls will help. We can all get to know you and you can get to know us a little better. And tomorrow, you will wake up feeling fresh and clean and you can start a brand new day in your new home."

They walked toward the garage and Maxine knew home was with Robin, not here with Juliette and Steven. But she wondered what waking up feeling fresh and clean would really feel like.

CHAPTER ONE

Maxine **rolled over in** the bed. As the blankets slipped off, she felt cool air on her shoulders. While her partially asleep brain pondered that, she tugged the sheets back up to cover herself and her ring caught a thread on the blanket.

Her ring?

Maxine's eyes flew open as memories of the night before flooded her mind. She whipped her head around and stared at the empty space in the bed next to her, the pillow indented from where her husband's head had lain.

Her husband!

Alone in the bedroom, she lifted her left hand and stared. There sat the ridiculously enormous, preposterously expensive platinum ring, encrusted with emeralds and diamonds, that the man with whom she had been engaged for less than two hours before their wedding ceremony had picked out for her. When he slipped it onto her finger, he'd said something about the color of her eyes. Seconds later, he'd kissed her.

After a cursory glance around the room to be certain she was actually alone and the bedroom door was shut, she threw off the covers and rushed to the closet, looking for anything at all to wear. She grabbed a pair of jeans and a sweater and dashed to the bathroom, shutting and locking the door behind her. She leaned against the closed door for a moment while her heart raced and her mind reeled.

What in the name of all things holy had they done? Rather, what had she done?

With a few flicks of her wrist, she turned the water on for a shower and stopped to look at herself in the mirror. She lifted her fingers to her mouth and traced lips swollen from his kisses. Her green eyes sparkled like the stones on her hand. She normally had straight black hair and olive skin, both traits inherited from her father, a nameless one-night stand her mother would only ever crudely and often drunkenly refer to as Crazy Horse. But this morning her hair was mussed all around her head and her cheeks looked rosy, flushed. She felt warm inside despite the morning chill.

In her entire adult life, no other man had ever even so much as kissed her. Not once. Many men had tried to taste her mouth, but whenever they'd gotten close enough, panic would rise up and make her push them away. That typically ended the relationship. The ones who suffered that humiliation soon learned that it wasn't a one-time thing and very quickly gave up trying. As she stepped under the warm spray of water, she thought back to the night before and to her complete lack of fear.

Her husband of less than twelve hours—her husband didn't frighten her at all. When he kissed her, it occurred to her that she felt absolutely none of her normal panic.

Instead, what she felt was warmth, excitement, attraction. He made her feel safe. He made her feel... loved.

"Husband and wife," the Elvis impersonating officiator had proclaimed with a shimmy and a shake. Then her husband had slowly leaned in, leaned close, and taken her lips with his strong, masculine mouth as if her lips were the most delicate rose petals. Her knees had vanished and she felt his arm around her waist, holding her up, lifting her, supporting her as she kissed his heavenly mouth.

Then, here, in this hotel suite last night, her husband had carefully led the way. It was as if he sensed that she needed to be able to control the pace of the activity. She never had to say anything to him or explain her fear. He just accepted her hesitations or kissed her through them. He slowly coaxed and guided and offered until she accepted. It had been so wonderful, so beautiful, that he had held her to him with her head cradled against his broad, thick chest and his strong arms around her while she wept at the beauty of it.

Her sister, Robin, was going to kill her. Reflecting on that for a moment, Maxine realized she didn't much care. She was excited, thrilled. Married!

She quickly finished showering and got dressed. After brushing her teeth and running a comb through her hair, she left the bathroom, again comforted by the solitude. Little nervous butterflies woke up in her stomach while she slipped into her shoes, the sight of the enormous ring on her finger distracting her with every motion of her hand.

Stalling, she straightened the bed. As she pulled the coverlet up, her ring caught the light. Running her hand over his pillow, she smiled and felt a warm rush of love flow through her heart, quelling the nervous butterflies.

When she could think of nothing else to do, she opened the bedroom door and stepped out into the living room. Seeing him standing there staring out into the sunrise brought back visions of every time she had seen his face in the last three years. She thought of every time she had sketched his face. She could not believe how much had happened in the last three weeks.

The thought stopped her. Three weeks? Had it only been that long since they put her brand new husband's first wife in the ground?

He turned as soon as she opened the door and their eyes met across the room. Maxine's smile froze at the stoic look on his face. "Hi." His voice sounded low, scratchy, thick. She wondered if he had slept at all.

"Hi." She smiled. She noticed the cup in his hand. "Is there coffee, too, or just tea?"

Using the cup, he gestured at the room service cart sitting next to the table and chairs. "I didn't know how to make the coffee, so I just ordered you some instead."

Warmth flooded her heart at his thoughtfulness. "Thank you." She crossed the room and poured herself a cup. Her hand shook a little bit. What did they do now? What did they talk about? How did she handle this first full day of being a wife? His wife? More than anything at all, she wanted to please him.

When she turned back around, she saw that he had silently moved and now stood next to the couch.

"Obviously, we need to talk."

She didn't like the sound of his voice. No warmth, nothing she had felt from him the night before existed in his tone. She gripped the cup so hard she was surprised it didn't break. "Yeah." Needing to ease her own tension, she teased, "Kind of a little late for that, isn't it?"

SIX WEEKS EARLIER...

BARRY Anderson sat on the bench behind the little kitchen table in the alcove of his kitchen. His former linebacker physique made the bench look like an ottoman and the table look like an end table. He stared at his reflection in the huge bay window that looked out into his back yard without really seeing his reflected piercing blue eyes, close cropped blonde hair, or stony expression.

A closed Bible sat next to a steaming cup of tea and his mobile phone kept buzzing with incoming texts. As recently as a few months ago, Barry would have pored over the scriptures for up to an hour before leaving for the office. His morning habit would have had him meditating and praying over the space of his commute. This morning, Barry ignored the Bible, the tea, and the phone as he had for weeks.

Instead, he let his mind wander.

Had someone pulled him aside twenty years ago and asked his twenty-year-old self what he thought marriage would be like, never in a million years would he have answered that marriage resembled his present reality. He could never have imagined he'd be living in separate bedrooms from a woman who treated him like something she wanted to clean off the bottom of her shoe.

He remembered when they had met their Freshman

year of college. He had worked hard for a football scholarship, and she had made the cheerleading squad. They were wed eighteen years ago, the day after graduation, with all their friends and family still in town. He couldn't imagine a more beautiful woman to be his wife. According to those present, they were a match made in heaven.

That heaven only lasted about five years. Now, six or seven months out of the year, Jacqueline barely uttered two words to him while coming and going at her leisure; taking summer trips with "friends," or enjoying extended vacations away from Boston—and away from Barry. Lately, Barry practically enjoyed the solitude during her absences and generally managed to ignore the special circumstances.

He threw himself into work and church activities and watched the occasional game with his best friend, Tony Viscolli, or Tony's sister-in-law, Maxine. Maxine knew more about football than most of his former coaches and was as passionate about the game as Barry himself.

So for about half the year, Barry coped with unwanted solitude and earnestly prayed that God would soften Jacqueline's heart and bring her back to him as his wife. However, when the leaves started turning, that time of year the couple typically established an informal truce. Football season for a former professional athlete was a very social time. The early winter holidays brought parties and more social occasions. Former college cheerleader, Jacqueline, craved that lifestyle. Since Barry required either a hostess or a date, and Jacqueline lived for the social lifestyle, it worked out for both of them.

Fall and winter fed her need for attention and fed him hope. Hope that this year, during their annual armistice, she would let herself love him again, or at least respect him, if even just a little.

In his memory, he replayed the last meaningful encounter he had with his wife, which had taken place just over a month ago. Football season had just started, and the New England Patriots had a home game that week. Barry and Jacqueline had maintained season tickets ever since Barry retired from professional football years ago, and they almost never missed a home game.

That September morning, his Bible sat open before him and he had occasionally taken of sip of his steaming hot tea while he refreshed his knowledge of Paul's letter to the church at Ephesus. A landscaper with a backpack blower had walked along the edge of the covered pool blowing leaves off the stretched canvas. Another worked in the far corner of the yard using a different machine to mulch a pile of leaves. The noise and the activity hadn't stolen Barry's attention from God's word.

He'd heard Jacqueline come into the kitchen and glanced at his watch. It was still early. Jacqueline never made an appearance before eleven, so a nine-thirty emergence threw him off his game.

With some concern, he had noted that she looked sick. Her normally immaculately coifed deep red hair lay stringy and flat against her head. Her pale face accented the deep circles she'd had under her eyes. With shaking hands, she pushed her hair out of her face.

"Good morning," he'd offered.

"Barry," was her rejoinder. Jacqueline had retrieved a bottle of water from the refrigerator, then surprised him by coming to the table and sitting down next to him. She'd pushed his Bible toward the center of the table and out of her way, propped her elbows on the table and cupped her chin in her palms, then announced, "We need to talk."

"Oh?" A million things they needed to talk about had cascaded through his mind like a waterfall of thought. They could rationally discuss the way their marriage had started crumbling the instant he turned down a new football contract and decided to practice law instead. They could discuss the emotional distance between them that stretched wider each day like a bottomless chasm. They could discuss the fact that she had flatly and repeatedly refused to join him in visiting a Christian marriage counselor.

"This doesn't have to be a fight," she'd snarled.

Keeping his voice calm, even soothing, he'd rhetorically asked, "Who's fighting?"

He'd watched her face relax from the snarl. "You're right." Then, unbelievably, she whispered, "I'm sorry."

I'm sorry. Barry had let the words sink in and started silently praying. *God, if she's finally coming to me to start to set this right, please keep me from messing it up.*

He'd turned on the bench to directly face her. "Okay. What do you think we need to talk about, Jacqui?"

As Jacqueline had taken a sip of her water, her hand shook so badly that some of it splashed out of the top of the bottle. She'd wiped her chin and tears filled her eyes. "I don't know where to start." Giant tears fell from her lashes and slid down her face.

Barry's heart had tightened in his chest and he reached for her. "Jacqui, baby, come here." When she'd slipped her arms around his neck and sat on his lap, he'd felt like he was transported back twenty years, to a time of love, life, happiness. He'd pulled her close in that moment.

Her tears had soaked the shoulder of his shirt. For a long time, he had just been content to hold his wife. *Please, God, soothe my wife. Soften her heart toward me. Let her hear your voice. Stir the waters in her heart and let her know that she needs You in her life. Let her know that I can help her come to You.*

"What is it, Jax?" He'd asked, using a private pet name he hadn't uttered in more than a decade. "What's wrong?"

Jacqueline had sat back and looked up at him. She'd looked absolutely exhausted and deathly pale. "I'm sorry," she'd said, pushing all the way away and standing up. "I don't know what came over me. I'm so emotional right now."

Barry had taken her hand. It always looked like a child's toy in his enormous grasp. "It's okay."

"No." With her other hand, she'd covered his, sandwiching his massive hand between her two small palms. "Barry, I'm pregnant."

For a heartbeat, his world had frozen. Even the buzzing sound of the leaf blower outside vanished from his senses. Barry had felt his heart stop, heard a roaring in his ears, and all at once, what she said struck him. Hard. "Is that a fact." It wasn't a question.

She'd nodded and then smiled. She'd smiled. She'd smiled just like she felt really happy. Like she had a right to be happy. Like ripping his heart to shreds gave her the right to be happy.

"We haven't—"

"I know, silly. Why do you have to act so dense all the time?"

Barry stood, then. Something about his movement

made her eyes widen. At six-nine, he easily towered over his wife. "Silly? Dense?"

For the first time in their marriage, he'd felt like lashing out in anger. Physically lashing out. Recognizing that, realizing that, he had crossed the room to put space between them. Jacqueline, apparently unaware of how close she had come to being knocked unconscious in her own kitchen, had followed him. She'd reached out and reclaimed his hand once more. He'd stared down their joined fingers, noting her long red nails and the giant diamond ring on her left hand. How could someone so small make him wish he were dead?

"Barry, I don't know what to do. Charles—" Her breath had hitched and she'd squeezed her hands together almost painfully gripping his. "He's married and he is really angry with me right now."

The roaring in his ears had distracted him. He'd had a hard time understanding what she was babbling about. "So you know who the father is, at least."

"Don't be nasty."

He had simply raised an eyebrow. "Asking kind of a lot right this second, aren't you, darling?"

"I said I was sorry, Barry."

She's sorry. That makes everything better. His voice had sounded icy even in his own ears. "And the father of your only begotten soon to arrive bundle of joy is angry, apparently."

Good thing someone's allowed to be angry, he thought.

Jacqueline had nodded. "Yeah. He thinks I should get rid of it. He won't have anything to do with me until I do. I just don't know what to do." She then stepped forward and put her hand on his cheek. "Can you help me?"

He'd thought, *Help her? HELP her? Is this God's sick way of saving my marriage?*

Barry had cleared his throat and stared down at his wife of eighteen years. His wife. His responsibility. Was God punishing him for not covering her? Not husbanding her? Leading her? Anger, betrayal, hurt, and deep humiliation warred with duty, honor, forgiveness, and love. He'd managed to strangle out, "Exactly how is it that you want me to help you, Mrs. Anderson?"

"Couldn't we just, I don't know, go back to the way it was?"

"The way it was?" he'd prompted.

"You know. Before we started fighting all the time."

"You mean like that time when we vowed in front of God and a church full of witnesses that we would love, honor, and cherish each other until death us do part?" He'd pushed her away. "Is that how far back you want to go?"

Jacqueline had buried her face in her hands and sobbed. "You're right," she'd wailed. "I've been awful. But can't we just put all that behind us for the sake of the baby?"

For the sake of the baby. Of another man's child. A married man, at that.

"I'm just not sure—"

Jacqueline then fell to her knees in front of him and grabbed the hem of his shirt. "Please, Barry. Please don't abandon me. Please. You've always wanted this. You've always wanted me to love you again. I'll do anything. Just don't make me go through this alone."

She was right. He desperately wanted nothing more than to have his wife back. But at this cost? At the cost of raising another man's child?

Maybe. With God's help, maybe he could.

"How long have you known?" His massive arms crossed across his broad chest. He'd felt his heart beating like a stampede beneath his forearm and he strained to keep his breathing even.

"I found out a week ago."

He'd snorted in disgust and wasn't even ashamed that he had audibly expressed his disdain. What frustrated him almost entirely was a very unexpected realization. Truth be told, no matter how bad things got, no matter how angry or ashamed or disappointed he felt, the ferocious and inescapable fact was that he loved his wife.

He'd felt the Holy Spirit telling him that he needed to keep her close, make her feel secure, help her feel safe. A tiny little part of him, a dark little part he wasn't exactly proud of, wanted to hurt her back and ignored the divine voice in his heart. She had pushed him away for a decade, belittled him, disrespected him, shunned him, and ultimately betrayed him. In the space of a heartbeat, Barry had surrendered to an overwhelming impulse to push her away and let her feel some of that same insecurity and uncertainty she had inflicted on him for years.

"Jacqueline, I need some time to think about all this." He'd tried to unclench his jaw and speak very calmly. He then bent down and helped her to her feet. "I need to process it. You've had a week. I need more than a few minutes. How about you go somewhere else. Give me some space so I can think about all this."

So it came down to trust. If she was sincere about a fresh start, she would have to prove it to him. He was going to give her a week or two of insecurity and see if she ran back to her married boyfriend or came back to her husband.

"Barry, I…"

At the sound of her voice, the fear and desperation, he'd taken a little bit of pity on her. "I'm done talking for now. I'll call you when I'm ready to talk again. Don't be here when I get home. I will call you, Jacqui." With that little bit of hope for reconciliation stated aloud, he'd turned and left the room, leaving his pregnant wife, his tea, and his Bible behind.

He had hoped and he had prayed for the last month and a half. The result? This morning, he set his tea cup atop the Bible he hadn't opened in weeks, snatched up his mobile phone, and headed to the office leaving his empty house behind.

CHAPTER TWO

The **Grand Ballroom of** the Viscolli hotel in downtown Boston stood empty, a clean slate ready for whatever the half-sisters, Maxine Bartlett and Sarah Thomas, could throw at it. They stood together in the center of the room, one of many huge chandeliers directly above them. Maxine idly tapped a fingernail against her lips as she spun in a circle.

Sarah, a fresh *cum laude* nursing school graduate and the newest member of the obstetrics team at St. Catherine's Hospital, wore her surgical scrubs and clasped hairpins in her teeth while she twisted her mass of strawberry blonde curls into some semblance of order.

Maxine stood next to her clad in a camel colored suede suit, the long skirt falling just to her calves and brushing against the tops of her brown leather boots. With the heels on the boots, Sarah barely came up to Maxine's shoulder.

"You know," Sarah said as she pinned the last pin, "most people do the planning before the day of the event." In twelve short hours, the room would fill with hundreds of people, friends and acquaintances of their elder sister, Robin Viscolli, and her husband Tony, all in celebration of the impending birth of the couple's first child. Tony, a self-made entrepreneur, owned this hotel along with many other businesses in Boston and beyond.

"I selected and ordered all the food and flowers, I just never worked it all into the room." Maxine glanced at her watch. She couldn't believe it was already seven in the morning. "I think the day snuck up on me. I'm going to blame Cassandra. She's the event coordinator here."

"Hard for her to sneak anything by Tony in his own hotel. Besides, the last time she tried to help you, you shot her down. I bet she figured you'd let her know what you needed."

"What makes you say that?"

Maxine turned to look at Sarah, who smiled a very sarcastic, sweet smile and said, "Because that's what I do."

"Yeah? What have you done for this party?" Maxine teased, knowing exactly how hard Sarah had worked.

"I mailed 500 invitations and logged RSVP's. Quite a bit more labor intensive than deciding between yellow roses or Gerbera daisies for the centerpieces."

Ignoring Sarah's sarcastic jab, Maxine checked her phone. "I still haven't heard from Jacqui."

Sarah frowned. "How are we going to run the games if she isn't here?"

"Maybe we just won't have games," Maxine said. "How were we going to do it with 500 people, anyway?"

"We ordered the supplies she needed, and we have the game instructions, so we'll just have to do it for her," Sarah said. "It's a baby shower. You have to have games. That's what you do."

Maxine spotted Derrick DiNunzio coming through the far door. "Derrick!" she called, waving her hand.

She crossed the carpeted floor with long, graceful strides. Sarah followed, almost at a run compared to Maxine's fast walk. Derrick nodded and lifted his hand in greeting. By the time they reached him, Maxine felt a huge grin on her face. She loved Derrick and had since the first day she met him.

Three years ago, Derrick had shown up at Tony's office with a worn business card in hand, following up on an employment promise Tony had made him. As good as his word, Tony took Derrick in and made him his protégé. At present, Derrick was finishing up college. Surrounded by the luxury of the Viscolli ballroom, wearing a thick cream colored sweater and navy slacks as easily as he wore a quiet inner strength and outer confidence, Maxine could not pick out anything about Derrick, his demeanor, his accent, or his countenance, that suggested he hadn't grown up surrounded by anything other than love and riches.

Though Derrick made eye contact with Maxine first, and though Maxine reached him first, it was Sarah to whom he first spoke with an ironic lift of a single eyebrow and an undeniable teasing tone in his voice. "Hiya, sweetheart."

After Robin and Tony's wedding, Sarah and Derrick had lived under the same roof with Tony and Robin for a full year while Sarah finished nursing school. Even so, instead of treating each other like acquaintances, they barely tolerated each other. Maxine watched in fascination as her younger sister's lip curled in unfeigned loathing, astonished by the force of her sister's reaction this morning. Sarah's increasing vehemence toward Derrick never ceased to amaze Maxine. The way Derrick invited it—nicknaming her petite half sister "sweetheart" for example—also presented a perpetual puzzle.

"I told you not to call me that." Sarah's voice came out low and laced with loathing.

Derrick appeared utterly oblivious to Sarah's venom. "Whatever you say, sweetheart." Before Maxine could give much more thought to the interplay between them, Derrick's grin grew wide and his eyes danced with genuine mirth as he took in the sight of her. "Maxi! You look like a hundred bucks."

Maxine laughed at his teasing and explained, "I've only had one cup of coffee so far."

Derrick's eyebrow quirked and he said, "We'll have to fix that."

Maxine opened her mouth to enthusiastically agree when Sarah unexpectedly piped up, "As if you could fix anything. Where's Cassandra?" Sarah crossed her arms and glared at Derrick from beneath her strawberry curls. Rather than making her appear threatening, her stance comically transformed her into a Little Orphan Annie double.

Instead of reacting, Derrick insinuatingly winked at Sarah before turning his attention back to Maxine. "I have an army of help ready to place tables and chairs where they need to go. I also have confirmation of a flower delivery at noon, and Chef Armand called up from the pastry kitchen to let you know that the cake is ready for you to view."

Maxine looked at her watch again and mentally structured her day. "Okay. I have a nine-thirty meeting in the restaurant here, so hopefully I can get everything organized and still be able to put in a couple of hours this afternoon at the office."

"My shift starts at eleven," Sarah said, pulling her phone out of her pocket to check the time. "So I can help until ten. My roommate is going to cover for me this afternoon, so I should be able to be back by four."

Derrick reached into the pocket of his slacks and pulled out several sheets of graph paper. "I knew you hadn't met with Cassandra yet, so I sketched a few possible ideas for the layout of the room." As Maxine took the sheets from him, he looked at Sarah. "How many people RSVP'd?"

"Four eighty-six," she said, "but there was also an announcement made at church. I'd count on at least fifty more."

"Maybe we should plan for six hundred."

"Maybe we should plan for five-forty," Sarah sneered. "Otherwise, you're going to end up with a bunch of empty tables."

"I think you're going to get more than fifty from an open invitation at a church that size."

"Why? Because the Viscollis are so amazing?"

Maxine watched Derrick's eyes look Sarah's petite body up and down. "Someone certainly is," he observed.

Sarah gasped as Derrick turned his attention back to Maxine once again. "Well?"

"Let's split the difference," she said. "Five-seventy?"

Derrick nodded and pulled a two-way radio from a clip on his belt. "Rubert? Five-seventy, as we discussed yesterday."

"As you discussed?" Maxine laughed.

Derrick waited for the confirmation from the catering department's head sous chef before turning the volume down on the radio and re-clipping it. He shrugged. "I guessed."

"Hotel and restaurant management was a good major for you to pick, then."

"Speaking of which," Sarah interrupted, "why aren't you in class? Playing hooky?"

"It's seven in the morning, sweetheart. Even BU doesn't start before nine." As if on cue, the double doors leading to the kitchen hall opened and a uniformed waitress pushed a room service cart into the room.

"Breakfast, ladies?" He gestured to the cart, "I even accounted for the herbivore," he said to Sarah, "with a fruit platter and some dairy-free, egg-free muffins."

Despite herself, Maxine shook her head and giggled, overcome by Derrick's relentless wit at Sarah's expense. "I'm dieting, but if there's coffee on that cart, I'll love you forever."

Derrick covered his heart with his hand. "Another conquest. And so easily won."

Two more waiters brought in a table and chairs, and the trio sat down to breakfast and coffee while they planned, and bickered, over the layout of the room.

ON the commute into work, Barry pondered how badly things had deteriorated since that day six weeks ago. In the time since that morning conversation with his wife, a great deal had changed.

Barry stopped reading his Bible, though it remained a fixture on his breakfast table. He stopped attending worship services. He started dodging calls from friends and family, and avoided seeing them in person as often as possible.

An irrational part of him felt that the humiliation of his personal life could be plainly seen by those who knew him best. So he didn't go to any friends with his problem. It seemed too enormous. He figured he knew what they would say, anyway, so why bother? Maxine would advise him to just ditch Jacqueline and all of the evil and drama Jacqueline constantly introduced into his life. Tony would counsel him to pray and seek the will of the Holy Spirit.

Barry kept it all inside and, after a few weeks, he called Jacqueline. They met and he told her he was willing to forgive her, raise her child as his, and love them both. His condition was that they begin living together as husband and wife with the same bedroom, the same vacations, and the same social activities.

He also asked her to begin attending church together with him every Sunday and, after services, spending time in fellowship with friends. He said that if she didn't think she could do these few things, they likely would have no way of working things out.

After he finished speaking, she had stared at him for a very long time. For the life of him, he could not read her expression.

At last, she had said, "Barry, I appreciate all the thought you've put into this. But the fact is that I just don't love you anymore. I'll tell you the truth for once. I don't know if I ever really did. If I ever did, I certainly haven't for a very long time. I think I just want a divorce. The thought of us playing house again after all this time, honestly, is disgusting to me. Charles and I have been talking and he is going to leave his wife. We're going to get married and have our baby."

This morning, he reflected on the fact that he had no idea where Jacqueline even was. The next time they met, he would hand her the divorce papers he had quietly drawn up and he fully expected she would sign them.

That fact, that fact alone, paralyzed Barry. He would be a divorcé—a childless divorcé. After nearly twenty years of marriage to the same woman, he had nothing to show for it. The shame of that burned his mind like hot coals. Ultimately, after all of his successes, he had utterly failed in his marriage.

God, he silently prayed, *if You are the author of this situation, then You already have a plan to spare me from any shame. Please spare me from this shame.*

His entire life all he had ever wanted to be was the very best husband and father he could be. Since he had married Jacqueline, the only thing on this earth he craved—more than the adoration of 20,000 cheering fans and more than the grateful praise of any of his clients—was to be seen as a hero by his wife.

Why did she have to ruin everything? Was his enduring love for this woman, his wife, was that just God mocking him for a fool? Just ripping his heart and life to shreds even as God had allowed Job to suffer?

Was it something as common as pride that made him want to reconcile with his wife? Was it just that base and banal? Or did he really love her?

The shame of it alone would crush him. The weight of

that shame loomed over his head like the sword of Damocles. For the first time in his Christian life, Barry felt a constant speck of mistrust in his relationship with the creator of the universe.

One thing was certain, Barry would never again let a woman undo him so completely.

CHAPTER THREE

Maxine unzipped her boots and slipped her feet out of them, thankful for the privacy of the hotel room that allowed her to grab a few hours of comfort before she had to put the boots back on.

Her meeting at nine-thirty ran over. It was originally intended to be an informal meeting. The client wasn't certain she wanted Maxine representing her as her advertiser for a local veterinary hospital, and Maxine wasn't really ready to put too much effort into a proposal that might or might not be selected. When the morning meeting turned into a lunch meeting, and they haggled over details and concepts and price, she left the meeting feeling like maybe she had won the client over.

After shooting a few e-mails from her phone to her secretary and adding another meeting later in the week with this almost-certain client, she secured a room at the Viscolli hotel to get back to party planning details.

She checked her watch, then dialed Jacqueline Anderson's number. Up until a few weeks ago, she'd been actively involved with Maxine and Sarah with the party planning and insisted on running the games for them. But for the last two weeks, she'd not returned Maxine's calls. Maxine couldn't figure out what kind of game she was playing. Where was she?

As close-knit as Maxine and Robin were, Jacqueline's position—as the wife of her brother-in-law's best friend— forced Barry's wife into her life far more often than Maxine enjoyed. She found the woman plastic, stuck up, and rude.

Maxine loved it when Jacqueline was out of town because Barry seemed to be happier, more relaxed, less on guard. He always seemed more open to watching a football game or talking about basketball scores or anything. Though the second Jacqueline showed up, he turned reticent, withdrawn, noncommunicative, and obviously unhappy. Maxine couldn't figure out how they'd stayed married for almost twenty years.

Every Sunday after church, family and friends gathered for lunch at the Viscolli home. Tony and Robin would have a soup and sandwich bar and they would eat and fellowship and rest before evening services. In the three years since Robin married Tony, that tradition had been something that kept Maxine going to church, even on her most "exhausted from the Saturday night before" Sunday mornings.

Tony and Robin had close friends at their church who joined them on a semi-regular basis, and almost always some pastor or visiting evangelist joined as well. In attendance without fail, in addition to Tony and Robin, one could nearly always count on: Derrick; Sarah and a few boyfriends here and there over the years; Barry, but rarely with Jacqueline; and an always unescorted Maxine.

In those three years of Sunday lunches, Maxine and Barry had become really good friends—great friends. They typically found a corner somewhere in the massive apartment and spent hours talking, laughing, planning lunches or, to Barry's dismay, golf outings. They both loved football and a few times when Jacqueline was on one of her regular out of town excursions, Maxine would head to Barry's house after Sunday evening services to watch the day's games that he'd recorded. He usually let her fast forward through the commercials and the endless game replays. She looked forward to that time with him and had really grown to count on his friendship.

Shaking her head at the train of her thoughts, she brought herself back to the present. Shooting Barry text number three of the day, worried about why he hadn't texted her back yet, asking him if he knew where Jacqueline was and how Maxine could reach her, she went ahead and placed a call to the kitchen and reconfirmed the schedule for the night ahead.

Checking her watch and calculating the time until the party, she determined she had about two hours to do some office work before she had to refocus on party work. She knew she owed the bulk of the party preparation credit to Derrick and the rest of Tony's staff. She wasn't even going to pretend that she could have done this without them.

Her phone rang, interrupting her thoughts. She caught a glimpse of the caller ID as she answered it. "Hey, Sarah."

"Hey. I got your text. Thanks for getting a room. My roommate is dropping my clothes off on her way in to cover for my shift."

"Awesome. I thought about what you said and I agree. I think it'll just be easier to have a command center here."

"Are you staying there tonight?"

Maxine looked around the luxury of the suite. "Probably. We'll be here rather late. What about you?"

"Definitely. It isn't every day I get to stay at the Viscolli." She laughed. "Any news from Jacqui?"

Maxine felt herself frown. "No. It's not like her not to be in the center of the party planning. I can't help but feel like something's wrong."

"It's possible she's just having too much fun to come back to town." Sarah answered drily.

"I can't even get Barry to return my calls," Maxine said.

"Well, the world must be coming to an end if Barry isn't calling you back," Sarah observed.

Maxine frowned. "I beg your pardon?"

"Nothing. Sorry. Did you read over the game instructions?"

Maxine sighed. "I did. They're easy and will be manageable with the size of crowd we have. Hopefully the wait staff will be available to help us."

"Since it's Tony's hotel and Tony's wife's baby shower, I'm sure the wait staff will be more than available," Sarah offered with a wry smile. "We can't spend a lot more time worrying about Jacqui." Maxine could hear noise happening around Sarah. "I have to run, Maxi. See you whenever Melissa gets here to relieve me. Love you!"

"Love you, too." Maxine hit the button to disconnect the call and frowned. Trying to ignore the sense of foreboding, she removed her laptop from her bag and turned it on, determined to get some work done before she had to go supervise the placement of the centerpieces.

BARRY didn't recognize the incoming number on his mobile phone's caller ID at 10:26 that morning. Since he was in the middle of a conference call with a client he ignored it and let it go to voice mail. Two minutes later at 10:28, he let the same number go to voice mail again.

A little over one minute later his secretary, Elizabeth, burst into his office. The look on her face alone silently informed him that he needed to end his conference call immediately. So he did.

As soon as his handset hit the receiver, he said, "My cell's been ringing constantly…"

Elizabeth interrupted, "Please pick up on line two, Barry."

Barry noted that she did not address him as "Mr. Anderson," or "Sir." He noted that she cut him off and heard the hint of anxiety in her voice as if it were a scream.

"What is it?"

Elizabeth shook her head. "It's the hospital up by your ski resort in the Berkshires. They won't tell me anything."

A cold, sinking feeling hit Barry in the pit of his stomach as he punched the blinking button and brought the phone to his ear. He heard his own voice, sounding numb and distant in his ears, saying, "This is Barry Anderson."

The cold, sinking feeling turned into a frozen ball of iron when he heard a distracted voice answer, "This is the Trauma Center. Can you hold please, Mr. Anderson?"

"Yes, I can hold." Barry didn't even complete the sentence. He began listening to canned hold music before the first word completely left his lips.

A few more heartbeats passed after which a new voice came on the line and asked, "Is this Jacqueline Anderson's husband?"

Barry paused before affirming, "Yes, this is Mr. Anderson."

The voice went into a kind of rehearsed speech mode. "Mr. Anderson, there's been an accident. Your wife sustained very serious injuries and was rushed here less than an hour ago. We've been treating her to the extent that we can within the limits of the law."

Barry suddenly realized how serious this conversation was. Out of all the conversations of his life on earth, this one might end up ranking in the top two, second only to when he had asked Christ Jesus to become the Lord and Master of his life as a youth.

The hospital representative continued to explain, "Your friend, Charles Mason, is here but can't legally sign the consent forms."

Barry thought, *Charles Mason? As in the married man I strongly suspect impregnated my wife, Charles Mason? That Charles Mason? Why exactly would THAT Charles Mason be at the trauma center in the Berkshires?*

Then an absolutely terrifying thought struck him and he blurted, "Is the baby okay?" He ignored the widening of Elizabeth's eyes and the sound of her gasp.

The voice kept talking. "Mr. Anderson, you're an attorney. You know I can't speak to that on the phone. We need you to get here as soon as possible so we can advise you as to the prognosis. Could you please allow me to record the remainder of our conversation while you grant me verbal consent to continue treatment?"

Again he heard his own voice, but he had no idea how he was speaking. "Please proceed. Whatever you need."

With the receiver of his desk telephone pressed into his ear by his massive shoulder, he listened to the questions and answered them. He wished he were on his cell phone so that he could start moving right now. He stated his full name as "Bartholomew James Anderson," and said, "I'm her husband," then he impatiently said, "Yes, I agree," three times. He leaned down, and years of habit made him pack his laptop and some paperwork into his briefcase before he shouldered it. Before hanging up, he said, "I'm on my way."

He caught Elizabeth's eye as he stalked out of his office, headed toward the elevators that would take him to the parking garage. Over his shoulder, he ordered, "Cancel the rest of my week."

THEY sat amongst the debris of the party. A few members of the staff set about removing furnishings and cleaning the room. They studiously avoided the little group stubbornly claiming the head table because the owner of the Viscolli Boston, Tony Viscolli, had arrived to retrieve Robin, his wife.

He sat with her feet in his lap, gently rubbing her arches. Maxine had her head back, reclining as best she could in the cloth-covered banquet chair. Sarah sat next to her, phone in hand, texting someone.

"You two did an amazing job. What a wonderful gift," Robin said.

"Speaking of," Maxine said, rolling her head on her shoulders, "what do you want to do with the presents people brought despite our request not to?"

Robin sighed. "I guess we need to open them. There are just so many, though."

Maxine's phone vibrated next to her elbow. Recognizing Barry's number, she snatched up the phone. "Barry, hi. If you're looking for Jacqui, she isn't here. Did you get my texts?"

Barry was silent for a few breaths. "I know where she is, Maxi. Is Tony with you? I've been trying to get him for the last hour."

Something was wrong. She could hear it in his voice. Wanting to ask, but feeling it wasn't her place, she held the phone out to her brother-in-law. "Tony? It's Barry. He says he's been trying to reach you."

Tony patted his jacket, then shook his head. "I left my phone in the car."

Robin smiled. "Miracle of miracles."

Picking up her hand, he gently kissed her knuckles. "I'm here with you, *cara*. What call would I want to take?" He smiled at her blush and took Maxine's phone. "Barry, *mio fratello*."

Maxine watched Tony's face fall as he sat straighter in his chair.

"*E' una tragedia*! Where are you right now?" Tony asked as he bolted to his feet. Maxine found herself standing with Tony. "I'll be there as soon as I can." He held the phone out to her and she saw his hand tremble as she retrieved it. "There's been an accident. Jacqui's dead."

Simultaneously, Maxine exclaimed, "What?" as Sarah

repeated, "Dead?" and Robin gasped, "When?"

Tony leaned down and kissed Robin's forehead. "I don't have all the details and I don't know when I'll be home. I'll call you as soon as I get there."

"Don't worry about me." She looked at Maxine. "Can you take me home?"

"Of course." Maxine assured. "Or you can stay with me here. Sarah and I have a suite upstairs. I'll sleep on the couch and you can take one of the beds."

Derrick quietly asked, "Should I come, too?"

Tony considered, then said, "Better if it's just me for now. But I'll let him know you asked about him." By way of answer, Derrick offered a single nod of understanding.

A well of panic bubbled up in Maxine's chest as she watched Tony march away. "Tony, wait!" He stopped and pivoted on his heel, a questioning eyebrow raised at the distraction.

Maxine rushed toward him. "Tell Barry…" She paused and felt her throat burn with tears. "Tell him to call me if he needs anything."

Tony cocked his head and his brown eyes searched her face before he answered, "I'll be sure to tell him, Maxine."

"Thank you." Maxine felt her cheeks burn with unidentified embarrassment as she slowly turned back toward her group. "I left my room key with the front desk so that I wouldn't have to keep up with it all night. I'll go get it."

Robin maneuvered herself to a standing position, rubbing her large belly. "I hate that our evening ended with such tragic news."

Sarah put one arm around Robin's back and with her other hand, rubbed Robin's stomach. "You okay?"

"I'm fine. I have some time yet." She patted Sarah's arm. "Just us three girls. Kind of like old times, huh?"

CHAPTER FOUR

The engine of the tiny green sports car hummed in perfect tune and all four tires left the pavement as it crested the hill. The tires chirped as the empty street, slick and glistening from a recent downpour, reached up and welcomed the vehicle back to earth. Maxine managed to continue accelerating, watching the speedometer climb as the clock on the dash remorselessly ticked away precious seconds.

The headlights cut through a sudden mist and spotlighted an unforeseen puddle less than a second before all four tires plowed through it, sending an almost artistic rooster-tail spray high into the air that Maxine could see in her rearview window. The engine whirred as she shifted gears and turned the wheels hard. A little bit of a fishtail sent her heart pounding. She regained control, straightened the car, and punched it.

Harsh music blared out of the speakers, a modern staccato rock beat with heavy emphasis on the bass. The music felt exciting, dangerous, thrilling. Maxine stabbed the knob to increase the volume even further as the swift car continued to whip down the interstate ramp. After what seemed like forever, but was actually mere minutes, the suburban exit appeared. Maxine hit the blinker to announce her intention to take that exit, then whipped into the left lane to pass three more cars before careening back to the right, barely missing the bumper of the car she just cut off as she downshifted in an attempt to slow down the little green bullet.

Barely pausing at the red light at the end of the exit, she made a quick right, a succession of a few turns into the heart of suburbia, and finally wheeled onto the street where she would find the big white church with the tall black steeple.

She forced herself to slow down. Nothing could be gained by the sound of screeching tires penetrating the walls of the building. She parked her car, double-parked it, technically, at the end of the parking lot and grabbed her little black purse that perfectly matched her sedate and stylish black suit. A quick check of her lipstick and she could go.

Few women could get away with that shade of red lipstick. Maxine considered herself one of the lucky few. Her straight black hair and olive skin, both traits inherited from her father, made the lipstick a perfect shade for her. She bared her teeth to the mirror to make sure no lipstick marks marred the white surfaces, then slipped out of the car.

The two sets of double-doors at the top of the stone steps were shut tight and no one remained outside the church. The December sky, pregnant with ominous looking gray clouds, silently spit out a few flakes of snow and Maxine shivered. Before quietly shutting the car door with her hip, she bent and reached inside and grabbed her long black trench coat and threw it over her shoulders as she dashed up the stairs.

She silently opened the giant wooden church door just wide enough to squeeze inside, and found herself standing in a huge vestibule with ceilings at least three stories high. Corridors branched off in either direction, with rest rooms on either side of the massive lobby. A large tripod supporting a poster sized framed headshot dominated the middle of the room. Maxine walked up to it and bit her lip to keep herself from snarling.

Jacqueline Mayfield Anderson's long, wavy red hair, her porcelain smooth skin, and her glowing blue eyes all mingled together to create a classically beautiful woman. The artist in Maxine allowed herself to admire Jacqueline's bone structure and cream cheese exterior.

Her personal knowledge of Jacqueline's character, however, identified a true wolf in sheep's clothing. Maxine hesitated to speak or even think uncharitably about the dead, but she also considered herself a realist. Her own mother had been murdered when Maxine was very young, and Maxine never minced words about the kind of woman she had been in life.

In life, Maxine had never, ever liked Jacqueline. In fact, she sometimes imagined some kind of slimy wormlike alien had inhabited Jacqueline's insides, feeding itself on her rudeness, carnality, and avarice. So unlike, she thought, the Spirit whose fruits include such things as kindness and self control.

Now, the woman was dead and had to answer to her Maker. The fact was that Maxine wasn't here for

Jacqueline. She was here for Barry. She started forward, stopped long enough to sign the registry, then quickly moved toward the usher who stood sentry by one of the several sets of massive double doors leading to the sanctuary of the church. Her heels made no sound on the carpeted floor.

The usher didn't return her smile, but opened the door for her. She slipped into the sanctuary and stopped.

Every seat appeared taken. She slipped back out again and spoke in low volumes to the usher, trying to determine if moving up to the balcony would prove worthwhile. In whispered tones, he informed her that she would find the balcony just as full as the main floor, so she slipped back into the room and stood against the back wall.

She could not see her family, but knew that the front rows on the left side were reserved for Barry's family. Tony would be seated as close to Barry's parents as possible since he was Barry's best friend. Maxine often felt the men acted like fraternal twin brothers. Tony considered Barry family in the same way he considered Robin's sisters family, and to him the differing last names meant absolutely nothing.

She decided to walk along the far left wall until she spotted them. She started to move to the far side of the room so that she could sneak along the wall, but just as she took her first steps, Barry took the podium.

At six-nine and nearly three hundred pounds of muscle, Barry looked like the professional football player that the Super Bowl ring on his left hand proclaimed, but Maxine knew football had only been Barry's shortest path to his law degree, and he had never looked back or regretted retiring from the game. Fitness was central to his life, though, and he still kept in very good shape. She could not help admiring the way he filled out his dark charcoal suit from his broad shoulders to his thick limbs.

Not wanting to distract him by walking to the front while he was speaking, she resumed her position against the back wall just beside the door and watched her best friend eulogize his late wife. As he faced the crowd, Maxine realized he'd shaved off his goatee, and she wasn't certain if she liked the clean-shaven look or not.

She hadn't seen him in weeks. She tried to remember the last time she'd talked to him. Mid-September, maybe. She'd called to see if he had a ticket to an upcoming Patriots game.

"I have a client who would probably give me his first born if I could get him tickets," she said.

Barry had been very abrupt and distracted. "No. Someone else has my tickets this week. I can't help you. I have to go."

Despite her occasionally trying to get in touch with him since then, she hadn't heard from him.

She watched Barry pull a small sheet of paper out of his jacket pocket. On either side of the massive stage, large screens provided a close-up view, and the person manning the camera zoomed in on Barry's face. Maxine couldn't help but stare at the handsome man, his strong features hard as stone. He raised one of his massive hands and rubbed his forehead. Maxine noted the Super Bowl ring he sported on his left ring finger in lieu of a wedding band.

She watched him close his eyes and take a deep breath before opening them again, focusing on some point in the crowd near the front. She almost gasped out loud, nearly tried to take a step back, at the intensity of his stare—even from a distance she could see it.

He cleared his throat and put away the paper. "I had a nice speech prepared. Something impassionate and just the right amount of emotional, but it's all just a bunch of hogwash."

A murmur rippled through the crowd as hundreds of people bent their heads together and started whispering. Barry gripped the podium with both hands and leaned down toward the microphone. "I would probably have kept up whatever pretense I needed to keep up to save my parents and sisters any kind of embarrassment, but marrying Jacqui eighteen years ago was probably embarrassment enough so that anything that happens now won't even faze them."

The murmur changed to a full gasp, and now people sat forward, on the edges of their seats, ready for more. "The truth is, I always loved my wife. Even when she gave me absolutely every possible imaginable reason to stop, I still loved her. I always prayed that she would come to know Christ, that I could witness to her. But God chose not to answer that prayer. I don't understand why. So, in that mission, I failed. I have absolutely no doubt that I will answer for that one day."

Barry bowed his head. Maxine felt her heart hurting for him. She could almost see the emotions he struggled to hold in check.

The population of the church murmured continuously. It sounded like a constant quiet hum. Maxine wasn't sure how much time passed before Barry said, with his head still bowed, "As you all sit out there in your funeral best, let me go ahead and confirm whatever rumors I must to keep this town in gossip for a few days. Yes, Jacqui was pregnant when she died." Suddenly, the church turned so silent it was almost a roar. Barry continued, ruthlessly, his voice even, a monotone. "Of course, the baby wasn't mine."

Maxine felt her knees turn to water. *Oh, Barry. What are you doing, Barry? Please stop, Barry. Please don't.*

He continued, "Apparently, she was really in love this time. Our divorce was quietly in the works. I have absolutely no business eulogizing her today. So I won't stand before you and say anything I don't mean. I won't be joining you at the graveside. In fact, I have just enough self respect left in me to turn the podium over to Charles Mason, the father of that unborn child and Jacqueline's future husband. Charles? You have the floor."

No one murmured as Barry stormed off the stage. The mood of the entire room was that of complete shock. The giant flew down the stairs. His footsteps clapped like nearby thunder in the deafening silence.

Maxine slipped back out the very same door she had entered and moved very quickly across the outer narthex to the double doors leading to the outside. She stepped into the cold December air and made it halfway down the church steps when she heard one of the doors above her slam open hard enough to hit the outer wall.

She looked behind her, but kept going down the steps just to keep her momentum going. "Hey, Barry," she said, holding up her car keys. "Need a getaway driver?"

He stopped—totally stopped—halfway down the stairs. She reached the bottom and turned fully around to look at him. "You probably have about three seconds left before my brother-in-law comes racing through those doors."

Barry glanced back, then took the last ten steps in three

massive strides. "Let's go," he urged. They reached Maxine's car as the doors to the church flew open again. As Maxine buckled up, she heard Tony calling Barry's name.

She pealed away, tires chirping on the cold pavement. She looked over at Barry, who grabbed the seat belt behind him and clicked it shut just as she turned onto the main road and darted into traffic. "Where to, big guy?"

Barry rubbed his face with both hands. "I don't care." He sat quietly for a moment, staring out the car window, then pointed at a restaurant sign. "That's fine, there. I haven't eaten today. Pull in and park around back so they don't see your car."

MAXINE parked the car behind the restaurant and grabbed her purse as she slid out of the car. Barry put a hand on the small of her back to lead her to the door. Catching their reflection in the glass, she thought they looked like a very serious, very handsome couple. She, in her long black funeral suit, he in his charcoal suit with crisp white shirt and staid gray tie—they matched well.

Even with her six feet of height and additional three-inch heels, Barry towered over her by several inches. Barry leaned around her and grabbed the door handle, scanning the street behind him as he opened the door for her.

They didn't speak as the hostess seated them and handed them menus and the waitress brought them ice water and took an order for coffee. Maxine's eyes skimmed over everything on the vinyl coated menu within seconds and she folded it and set it aside. She ran her finger over the condensation on her water glass as she leaned back in the booth and looked at Barry. He looked very tired. His blue eyes seemed a little dull, his mouth a bit pinched, his color off.

"I've missed you the last few weeks," she murmured just to break the silence.

He peered at her over the rim of the menu before tossing it down. He propped his elbows on the table and rubbed his face, then ran his hands through his close cropped blond hair. "It's been a difficult time."

Maxine nodded. "I gathered."

He leaned back against the booth and crossed his arms over his massive chest. He released a deep breath. "We'd been living separate lives for years; different bedrooms; different holiday plans…"

Maxine raised an eyebrow. "Why?"

Barry shrugged. "I don't know. I needed a wife or a hostess sometimes. She needed money to support her lifestyle. She could throw a killer dinner party, and that kind of networking really helped my law firm." He sighed and threw an arm over the back of the booth. "It worked for us. When she told me she was pregnant, I just kind of shut off."

Maxine could hear the hurt in his voice. Deep hurt. Her heart twisted and she felt tears burn the back of her throat. Barry continued, "I realized that there'd been some small hope inside me—for years now—that if I lived a righteous enough life and if my righteous life witnessed to her, that one day she'd come to know the Lord and that would change things. We could really be married and start a family together."

She watched his finger tap to the beat of an unheard rhythm on the back of the booth. "At first, we tried to reconcile. For the sake of the baby, I was willing to forgive. I was making plans about how we could work it out. Then the baby's father decided he was really in love with her. He left his wife and Jacqui went running to him without looking back. He was there when she died."

The waitress started toward the table, but Maxine lifted a finger and gave a brief shake of her head to ward her off. Barry continued, "Probably once a year I would read the commands of God for husbands and realize that I wasn't where I should be, and I'd pray for help. But it seems like whenever I did that, she'd flaunt some lover in my face and I'd go right back to apathy."

Maxine tried to grasp the extent of what he was saying, but she couldn't. As deeply faithful to God as her sister and husband were, as deeply faithful as Barry had always been, Maxine simply didn't feel it. She liked church, she prayed at family meals, she attended church functions, but this abounding faith that those around her professed to have seemed to have missed the boat with her. Not knowing what else to say, she simply said, "I'm sorry."

"Yeah." He met her eyes and smiled. "Everyone's very sorry." His smile turned into a wry smile. "I'll probably be sorrier when the impact of what I did today sets in."

Maxine sat back and gripped her hands in her lap, strangely wanting to reach out to him and comfort him with just a touch of her hand. "If you were trying to avoid gossip, you kind of managed the opposite of your intent."

"Everyone knew. Why keep up such an absurd pretense?" Barry looked over his shoulder and caught the waitress' eye. He waved her over. "I saw him sitting there and realized that he was the one really mourning. Apparently, they were really in love and all gaga over the baby."

"Does he have kids?" Maxine wondered.

Barry nodded. "I understand he has two, but they're both teens. Still, makes you wonder."

Maxine had no idea what it was supposed to make her wonder about, but she nodded in agreement anyway. The waitress approached, pad and pencil in hand. "What can I get you?"

Barry gestured with his hands. "I want a huge steak—the biggest you have. And some grilled vegetables. Do a double order if you need to. And an iced tea. No sweetener."

The waitress looked at Maxine, who smiled. "Just a plain salad, no meat, with some oil and vinegar on the side."

When the waitress left, Barry raised an eyebrow. "What's with the rabbit food?"

Shrugging, Maxine took a sip of water. "I eat like a rabbit and workout five days a week and still seem to be losing a battle with something. Nature, I guess."

If she'd been standing, he would have looked her up and down. She could tell the way his eyes moved over her that he was processing her size and shape. "I'm sorry, Maxi, but I'm not seeing you losing a battle with anything."

She felt a flush of heat tinge the tops of her cheeks. "Well, working out helps."

"What kind of working out?"

Maxine knew Barry had a private gym in his home that

could rival any fitness club's setup. "Twice a week, I go to a spinning class, and twice a week I do a cardio-kick class."

He snorted and smiled his first genuine smile since they sat down. "Cardio- kick?"

"Sure. It's like kick boxing and aerobics rolled into one."

He started laughing and repeated, "Cardio-kick?"

Maxine felt herself getting a little irritated at it. "Yeah. Why?"

He smiled as he spoke. "Nothing, I guess. If you want to prance around in a decorative leotard and look good for your trainer, then nothing."

"Prance around?" Thinking of the hours and hours of grueling sweaty kicking being called prancing around just made her anger rise. "What would you suggest?"

"I'd suggest working out."

"That's not working out?"

He snorted again. She thought if he did that one more time she'd have to throw her ice water right in his face. "No. It's not working out."

Running her tongue over her teeth, she raised an eyebrow. "You could teach me how?"

She could swear he looked her up and down again. "Oh yeah. You bet I could."

Ignoring the double entendre, she tapped the top of the table. "Then show me."

He paused and cocked his head. "Okay. Be at my house…"

This time Maxine laughed. "No way, big guy. Come to my gym and show me how to work out for real. Teach me how to properly work out on equipment I can access anytime."

He straightened and grabbed his napkin wrapped silverware as the waitress approached with a platter mounded with meat, squash, and carrots. "Sure. When?"

Maxine eyed the wilted iceberg lettuce and dried out carrots on her plate and resignedly reached for the oil and vinegar containers that the waitress set next to her plate. "Monday morning at six sound good?"

A look of surprise crossed Barry's face about two seconds after he agreed to meet her. Maxine was curious about the little flutter of excitement that began in the pit of her stomach at the confirmation of the—her mind purposefully skipped over the word date and replaced it with—appointment.

CHAPTER FIVE

Barry **found himself sitting** in his Jeep at five-fifteen on Newbury Street outside a designer gym four buildings down from Maxine's apartment Monday morning. Part of him wondered why. Another part knew exactly why.

He got out of his Jeep and snugged his ski cap down over his ears. The December air took his breath away. He reached into the back seat and grabbed a pair of wool gloves. Checking his watch to confirm his starting time, he set out in a slow jog. He would run four or five miles and arrive back in time to meet Maxine at six.

He kept his pace careful, not wanting to slip on any unseen ice. Another couple of weeks and he would be stuck running on a treadmill for the rest of the winter. He didn't enjoy that as much. It just didn't feel like a good run under the bright fluorescent lights while watching the morning news.

As he passed a restaurant, he saw the lights flicker on, flooding the sidewalk with their glow. The day was starting.

He sighed inwardly. Today would prove to be a very tiresome day. After Maxine dropped him at a car rental place on Thursday, he rented a car and drove to the Cape, where he had hidden out in a no-tell-motel for three days. He'd left his cell and laptop in his Jeep at the church. No one could reach him and he didn't feel obligated to contact anyone. He wondered, briefly, how Maxine handled the family after acting as his accomplice in the getaway.

What he hoped would happen likely would not. It seemed hugely unlikely that everyone would ignore the whole thing and get on with their lives. He knew Tony too well. He knew his mother, too. And his sisters. No. No one would ignore anything.

After three days of solitude, Barry still didn't understand his motivations on Thursday. Why in the world had he done that? Maybe he couldn't bear the thought of one more pretense, one more lie, in a marriage that had been built on nothing but pretenses and lies.

It felt good, whatever the reason. Internally, the part of him that knew the sinfulness of his emotions recoiled from this newer, more dominant part of himself. His dark persona had put his wife away as soon as he realized that their marriage could never be saved. This alter ego had discovered that Jacqueline's lover had spent the past few months destroying his own wife with a divorce while wooing back the pregnant Mrs. Anderson.

Barry had changed so radically that just five short days after his wife broke her neck and died while skiing next to the father of her unborn child, he couldn't wait to see what kind of outfit Maxine wore to workout with him this morning. She always dressed perfectly to the nine's for any occasion, which told him he was in for a treat.

He knew that most people would think his thoughts weren't appropriate. As a rule, Barry had never cared overly much what most people thought, and this stood as no exception to the rule. He wondered, though, if Maxine would find his attraction improper. That thought gave him pause. He almost didn't recognize himself lately. Angry dark thoughts occupied his mind, and he found himself occasionally fighting feelings of despair. He was learning how to shut it out, to feel nothing, to function with total apathy.

Barry worked his way through the beautiful downtown area as the restaurants and flower shops turned on their lights and opened their doors, as delivery truck drivers cautiously guided their oversized vehicles through the mazes of the wet streets. He listened to the voices calling greetings and the hard clanging of loading dock doors, smelled the heavenly scents drifting out from bakeries. The sights, sounds, and smells struck him in stark contrast to his normal jog at this time of the morning in the total seclusion and near silence of suburbia.

He made it back to his Jeep with about five minutes to spare. He opened the back door and dug through the gym bag he'd packed last night, finding a clean towel and a bottle of water. A spicy, citrus smell wafting on the breeze teased his nostrils, and he knew Maxine stood behind him as he closed the back door.

"Hey, big guy," she greeted as he turned to face her.

The first time Barry had ever seen Maxine, even before he grew to know and like and respect her, he thought that perhaps he had never met a more classically beautiful woman. Her oval face, full lips, and high cheekbones all formed this perfect, beautiful visage that framed almond shaped eyes the most striking color of green he had ever seen. She had long limbs and long straight black hair that reached her waist. He had always appreciated her beauty in a detached, faithfully married kind of way.

"Good morning," he said, eyeing her blue spandex pants and white sweatshirt. She wore designer tennis shoes the color of red hots and he realized that she'd pieced together the colors of their favorite football team.

"I wondered if you'd show."

He chugged half the water then tossed it in the bag he'd slung over his shoulder. "Why?"

"Because you weren't exactly in a normal frame of mind on Thursday. Then you pulled a Houdini." She reached up behind her head and gathered her long, long hair into her hand. She made a rubber band magically appear and expertly twisted the strands until she had completely contained them at the base of her neck. "Thanks for that, by the way. That was a lot of fun."

Barry winced. "Pretty bad, huh?"

They walked together to the door of the gym. Barry reached around her and grabbed the handle before she could. Opening the door, he let her precede him inside. Bright lights, shiny equipment, a local radio station morning show pumped through cheap speakers, a sweaty smell beneath some designer scent intended to cover it; the place was exactly what he'd expected.

At the desk, Maxine pulled a key chain out of another hidden pocket and scanned the key tag. To the ridiculously muscled attendant with the one size-too-small muscle tank top and the moussed-up hair, she announced, "He's my guest this morning."

The attendant sidled up to the desk and leaned in, angling his body to show just the right amount of chest and biceps. Barry laughed inwardly. Maxine, as usual, acted oblivious. He wondered if she could possibly always be that unaware of the way men reacted to her. "Sure thing, Miss Bartlett," he said. "I'll take care of it for you."

He said it like he was doing her a favor instead of his job, and Barry rolled his eyes at the ridiculousness of it. Maxine simply smiled in thanks and turned to Barry. "What first, big guy?"

He looked around before pointing to the corner. "First, we stretch." He led the way to the far corner. He set his bag down and turned to her. "We're going to stretch, do some sit-ups, a few warm-up exercises, then we'll utilize some of the machines." While he explained the way she needed to stretch and the gradual escalation in the warm-up, she took off her sweatshirt, revealing a Patriots T-shirt... a loose-fitting Patriots T-shirt. With a silent thank you for little blessings, Barry counted off to eight then started back again for the cycle to twenty reps of eight. "How bad?" he asked, continuing their conversation from earlier.

"Tony was cool," Maxine said, shifting her body as she stretched her hamstring. "Robin was mad. She couldn't believe that I helped you get away from everyone."

"I appreciated it."

"I'm just glad I was running late." She grinned as she shifted again. "I couldn't believe I was late for your wife's funeral. That's terrible."

"I doubt she minded," Barry observed dryly. When they finished that rep of twenty, they moved to the floor so he could hold her feet while she knocked out some sit-ups. "I'm sure they have a setup where you can do this alone," he said, "But I'm comfortable here." He glanced up, noticing how full the gym had become in the last twenty minutes. "Popular place."

Maxine effortlessly pulled her body up, then lay back against the mat before pulling herself back up again. "Yeah. It seems like a good place."

"Lots of bells and whistles."

She grinned, making her eyes dance like jewels. "Women need bells." She huffed up and back down again. "And whistles."

"About your diet," he said. This time when her shoulders touched the mat, she didn't immediately pull herself back up. He watched her hesitate. "Come on, Maxi. Three more."

"What about my diet?" she asked, closing her eyes and drawing her body up then back down again.

"Rabbit food won't cut it."

With a grunt, she finished the last two reps. "What else is there?"

He put a hand on the side of her bent knee and squeezed, signaling in silence the end of that exercise. He silently acknowledged how she tensed up then jerked away from the touch and mentally filed that away. He fished another bottle of water out of his bag and tossed it to her. "High protein, whole grains, eating small portions every couple of hours, but eating the right foods." While she drank the water, he pulled a book out of the bag. "This book will tell you what to eat, how to eat it, and when. The guy who wrote it knows what he's talking about."

Maxine eyed the book suspiciously, but took it from him. "I'll give it a look."

"Do more than that. Get on this starting right now. You should see noticeable changes in your energy and concentration levels in about 10 days. It requires a lifestyle change in your eating habits. You need to approach it in a disciplined manner."

Maxine couldn't stop herself from grinning. "Yes, coach." She pushed herself to her feet. "What now?"

AN hour later, Maxine sat across from Barry in a little bakery next door to the gym. Her muscles felt rubbery and very tired. As she sat there, she could still feel her thighs burning from that one last repetition. She felt like she'd worked more muscles in her body in the forty-five minutes with Barry than in a week's worth of aerobic classes.

She took a sip of hazelnut flavored coffee and closed her eyes in ecstasy. "If coffee is disallowed by that diet book, I'm not reading it."

He wrinkled his nose and dunked his tea bag in the hot water in his cup. "It's allowed."

"Yet you obviously disapprove."

As he shrugged, she wondered if his huge frame would crush the little filigreed café chair in which he sat. "There are too many ways to naturally generate energy without requiring a drug."

"Man, you are still on that kick. There's a difference between God-given caffeine in coffee and laboratory made industrial grade steroids, you know." She sipped.

Barry shrugged again, this time as if to announce that nothing would change his mind in this conversation that was months old between them. "What those men did hurt more than the team. It hurt the League and it hurt every kid in the world who looked up to them as role-models."

Hoping the little plastic knife wouldn't break under the weight of the cream cheese, she carefully applied it to her whole grain bagel. "Coffee was put on this earth to provide pleasure and ecstasy, especially hazelnut flavored coffee on cold December mornings."

Barry reached into that never ending bottomless gym bag that hung on the back of the metal chair and pulled out a plastic drink container. When he opened the lid to take a sip, she caught a glimpse of something thick and gray. He took a long swallow, then used a paper napkin to wipe the sludge off of his lips. Maxine pushed back any curiosity as to what ingredients might possibly be found in nature to produce a concoction of that particular color for fear he would offer to share. Instead, she took a small bite of bagel and thought she much preferred this focus Barry had on protein, such as this cream cheese, over her usual breakfast of a banana.

Using his drink container, Barry gestured at her shirt. "Catch the game yesterday?"

"Not until I got home last night at seven. I don't know how I managed to get through the day without hearing anything about it, but I'm so glad I went into that third quarter completely ignorant of just what excitement awaited me." She took another bite and washed it down with coffee. "I imagined you couldn't even sit down."

"I had to pay for my room for Sunday night, too, so that I could stay and watch the game. Worth every single dime." Barry shook his head while he grinned. "It was crazy. I thought they'd kick me out of the hotel. I kept screaming at the television."

"It's really turning out to be a great season."

Barry took another long pull of the drink, then put the lid back on and tossed it in his bag. He picked up his own bagel and ripped it in half, then bit into it and gestured with the remaining piece. "Hey. You want to go to the game with me this Sunday?"

Maxine raised an eyebrow and ran her tongue over her teeth. It took her about a second and a half to grin and agree. "Heck yeah, I want to go."

"Great." He glanced at the massive watch that he sported on his left wrist. Maxine couldn't help noticing that it didn't look too massive on his arm. It would swamp most men. "I have to go. I have to be at the courthouse at eight-thirty. I'll be outside the gym at six Wednesday morning if that works for you."

Maxine raised an eyebrow. "You will?"

"Of course." Barry stood with a grace a man his size shouldn't have. "You didn't think today was it, did you?"

She'd hoped not, but didn't dare ask. "I didn't think about it, honestly."

His face became very intense as he put both of his massive hands on the little round table and leaned forward. "We just breached the bare surface. There are so many things that you could do that you don't, that you should do that you don't know about. First of all, start eating right today. Maxine, diet is 90 percent of the whole thing. If you're serious about wanting to get fit and healthy…"

Maxine nodded and interrupted. "Of course I'm

serious."

Barry straightened and pulled a ski cap out of the pocket of his pants. "Then I'll see you at six on Wednesday." He slung the bag over his shoulder and started to leave the bakery but paused and turned around. "Thank you." With eyes turning very serious and very somber, he said it again. "Thank you for Thursday. I needed that."

Maxi tilted her head and gave a slight nod. "Glad I could help."

He paused for a long time, two heartbeats, then three, before pushing open the door and walking away. The bell on the door jingled as it shut behind him, sending a draft of cold air toward Maxine's table. She couldn't take a sip of her coffee until she quit smiling the ridiculous smile that had somehow taken occupancy on her lips, but she just honestly couldn't help it.

CHAPTER SIX

A hard rock "hair band" from several decades earlier beat a frantic rhythm and exclaimed that it had been a long time since they'd rocked and rolled while Maxine played with the background color of the template she had designed on her computer. She lifted a finger to adjust the earbud of her MP3 player while she clicked between a violet and a blue-violet, trying to decide the best interior wall colors for a set for a bedroom furniture commercial that would shoot next month. The white headboard and bedding would really pop in front of purple walls.

She'd used the MP3 player since she'd worked in a cubicle as an intern and needed to isolate herself from the world. For the last year, she'd worked from the privacy of her own office complete with the services of a secretary she shared with three other associates. Even though she could shut the door and play music at a somewhat reasonable level, the habit of total isolation had long been established and she found she worked better with it.

As she reviewed her notes to make sure she had incorporated all of the elements in the original design, the song ended. Before the next one could shuffle forward, her door opened. Maxine popped the earbuds out of her ears before her rather eclectic secretary could wave her bejeweled arms to get her attention.

"Mike Robison is on six," she said, as the sound of a dozen bracelets clinking together preceded her handing Maxine a stack of messages. "You said to flag you when he called. And your meeting with the design department for that," she gestured to the computer, "has been pushed back an hour. The director is tied up somewhere else."

"Thanks, Julie." As her secretary turned to go, Maxine called her back. "Hey, Julie. Violet or blue violet?" she asked, pointing to the computer monitors on the credenza behind her.

Julie raised a hand to her bangs. "My hair? It's more like an eggplant, don't you think?"

With a chuckle, Maxine shook her head. "I like the eggplant. It works well. I'm talking about the walls of the bedroom."

Julie walked around the side of the desk to peer closer at the monitors. "I'm not seeing a difference," she said when she straightened.

Maxine laughed as she picked up the phone and hit the flashing light for line six. "No biggie. Thanks."

"Sure." With a swoosh of her long fuchsia skirts, Julie left the room.

"Mike," Maxine said, "thanks for calling me back."

She could hear the sound of the police station in the background of the phone. "Sure," he said. "We still on for tonight?"

Opening her desk drawer, she drew out a new pack of raw almonds, recommended by Barry's book as an in-between meals snack, and used her letter opener to break the seal on the package. "That's why I called. I have to cancel."

"Why?"

The incredulous tone had her frowning. She grabbed a handful of nuts and piled them on her desk before putting the package back in her drawer. "Something else came up."

"What could possibly come up instead of Monday night football at O-Leary's pub?"

Absolutely nothing could possibly come up. Even the atmosphere at O'Leary's didn't appeal to her if she had to go with Mike. She hadn't enjoyed spending time with him for the last few weeks, and decided that it was time to end it. After a few weeks, every man she'd ever dated wanted to take their relationship to the next level, to the physical level, and Maxine just didn't do physical. Ever.

She found it best to just end it instead of trying to explain that, *yes, I like you*, and *thank you for dinner*, but, *no*, I'm not going to hold your hand or kiss you good night or sleep with you and thank you for *not touching me*. Even thinking about a man's touch made her stomach crawl and her blood run cold. The two times in her past when she'd actually tried to explain the why's just didn't go well, and were experiences she personally never wanted to relive.

Julie cracked open her office door and gestured at the phone, mouthing the word, "Robin," and held up four fingers. Maxine closed her eyes and sighed. "I have to go, Mike. Have fun tonight."

Without waiting for a response, she disconnected and hit the button for line four. "Hey."

Little fingers of anticipation danced up her spine, tightening the muscles on her neck. She wondered if Robin was still really mad at her. "Hey. Can we have lunch?"

"Of course," Maxine said in a rush, wishing she could read more into the tone. "Where?"

"Hank's if you can make it out here. If not, tell me where to meet you."

Closing her eyes and thanking God for the shift in the meeting with the set people, she agreed to meet at Hank's in an hour. With Monday traffic, Maxine decided she probably needed to start heading in that direction. Her sister's restaurant was well outside the city limits, closer to one of the colleges, and the spits of snow out there would make traffic beastly.

MAXINE tapped on the frosted glass of the door leading to Robin's office. With Hank's not open on Mondays, Robin would be in there doing whatever she did to manage one of the best family restaurants in the Boston area, if the food critics could be believed.

Robin's voice beckoned her inside. When she opened the door, she found her older sister standing by the tall bookshelf stretching her lower back, rubbing one hand over her incredibly pregnant belly. An open cardboard box lay at her feet, and a picture of her and Tony on their honeymoon in Italy lay on a piece of newspaper on the corner of her desk.

"Moving day?" Maxine asked.

"It is. Our new manager starts Wednesday. I needed to take a break from working on the computer and move around some." She gestured at her desk. "Casey made us some hamburgers."

"That's awesome. I'm starving." She couldn't understand why she was so hungry since she'd been eating every two hours following Barry's book, but the sight of the hamburger with melting Swiss cheese sitting on two sourdough buns made her mouth water and her stomach grumble with anticipation.

Robin met Tony when he bought Hank's place back when she worked there as a bartender. He promoted her to manager when they pulled the bar out and added more seating. Maxine knew that Robin didn't intend to work once the baby came.

Robin finished stretching and came forward the three steps to hug Maxine. As she released her and stepped back, Maxine put her hands on either side of her sister's swelling stomach, leaning her face close enough that her nose touched it. "Hello little niece or nephew." She smiled as she received a kick in the nose. "Hey, let's sit. You can put your feet in my lap."

Robin smiled as they took a seat at the desk. "I don't need to put my feet up, but thank you." She held her hand out and Maxine took it and bowed her head. Robin blessed the meal, thanking God for the food and for the relationship that only sisters could share.

Maxine felt the sting of tears in her throat when it was over. It wasn't until she chewed and swallowed the first heavenly bite that she asked, "What did you want to talk about?"

Robin washed down her own bite of hamburger with a long pull of water before answering. "I want to start off by apologizing for getting so angry with you. That was wrong of me. Please forgive me."

Maxine cocked an eyebrow. "Sure."

Robin put a hand on the side of her stomach and shifted. "Secondly, I want to ask just what you're doing."

"I'm sharing lunch with my sister. What do you think I'm doing?"

"I don't know. I've never been a big fan of your closeness with Barry. He is..." she paused and corrected herself, "... was married and you two spent an awful lot of time alone."

Maxine felt some heat creep into her cheeks. "Alone while his wife was..."

"There's no reason that one person's wrong should justify another's."

"Barry and I were only friends. It never went further."

"I understand that. But you just used past tense, and now that there isn't a wife in the picture, will it stay that way?"

"How should I know the answer to that?" Maxine surged to her feet and grabbed an empty box. She snatched a picture frame off the desk and shoved it into the box.

"Maxi..."

A paperweight and a stress ball followed. "No. I'm not listening to anymore. I admire Barry's ability to have worked at being faithful to that—that woman he was married to. I don't know what will happen in my future or his future. I just know that he is one of my best friends and

I have always enjoyed spending time with him. I realize that you've never understood my relationship with men and that you condemn it in your mind, but I can watch a football game with a widower and not end up like our mother!"

Robin's eyes widened. "Is that what you think this is about?"

"What else is there?"

Robin teetered her way out of the chair and put a hand on her lower back. "Maxi, I'm concerned about you. Not because our mother was a drug addict who moved from dealer to pusher and hauled us with her. I'm concerned because Barry has been pulling away from God, and I'm worried about his anger right now."

All of the steam left Maxine and her hands stilled. "His anger?"

"His anger. He's spent weeks pushing everyone aside. He won't even talk with Tony or pray with Tony about it. He is full of anger about Jacqueline's pregnancy, his marriage, her death. I'm worried that he's going to go through some all out rebellion and take you with him." Her eyes filled with tears and she dashed them away with jerky movements.

Maxine rushed forward and took Robin's hand. "You don't have to worry about me."

"Maxi, I know you believe in God. But I also know that you go to church to please me and Sarah. I know that. I know you don't have the zest I have. But I also know that you will. One day, the Holy Spirit is going to knock you in the head with a two by four and you'll not be able to deny it. But starting a relationship with a man who is so angry will pull you away from God."

Maxine couldn't fathom why Robin was so upset. It didn't make sense to her. She put her hands on either side of Robin's belly. "You have so much going on right now that worrying about whether I will start a relationship with Barry Anderson should be at the bottom of the list." She pulled her close and hugged her. "I love you. And I so appreciate how much you love me. Did you know that?"

"I know you do." She pulled back and looked deeply into Maxine's eyes. "But, please. Keep this conversation in mind as you go forward from this day."

To make Robin feel better, she smiled. "Of course." Gesturing back to the desk, she said, "Let's get that meal eaten. I'd hate to face Casey's wrath if we sent back plates with just one bite out of each burger."

"After work tonight, can you help me run an errand?"

"Sure." Maxine sat back down in her chair and picked up her hamburger. "Where are we going?" She took a big bite of the delicious sandwich.

"I have a box of Bibles and hymnals I need to take to Craig at the prison. Tony usually goes with me, but he's not free tonight, and they need them for a worship service Craig's leading tomorrow."

Craig Bartlett was Robin's biological father who was currently serving the remainder of a 20 year sentence for a double homicide committed decades in the past. One of the lives he had taken had been their mother.

Maxine nodded and swallowed. "Glad to help," she said.

Robin put a hand on her shoulder and squeezed. "Thank you."

CHAPTER SEVEN

Barry didn't know what to expect when he walked into his offices after court on Monday afternoon. He felt a very real uncertainty about how people would treat him. Almost all of the staff had attended the funeral, and those who hadn't attended had most certainly heard about his outburst by now. So if he felt a bit of trepidation as he stepped off the elevator, certainly some justification for that feeling existed.

The receptionist's face flushed and she stammered as she bid him good afternoon. He thought she would actually thank God outright when the phone interrupted them. As he walked through the outer area and past secretaries' cubicles and desks, a wake of first silence then murmuring and whispering followed. When he finally made it to his office area, his own secretary quickly hung up the phone and stood. "Mr. Anderson," she said, grabbing at a stack of messages. "I wasn't sure if you were going to be in or not today."

A war widow with two teenage sons, his secretary,

Elizabeth, had worked for him since he opened his own practice. Her knowledge of the law often rivaled his junior associates, and he occasionally wondered why she didn't bite the bullet and take her husband's pension to attend law school herself. She typically dressed in conservative pantsuits and wore cross necklaces in all different styles and colors—whatever matched her suit of the day. She wore her hair in a long braid every day, and had never removed her wedding ring.

He paused beside her desk and set his briefcase on the floor by his feet and his travel mug of herbal tea on the corner of her desk so that he could thumb through the messages. "There's no reason for me not to work today," he said.

As he thumbed through the dozens of messages, she let out a breath. "I'm not quite sure what to say about that."

The wall of callous defense he'd shorn up before entering the building fell at the look on her face. He immediately felt like an inhuman heel. "I apologize. I think I was prepared for this to all be a bad experience. I was defensive before there was cause, and that made me rude."

"May I say something?"

"Of course." He gripped the messages and mug in one hand and bent to pick up his briefcase.

"I realize that your marriage to Mrs. Anderson has—had—been strained for some time. But despite that, she was a human being whom you shared a house with, if not a portion of your life. If you don't allow some grieving, despite everything, you're going to regret it at some point."

"I appreciate that, Elizabeth. Thank you." He gave her a slight nod. "Now I have work piled up from the last week, I'm sure, and I need to get to it."

He left her standing there, gripping her necklace. He imagined her thinking about her late husband and wished that anything to do with his late wife wouldn't cause her any pain. Elizabeth didn't deserve any pain for anything.

Shutting the door behind him, a signal to everyone in his firm not to bother him, he entered his office. A decorator had taken the former football player persona to the extreme, but he'd never had it redone. People who came to see him because of his past life expected the decor to be what it was, so it did no harm. The dark green walls with stark white trim held shadow boxes of signed footballs, autographed photos, and Super Bowl posters. The hardwood floor had scattered rugs that mingled the colors of his former team with the colors of the wall, and flowers and knickknacks around the room drew it all together.

In one corner of the large expanse, a leather sofa and two leather wing-backed chairs formed a sitting area around a heavy wood coffee table. He often met with clients there. Removing the barrier of the desk lowered defenses and in many cases, fear. In the opposite corner and closest to the door, a conference table that comfortably seated eight crouched beneath a crystal chandelier. His huge desk, especially designed and customized to accommodate his large size, filled the other half of the room. It sat in front of a picture window that overlooked the water and the financial skyline. He purposefully picked the location of his offices for an easy walk to the courthouse. Credenzas on either side of his desk held the customary law journals and business books. He rarely opened them. He much preferred the ease of research using the slim laptop that he pulled out of his briefcase when he reached his desk.

Along with the half dozen messages she'd left on his cell phone and home phone voice mails, his mother had called here twice. He needed to go ahead and call her and get that out of the way. As he picked up the receiver of his phone, he sorted the messages between personal and business. The business stack was very small compared to the personal stack.

He quickly dialed his parents' home and his mother answered on the first ring. "Hi, mom," he said, sitting in his chair and swiveling it around to look out over the water.

"Barry." She made the word a whole sentence. "I'm glad you're okay."

"I'm just fine, mom."

From her end, a deep breath punctuated a long pause. "As long as you are. Do you need anything?"

Barry closed his eyes and felt an unfamiliar rush of emotion. He needed something. He needed to erase the last twenty years and hit restart. "I just want to get the next few days out of the way so that everyone and everything can go back to normal."

Another long pause. "Okay. Fair enough. Do you want to come to dinner Sunday?"

"I would, but I'm going to the game. How about Saturday?"

"Your sisters will be here."

With a short laugh, he thought of his three older sisters and shook his head. "Might as well get it all over with at one time."

He could hear the smile in her voice. "Saturday it is then. See you at six."

"Yes, ma'am," he agreed as he hung up the phone. He scribbled a note on the message slip which would later go into his laptop calendar just to ensure he would not forget. He knew that absolutely no excuse, no matter how grand, would allow him to duck out of that dinner.

Feeling a huge weight lifted by walking into his offices and then that simple phone call, he ignored the stack of personal calls and started making his way through the business calls. As he ended his third call, he pulled his laptop out of the briefcase and docked it, connecting it to its various plugs and ports, connecting the battery to power and the network card to hard wired connectivity. He didn't yet trust wireless networks to keep his client's information totally secure.

While concluding typing in the notes from the last call, his office door flew open and Tony Viscolli marched in. At his heels, Elizabeth looked surprised and a little bit angry. Tony turned around and gave her a smile. "Don't worry, Liz. He'll be fine with the interruption." He shut the door in her face and came all the way into the room.

Tony always looked like the cover model of a men's fashion magazine, whether he was going to a business meeting in some handmade Italian silk suit or sailing in the harbor in white Dockers and a cable knit sweater. This morning proved no exception. His gray suit, light blue shirt, and dark blue tie authoritatively announced confidence and business acumen. His dark hair and Sicilian features perfectly complemented the light fabric.

Barry didn't stand. Instead, he leaned back in his chair. "Good afternoon."

Tony sat in one of the chairs opposite Barry. "Is it?"

Barry rubbed his face with his hands and sat forward. "Not particularly."

"Didn't think so."

Tony rarely came to Barry's office. Barry typically went to Tony, which was fair since Tony paid him. He pretty much only came when there was a third party meeting on a legal level that required a neutral environment. "Are you here on business?" Barry asked hopefully.

"What gave you that idea?" Tony answered, leaning back in his chair.

Barry grinned. Anyone else, even a client as important as Tony Viscolli, he would have dismissed at that point. Of course they shared business interests. He and Tony, though, had a relationship much more like brothers than close business partners. Around his ironic grin, he asked, "Why are you here, then?"

Tony cocked an eyebrow and tilted his head as if to look at Barry from a different angle. "Because I love you."

Barry nodded. "So my not calling you back didn't tell you that what I really need is some time alone and some emotional space?"

"Well, you've been pulling away from me for weeks now. I think I've given you all of the space you can handle."

Barry felt a little tickle of annoyance. "What does that mean?"

Tony sat forward. "It means that when I gave you the space you so clearly projected you needed, I watched you withdraw from everything normal and become quite rude in the process." As Barry prepared a retort, Tony held up a finger. "Maybe rude is the wrong word. Abrupt? Terse? I think the stress Jacqueline constantly brought to your doorstep contributed to that. But you have also been pulling away from church and men's groups, and that greatly concerns me."

Barry started feeling a little antsy. He slowly drummed his fingers on his desk. "Why?"

"Because I wonder if you've pulled away from your relationship with God the same way you've pulled away from everything else."

Defensiveness surged through him in a hot, painful flicker of flame. He wanted this conversation over and he wanted Tony out of his office. "Is that any of your business?"

Tony's eyes hardened and his mouth firmed. "Barry. What is wrong? What happened?"

Pushing the negative feelings aside, Barry leaned back again in his seat and covered his eyes with the heels of his hands. "I don't know what happened, Tony. I spent two decades trying to do the right—the Christian thing—with Jacqui. I stayed faithful. I stayed loving. I prayed for her. I prayed a lot. You prayed with me on more than a few occasions. I never gave up on her."

"I know…"

Barry sat forward quickly and slammed a hand on the desk. "No you do not know, Tony. Don't even try to say you know. You don't know what it was like. You don't know what she was like. You don't know how I felt." He let out a breath and felt energy drain from his body. "Toward the end she didn't even pretend to hide her lovers anymore. Then she met this guy and was suddenly in love."

He felt his lip curl. "As if that makes everything okay."

"Bear…"

Barry closed his eyes and massaged the bridge of his nose with his giant fingers. "I just wanted to do the right thing. I just wanted to get to heaven one day and have God say to me, 'Good game, Barry. You played well. Head to the locker room.'" He opened his eyes and looked at his best friend, someone from whom he'd shielded all of this misery. Or tried to, anyway. "Then she got pregnant."

Tony waited out the silence, then finally said, "Why did you never say anything?"

"What is there to say? You wouldn't understand it. You and Robin have this magical perfection, and here I am, married for eighteen years and my wife gets pregnant by one of her many lovers. How do I talk about that with you? How do I talk about that with anyone?"

"There's someone you could have talked to, who always understands."

Barry barked out a laugh. "God?" Unable to contain the energy anymore, Barry surged to his feet. He turned his back to Tony and looked out over the expanse of water below. His very view screamed success, but in his heart he knew he had no real accomplishment to stand upon. What would his legacy be? To whom could he leave it? He put both of his hands on the glass and pressed against it with his body. "You want to know what I said to God?"

"Yes, I do," Tony answered quietly.

"For years, I said to God, 'Please fix whatever's wrong with my wife. She's sadistic and evil.' Years and years went by. Then she came to me all weepy and pregnant asking me to help her. It took me a while to finally agree to it."

Tears burned his throat, but he would not give in to the emotion. Pushing it back, finding the balance of feeling absolutely nothing, he continued his story. "Then Jacqui didn't want that anymore. He'd left his wife, filed for divorce, and asked Jacqui to marry him. He asked *my* wife to marry him." Barry stared out the window, at the business of the street far below, at the people going through their lives like nothing different had happened in the world. "So then, I hit my knees and I said to God, 'Please, God. Spare me this embarrassment. Spare me the humiliation. Spare me from the world finding out she's pregnant by another man.'"

He heard Tony get out of his chair. He heard the tap of Tony's shoes on the wooden floor. He felt the comforting hand on his shoulder, but he didn't turn his head to look at his best friend as he continued, "Last week, on a trip to celebrate her finally feeling better, their coming nuptials and baby, she tumbled down a slope in the Berkshires, and broke her neck."

"*Amico…*"

Barry formed both hands into fists and punched at the glass. The safety glass didn't break, but it shook with the force. "No! Don't even try to hand me platitudes. I'm quite over it. I don't know what I did. I don't know how I've gone into every single situation in my life, including my marriage to that woman, in prayer and supplication and still managed to have what I had. Then the only prayer in eighteen years about her that gets answered ends up killing her and taking an innocent life. Spare me whatever it is that you're about to say, Tony. I don't care about any of it."

He turned around and fully faced Tony. "I love you. You're my best friend, and my brother. But if you're going to tell me you're praying for me or God will fix it or whatever it is that you're about to tell me, please just don't."

Tony raised an eyebrow. "I was simply going to say, *il mio amico*, that anything you need at all, you can call me. You need to vent, you need to play a game of chess, you need a boxing partner—just call me. Don't shut me out of your life, because I need you in mine. You are my best friend, and my brother, too."

Barry stared at Tony for several seconds, then felt his hands unfist. He rubbed his face and nodded. "Okay. Thank you."

Tony looked at his watch. "Now I must go, Bear. Robin has an ultrasound this morning."

Clearing his throat, Barry shoved his hands in his pockets. "How's she feeling?"

"Very large." Tony smiled. "But anticipatory. She is ready for the next few weeks to come and go."

"And you?"

"I could not be better. God is awesome." Tony held up both hands in a defensive move. "And before you take me up on that boxing, I will leave."

"Hey." Tony paused with his hand on the doorknob and turned to look directly at Barry. "Thanks," Barry said, swallowing emotion.

"*Sei benvenuto.*" He started to leave, but stopped. "Robin will be occupied with her sisters tomorrow night. She is doing thank-you cards for her shower gifts. Do you want to get dinner?"

Barry paused, but then nodded. "That sounds great. Sure."

"One more thing, Barry. Think about this. You prayed for God to spare you from the world learning that your wife had been faithless, that she was carrying another man's child. You are angry that God answered your prayer. But Barry, everyone in your world knows. Did God really answer your prayer?" Tony held up a hand to forestall any answer. "Just think about it. I'll see you tomorrow."

Long after the door shut behind Tony, Barry stood at the window, looking out over the buildings in his field of view. He watched the birds swoop and dive over the water, watched snow spit in the rain. Finally, he shook his head as if to clear it and turned back to his desk, to his work, to the one area of success in his life. He opened his laptop and shot Elizabeth an instant message asking her to bring him water when she had a free minute. Then he pulled up a client file and reviewed some notes before he picked up the telephone again.

CHAPTER EIGHT

"**A**re you cold?" **Barry** yelled against Maxine's ear to be heard above the roar of the crowd. Maxine grinned and shook her head, but didn't try to speak over the noise of the crowd. Seventy thousand fans cheered the Patriots down the field and she knew her voice would never make it to his ear.

When they sat back down and the noise returned to a better level, he leaned down again. "We can go into the deck if you want," he said.

She tore her eyes from the field as the teams broke away for a time-out. Looking Barry in the eye, she said, "Why in the world would I want to go into an isolated deck to watch the game? If I wanted to sip a drink from a real glass and eat finger sandwiches, I'd be watching the game from my living room couch." She narrowed her eyes. "And why are you so worried about me?"

Barry grinned. His face relaxed and he settled back comfortably in his seat. "I totally agree with you. I just wanted to make sure you didn't expect to go into the lounge and watch from the high life."

"Why would I want to do that?"

With a shrug, he said, "I don't know. It's been a while since I took another girl to a game."

Maxine felt her eyes widen as she realized what he meant. "Don't worry about me, big guy. Whenever you wonder about what I'd prefer, just go with the opposite of what Jacqui would have preferred. That should cover all the bases."

For a moment, Maxine felt horror that she'd said that aloud. Then, when a slow smile gradually took over Barry's face before he threw his head back and laughed, she knew she hadn't crossed some invisible faux pas boundary.

After that, he relaxed. They shivered in their seats, never realizing they felt the cold, while their team stomped the other team into the ground. They yelled and cheered and talked back to the field until Maxine's scratchy throat sounded hoarse.

At the end of the game, she wrapped her Patriots scarf tight around her neck and pulled her Patriots hat low on her forehead and followed closely behind Barry, who muscled his way through the crowd. It took quite some time to reach Barry's Jeep, but they chatted the whole way and she didn't mind. The crowds and parking lot and traffic were part of the whole package.

When they finally left the stadium parking lot and turned onto a main road, Barry looked over at her. "Where to?"

Maxine had to clear her throat a couple of times to get any sound out at all. "Tony and Robin's, I guess. We missed lunch. Might as well go graze before church."

Barry tapped his finger on the clock on his dashboard. "Too late. They'd be gone by the time we got there."

"Well, hmm," Maxine said, pursing her lips and tapping her chin. "I guess we could go straight to church."

"Why don't we stop at this pub I know and grab a sandwich and watch one of the west coast games?"

It possibly ought to have taken her more than half a second to decide to agree to go. In that half second, she wondered, pondered, contemplated whether she should press the church issue. Her conversation with Robin crept into the front of her brain somehow, and she had a brief moment of worry about Barry's avoidance of all things normal and typical for him. However, despite Robin's fears that Barry would pull Maxine away from God with his anger, Maxine didn't find him angry. She found him happy, even relaxed. An element that always held him back no longer existed, and she'd enjoyed watching him start to unfurl his wings a little bit in the last week.

Barry and Maxine had worked out together four mornings in the last week, and shared breakfast after every muscle searing session. They hadn't yet found a conversation they didn't enjoy, and Maxine hated to see the clock strike eight those mornings. That's when Barry lifted his immense frame out of the little scrolly iron chair, pulled a ski cap down over his ears, and smiled at her as he told her good-bye. The smile always made her heart skip a little beat, and the good-bye made her wish the next twenty-two hours would go by really fast.

She had looked forward to Sunday all week, knowing that they'd get back into their football watching schedule that they'd shared for the last few years. When he pulled tickets out of his pocket Thursday morning, Maxine laughed with delight and snatched them from his hand. Friday morning, he had a breakfast meeting and couldn't work out with her. She didn't enjoy doing it alone, but the anticipation of Sunday made the time go by much quicker than usual.

They reached the little pub in short order. Once they left the football traffic behind them, they encountered very few cars. Set outside the city limits, more toward Barry's neighborhood, the little pub had a very full parking lot.

Barry held her door open as she got out of the Jeep and stepped into the cold air. Maxine shoved her hands into her pockets and rushed toward the door while the wind cut through her jacket and fleece pullover. Walking into the welcoming warmth of the building, she pushed her cap off her head and unwound her scarf. Barry stood above her, scanning the room, and nodded in the direction of a couple standing near a booth putting on their coats. "Let's grab that table," he said, putting a hand on the small of her back to guide her. Maxine inched forward as much as possible, hoping to create a space between his hand and her back.

As they maneuvered their way through the full crowd, a cheer erupted around them. Maxine looked at one of the many wide-screened televisions that seemed to cover every spare inch of wall space and saw the game everyone else seemed to be watching. She noticed that the booth would offer no good view of that game, but it beat sitting at the bar.

Barry took her jacket from her before she slid into the booth, and he set their coats next to him as he sat across from her. They both gathered plates and glasses and stacked them at the end of the table. As Maxine used a paper napkin to wipe water rings from the table, the waitress approached. "What can I get you?"

Barry pointed at Maxine, who shrugged and said, "Anything seared meat."

He smiled and ordered. "Two Reubens, double meat. Instead of fries, we'll take carrot sticks and celery with some Ranch and Blue Cheese. And two waters, with lemon if you have it." The waitress jotted her shorthand quickly on her pad, then took as many of the dishes as she could. "I'll come back for the rest," she said.

Once she left, Maxine scanned the televisions in her view and decided that none of the games held her interest much. Instead, she focused on Barry. "Thank you for taking me to the game today."

He grinned. "Good game."

"Do you miss it?"

The shake of his head happened suddenly, like a reflex. "Never have. I didn't ever have a passion for it. I simply used it as a tool to get me through law school without having to pay back student loans for a decade." He fiddled with the Super Bowl ring on his hand. Maxine noticed that he'd moved it from his left ring finger to his right ring finger. She wondered when he did that. "I played third string—took a beating from the first and second string players at practice and hardly left the bench during the regular games."

The waitress rushed by their table and slid their waters toward them with barely a pause. She did reach into the small apron she wore on her hip and grabbed a handful of straws, two of which she tossed on their table, then grabbed the remaining dishes.

"What was playing in the Super Bowl like?"

The grin covered his face quickly. "Thrilling. More than I'd like to admit."

Her chuckle flowed over him, through him. "Why more? Isn't it every man's dream?"

He casually shrugged. "I'd just passed the bar and it was the end of my contract. I never had to put the uniform on again. But that game, we had three touchdowns the first quarter. By the third quarter, we were ahead by twenty points. Their offensive line decided that they needed to break down our defense. I was a defensive lineman, but our first string was the best in the country, which is why I rarely played."

"Did you get to play?"

With a smile, he twisted the ring on his finger. "Yeah. Four of our guys were on stretchers in the locker room at the half and two of them on the bench with ice packs or bandages by the fourth quarter. By then I was angry. They weren't playing football, they'd decided to go to war. They'd managed to push the score up to just a six-point spread and by then we were in the second half of the fourth quarter. The crowd was insane. It was cold and rainy, but I was so mad, I didn't even care. Without ever even speaking the words, we decided to give back. Only we didn't hit their offensive line. We went straight for the jugular."

Maxine turned her body so that her back was in the corner of the booth and she could stretch her long legs along the bench. She played with the straw in her water and enjoyed watching him talk. She could almost feel the cold, hear the roar of the crowd. "You went after the quarterback," she said with a smile.

"Yes. And he knew it. He started getting scared. They kept losing yardage, because he'd fall back so far, trying to get as far away from us as possible. But most of us on the line were fresh. We hadn't been playing for hours, and they'd hurt our guys, not just as part of the game, but intentionally tried to wreck a few careers, so we started playing for blood."

"What happened?"

"We sacked him three times in five minutes."

"You did that?"

He gave her a quick, heart stopping grin. "Once." His eyes shone with the memory he relived in his mind. "And as you know, we won. It was amazing. The crowd was so loud you could feel them inside of your chest."

She smiled. "Then what happened?"

His shrug wasn't as casual this time. "Then the season was over, I turned down another contract with a huge signing bonus, and Jacqueline never forgave me."

Maxine didn't want to breach Jacqueline territory just yet. "So what was next?"

"I took the money I earned from playing football and paid back my student loans. I had enough money left over to rent a little office in downtown Boston and hang a shingle on the door. Ten days later, this street-tough kid named Antonio Viscolli, barely twenty-one, walks into my office full of God and genius and says he needs a lawyer for a big business deal he was about to venture into."

Maxine straightened in her seat as the waitress came to their table with platters of food. "And history was made."

Barry helped the waitress set plates of food and bowls of dressings on the table then nodded his thanks. "No, that day it was just forged. One month later, the green attorney and the street rat bought a boat engine manufacturing plant for one quarter of its net worth."

"Ah," she said as she dipped a carrot stick in some Blue Cheese dressing and took a big bite. "That sealed it. That's awesome." She waited to see if he intended to pray over the meal, but he simply picked his sandwich up and started eating so she followed suit. It made her a little uncomfortable. She'd known Barry for a few years. While they hadn't been praying over coffee and tea and croissants, she'd never shared a real meal with him, other than the day of Jacqueline's funeral, when he also didn't ask God to bless the meal. Again, Robin's worries whispered through her subconscious, but she shrugged it off. "I'm glad you still like to watch football, though."

He ripped a paper napkin out of the holder before responding. "Yeah? Why is that?"

She didn't realize she'd spoken out loud. Taking a pull of her water, she formed her response carefully. "Because it brought us together and made us friends when we first met."

Barry paused eating and stared at her for the space of several heartbeats. Maxine felt a rush from her heart spread through her veins and up her neck in a warm flush. He finally spoke. "Yeah." Maxine wondered if he meant as much in that one syllable word as she hoped he meant. He broke the stare and picked up a celery stick. "I love to watch. It's why I didn't mind sitting on the bench. I've always had the tickets I have. I rarely miss a home game. And some buddies of mine and I always pick a bowl game to go to every year. We take our wives and make a big weekend of it." He froze, obviously realizing what he'd said.

Maxine let it slide. You couldn't spend the better part of two decades of your life with someone and have them gone in an instant and not trip up occasionally. She wished he'd realize that. "Where are you going this year?"

"MAACO." He cleared his throat and relaxed again. "Christmas week in Las Vegas."

With a smile, Maxine took a small bite of her sandwich. "Talk about Christmas lights."

"It's going to be fantastic."

"You probably had to use every string you have to get those tickets."

"You know it." He smiled. "Want to come?"

As he asked, she swallowed, then promptly choked. Her eyes watered and she couldn't catch her breath. Finally, with the help of the water and God, she managed to get the little piece of corned beef dislodged from her windpipe and swallowed properly. She wiped her eyes with a fresh napkin and looked at him. "What?"

"Well," he drawled, "I have this extra ticket. I thought about asking my dad if he wanted to go, but I bet you'd get a kick out of it. Vegas at Christmas is a hard place to beat."

"I don't think…"

He leaned forward and reached for her hand. She saw him coming and put both of her hands in her lap, so instead he just rested his large palm on the table in front of her. "Come on, Maxi. I have a suite—two bedrooms and a living room. It would be perfectly respectable. And, it's MAACO. Don't tell me you've never wished you could go to one of those holiday bowl games."

With a grin, she picked up a carrot stick and nervously broke it into pieces. "You're right. I have wished I could go."

"But…?"

"But Robin…"

"Robin has Tony and Sarah. Sarah's a nurse. An OB nurse. There's nothing that you could do for her in the three days you'd be gone that one of them couldn't do."

As she wavered between really-really wanting to go and really-really knowing she shouldn't go at all, he pressed forward. "It will be so much fun. We'd fly out the day before and come back the day after. Tony's loaning us the Viscolli G-5 so we wouldn't even have to deal with the crazy holiday travel at the airport."

All of her instincts screamed in panic to turn him down. She didn't go on out of town trips with men. She didn't share hotel suites with men. She didn't do anything with a man that would lead him to think that she'd be willing to…

But this was Barry. He didn't buy the tickets or get the hotel room in order to set a scene with her. He didn't have any preconceived ideas of what the trip would bring.

Against her own will, her mouth formed the words, "Sure. That would be a lot of fun." To hide her nervousness over what she just said, she picked up her sandwich and took a bite.

He relaxed and leaned back in his seat. "Really? That's great. We're going to have such a great time."

She held up a hand. "As long as you get two hotel rooms. Suite or not, I want separate rooms."

Barry nodded. "I'll see what I can do."

Maxine just smiled and took another bite and wondered, really, what she'd just gotten herself into.

CHAPTER NINE

Steven Tyler appealed to Maxine to dream on while her paintbrush maneuvered in time to the music, rapidly dotting the green landscape she had created with Scottish heather on the stretched canvas before her. Gray mountains rose in the distance and the gold of the rising sun reflected off the scabbard of the lone armor clad horseman riding wearily toward the keep.

One final stroke of her brush marked the end of the song and the completion of the painting. Maxine, barefoot in ripped jeans and a half-top, stepped back from the canvas and narrowed her eyes, seeking any flaw in the oils. As she shifted her eyes, the mirrored wall across from her caught her attention. Something about her stance made her look primitive, primal, elemental. She shook her head to clear the image of another painting as a mandolin heralded the next song, and Robert Plant began singing about the Queen of Light.

Satisfied, Maxine set her palette and brush down and rubbed the back of her neck with paint splotched fingertips. She felt drained, sucked dry, like she felt every time she finished a painting, but it was in no way a bad thing. In fact, she sought this feeling, this cleansing, perhaps, as her chief goal.

With natural grace, she slid across the hardwood floor of her studio and silenced the music. She rolled her head on her neck as she walked back into the main apartment.

Long before Tony entered their lives, Robin had worked two jobs to put Maxine and Sarah through college. Maxine lived with her even after college and after securing a good job with an advertising agency. While she tried to help Robin pay for tuition or living expenses or even food, Robin thwarted every attempt until Maxine just decided to start banking the money with the intent of handing Robin a paid tuition package the year after Sarah graduated. Before that could happen, Robin married Tony. So, Maxine had a large portfolio and no plans for it.

With Tony's sharp business mind, he took half of her savings and taught her how to invest it. With the other half, she purchased the top floor of a brownstone on Newbury Street. The two large apartments on that floor easily converted to one large apartment and one studio. With the help of a contracting company that Tony owned, she soundproofed the studio and installed a state-of-the art stereo system that played music with enough volume that she could feel the beat in her pulse, but kept the noise contained so as not to disturb everyone within a three-block radius.

She often found herself pulling all-nighters, rushing home from work, kicking off her heels, slipping out of the suit of the day, throwing on torn and tattered jeans and an old football jersey or sweatshirt from her college days and just painting and painting until the sun peaked through the blinds. Despite the artistic outlet her job afforded, she resented its intrusion on her purely creative side and often wondered, "when?"

When would she feel comfortable enough with her portfolio to quit that high paying job with the newly acquired office and shared secretary and just give in to her dreams of simply painting? Painting; the passion of her life; the succor her jaded soul required; the solace her troubled heart sought. When could she just paint?

Tony's guidance and mentorship had allowed her portfolio to grow and grow. Every quarter, Maxine watched the numbers and had almost reached her comfort level. She owned her apartment, she owned her car, and she owed no one anything. Maybe in another three months, she'd have the magic number savings that would allow her to quit her job and rely fully on her painting for the rest of her days. The very thought made fear and anxiety form into a tight little ball in her stomach. What if she couldn't succeed?

Maybe she needed to raise the number a little higher. Growing up the daughter of a drug addict who pimped herself out to whatever druggie boyfriend would take in her and her three girls made security extremely important to Maxine. So many nights she'd lay on her bare mattress or on dirty sheets next to one or both of her sisters and her stomach would growl with such intensity that the pain of hunger would claw through her body. The first twelve years of her life revolved around terror and hunger and pain. She needed that cushion of self-sufficiency to back her so that no matter what happened, no matter if she ended up completely alone and isolated from everyone she loved, she would still never be hungry again.

Maxine moved through her apartment. A brick wall on the far end made the room feel very "Newbury" Street to her. She loved it and had installed it, brick-by-brick, herself.

Her big red leather couch sat against that wall covered in bright pillows designed with stripes, polka-dots, zigzags—it didn't matter to Maxine. She sought a hodgepodge look with the patterns and kept a similar color scheme going. Angled with the couch sat a love seat in a red and blue with yellow floral design. Maxine found it at a flea market and fell in love with it so instantly that she sat on it while bargaining over the price because she worried someone else would come and take the treasure away before she could complete the deal. A large area rug with a large, modern floral design in muted reds and blues and soft yellows sat on the hardwood floor between the two couches. She covered the walls with her art, picking up little details from the furniture pillows or rugs or bright knickknacks and painting them to tie all of the room together.

Against the picture window looking out onto the street she dearly loved sat her Christmas tree. She surprised herself by going traditional with it—a green tree with reds and golds and silvers. She had it decorated with angels and stars. On the top of the tree sat a tacky plastic lit-up star covered in worn-out gold tinsel. Robin bought that to go on top of their very first Christmas tree when Maxine was sixteen. She'd been with Robin for just a few months, then, after being separated from her for two long years. As they put that cheap little star on the top of their sad little tree, they vowed that no matter what, they would win. They would win in this battle they called life—the pitiful hands they'd been dealt would win the house.

The first Christmas after Robin and Tony married, she and Maxine fought over who got to keep the star. They ended up drawing straws for it. Maxine won, and in the subsequent three Christmases, she had her sisters over for dinner and together the three of them decorated her tree and topped it with that star.

She moved past her living room and through her dining room with the stark black table and Amish backed-chairs. A flat gold bowl of red ornaments sat in the center of the table.

Maxine had remodeled the kitchen almost immediately upon completion of the studio. She loved to cook and loved to entertain, so she had a large island work station installed along with a commercial-grade stainless steel stove, double ovens in the wall, a massive refrigerator, and deep steel sinks. She could spend hours in the kitchen, preparing recipes, making big trays of perfect little hors d'oeuvres, applying frosting to a sister's birthday cake. She loved the whole art of preparing food and often hosted dinner parties with church friends or work colleagues.

She reached the sink and used the back of her hand to flip the handle to open up a stream of warm water. Before going to her studio to paint, she'd left a dish of olive oil by the sink. She dipped her hands in it and started scrubbing the paint off. The oil worked the oil paint off her hands in no time. Then she used a light soap to remove the oil.

Grabbing the towel she'd lain out for herself, she went back through the dining room and living room to enter her bedroom. This room she'd decorated in grays and turquoise. A thick gray rug covered the floor, a shade lighter than the walls. A turquoise spread covered the bed accented with dark and light gray pillows.

The open suitcase on the bed made her stop. Little butterflies of anticipation reawakened in her stomach and started fluttering around. Her heart beat a little bit faster and sweat beaded her upper lip. Why in the world had she agreed to go with Barry to Las Vegas?

Shopping bags covered the bed. For some reason, her extensive wardrobe didn't seem to suit for this trip. In a fit of nervous energy, she'd left work last night and gone straight to her favorite mall. New boots, new pants, new sweaters—Christmas and plain—new pajamas… they all lay on the bright spread while she put together outfits and tried to think of what else she'd need. Maxine knew they would be with friends, so she assumed there would be dinners out and such. That in mind, she tried to add some dressy and some casual until she just wanted to call him and cancel the whole thing.

Yet she knew, deep down, that clothes weren't the problem. The problem lay in the fact that she preferred to never be alone with a man, and somehow she'd managed to allow herself to agree to be alone with a man for several days, thousands of miles from home, and completely out of her element.

Maxine had always liked Barry. For some reason his immense size had never intimidated her. Now she realized that not only was he big, he was incredibly strong, and had spent a good portion of his life knocking down men at least as big and strong as him. If he wanted to…

The butterflies flew together and formed a ball of nausea. Maxine fisted her hand and pressed it against her stomach, pushing back old memories. Memories that had sent her racing to her studio to mindlessly paint for the last six hours. He wouldn't want to. He wouldn't force. He wouldn't do anything. Maxine could trust Barry. She had to make herself trust him.

Because if she couldn't trust him that would mean that she didn't win this hand she was dealt, no matter what.

The ringing of her phone brought her out of her little panicked moment. She snatched up the extension next to her bed. "Hello?"

Robin's voice answered. "Hi."

"Hey, sis. How's my niece?"

"Your nephew's still there. I think he's going to take up permanent residence."

Maxine chuckled as she opened her nightstand and pulled out a small pair of scissors. "You're not due for another two weeks."

"I know. I just kept hoping that maybe he or she would get tired of hanging out in my stomach and get ready to meet the world."

Maxine picked up a sweater and carefully cut off the tags. "As long as we aren't a Christmas baby, all will be good."

"I know. I've been dreading this week coming up." As Maxine folded the sweater and laid it in her suitcase, Robin continued. "I hear you're taking a couple of days off."

Maxine's busy hands stilled and she closed her eyes. "You heard about that, did you?"

"Can I ask you something?"

"Of course." Opening her eyes, she picked up the scissors again and methodically removed the tags. "As long as it's a question and not a lecture."

"No lecture. Question: Is there an end game in sight here?"

"How so?"

"Are you just going with the flow, or do you have an objective in mind?"

For the first time in her life, Maxine started to feel anger toward Robin. Robin, her sister, the one who saved her from unspeakable horror, the one who worked two jobs to put her through college—made her angry with this line of questioning. "I don't know what you think my objective might be."

She heard her sister sigh. "Listen. I just feel like you're getting involved in a situation that is going to get out of control."

"Oh, really? How?"

"Barry is really hurting right now. You are beautiful and wonderful and outgoing and nice. Most of all, you're nice. Kind of the antithesis of his late wife. I'm worried that he's going to rebound and end up getting hurt even more."

Anger spread across her shoulder blades and down her hands, where her palms started sweating. "I'm just a rebound, huh? Maxine, who bounces from man to man like a flighty little hummingbird. You think I'm not worthy of a real relationship because I don't ever have them? Is that it?"

Robin's response came very quickly, very hurriedly. "No. No, Maxi."

"So you're just saying that I am bound to hurt Barry?"

"No! That's not what I'm saying. I don't want either one of you to get hurt and I'm just worried that…"

"You're worried that he'll rebound and fall madly in love with me and I'll dump him after a couple of weeks, as is my normal pattern, and then both of us will be depressed lumps that you'll then have to contend with."

"Maxi, please. I just…"

"No. You listen. Barry and I are friends. Just friends. He had an extra ticket to this game because his wife will not be able to attend. And, despite MACCO and the holiday, he managed to swing getting an extra hotel room. You don't have to worry about Barry's virtue or his heart or anything. We've been friends for a long time and there's nothing wrong with that. Does it occur to anyone that Barry might need my friendship right now? That being able to count on it might help him through this season of his life?" She folded a pair of pants very precisely. When the seam wouldn't line up, she unfolded them and started over. "You know what? I have some packing to do. I love you. Have a great week and I'll see you Christmas Eve."

When she hung up the phone with shaking hands, she realized that wet tears streamed down her face. Beyond anger lay hurt; hurt feelings because Robin obviously thought so poorly of her. She went into her connecting bathroom and turned on the faucet. Looking in the mirror, she could see the fatigue from painting. Her eyes, normally a very bright green, stared dully back at her, wet with tears, rimmed in red. She broke eye contact with herself and leaned down to splash cold water on her face. As she dried her face with a soft towel the color of her bedroom rug, she went back to the bed and the suitcase and the clothes.

Fear didn't paralyze her from packing anymore. Instead, umbrage drove her to pack perfectly, completely, precisely—she went through her written list and managed to get it all packed in a short amount of time and all in one suitcase.

After changing into a soft flannel nightshirt, she brushed her teeth and left the list on her bathroom sink ready to pack the toiletries. It was late, almost midnight, and she had to meet Barry at the airport at nine. She set her alarm because she knew the traffic would be horrendous. She had no desire to keep Barry or his friends waiting in the morning.

The painting session, combined with the strong emotions, combined with the restless emotions of the last few days, lent to her exhaustion and she fell right to sleep.

CHAPTER TEN

Maxine enjoyed the plane ride. She got along well with Barry's friends and their wives. Dealing with clients on a regular basis made her feel at ease in social settings, and since this trip had the goal of attending a major football bowl game, she boarded the plane knowing she would enjoy the conversation with people whom she had at least that one thing in common.

When she first boarded, she met Bart and Melanie Jacobs. He was an attorney on the floor above Barry's. He had shocking red hair and pale blue eyes, and she had blonde frosted hair and green eyes. She immediately grabbed Maxine's arm and pulled her down onto the sofa next to her where she launched into a conversation about a little boutique on Newbury Street that Maxine knew well.

Right on their heels, Terrence and Kisha Lee boarded. He was a large man with skin the color of warm cocoa. From what Maxine knew from her conversation with Barry on their way to the airport, he had played with Barry for part of a season before an injury brought a promising career to a sudden halt. His wife spoke with a strong accent that Maxine identified as Haitian. Maxine soon found out that she owned a French restaurant in the art district and found herself as passionately engaged in conversation about cooking as she had been about shopping.

About two minutes before they would have to shut the door and leave them behind, Justin and Caitlyn Meyers rushed on board. Maxine knew that a decade earlier he had been a client of Barry's. He was tall and thin, his bald head shaved. She had curly strawberry-blonde hair and freckles. Caitlyn sat quietly until Maxine asked her what she did. When she found out that she was a homemaker with three kids, Maxine talked about Robin's impending birth and Sarah's occupation and discovered that Sarah had helped deliver Caitlyn's third baby.

Maxine didn't realize the level of apprehension she had over how they would treat her in Jacqueline's absence until it appeared that the apprehension had no place. All of Barry's friends treated her with warmth and courtesy and she immediately relaxed in their presence. The camaraderie of the men made the flight go quickly. They talked and laughed about old bowl games they'd seen, and in between her conversations with the wives, Maxine smiled and learned and enjoyed watching Barry interact with his friends.

She watched him talk, watched him gesture with his hands as he replayed some old college football play and felt her heart skip a beat. She wasn't there as his wife, but still felt strangely proud to be with him.

The plane ride ended quicker than she anticipated, and the cab ride from the airport to the hotel was incredible. Maxine had never been to Las Vegas before, and she couldn't look fast enough to see everything on The Vegas Strip that she'd like to see. Too quickly, they pulled up in front of the hotel.

The beautiful hotel had a spacious lobby that led to the entrance of the casino on one end and a line of restaurants and shops on the other. A massive Christmas tree dominated the center of the lobby and Maxine caught the wonderful smell of the pine sap as they went by it. The jingling sound of the slot machines interfered slightly with the Christmas music playing over the speaker system, but it made Maxine smile.

As they approached the desk, the concierge waved a hand and four bell hops appeared almost immediately, taking bags and suitcases up to the respective rooms. He greeted them all by name as he welcomed them to the hotel and handed the men gold keycards to the suites of rooms. All four couples shared an elevator to the top floor where they had five of the six suites on the floor. They agreed to freshen up and meet in one of the restaurants in an hour to get lunch.

Barry handed Maxine her own key card and pointed to her room. "I'm here," he said, tapping the door.

"I really appreciate you getting an extra room. I imagine between Christmas and the game, they've probably been booked since the game schedule was announced."

"It wasn't a problem. They had a last minute cancellation, so it worked out." Barry looked at his watch. "How long do you need to freshen up?"

"I just need to unpack. Is fifteen minutes okay with you?"

Barry shrugged. "No problem. I'll see you then."

Maxine went to her own room. She stepped into a small foyer with a low table against the wall that held a vase of fresh flowers in bright reds and soft creams. As she moved through the foyer into the living room, she smiled at the Christmas tree in the corner, decorated in a theme that matched the casino's. It even had some miniaturized house chips as ornaments. A bar separated a small kitchen from the room, and on either side of the room stood a door. The far wall had a glass door that opened up to a patio that overlooked the Vegas strip.

Maxine crossed the room and opened one of the doors. She saw a large four-poster bed and an adjoining bath. A quick rap on the door signaled the arrival of the luggage. While the twenty-something man in the cheap tuxedo carried her bags to the bedroom, she grabbed the purse she'd thrown on the couch and looked through it for a tip.

Once she was alone in the suite, she locked the door and slipped her shoes off. Maxine wandered around, examining the other bedroom—which was identical to the one she'd picked out—and the bathroom with the garden tub. She had a patio off her room, too, and stepped out into the cold, dry air to look down at the traffic below.

When she returned to her room, she quickly unpacked just in time for the rap of knuckles on her door. She opened it to find Barry standing in the doorway. With a smile, she invited him in. "What shall we do first, big guy?"

He slipped his hands into his slacks and rocked back on his heels. "Want to go play some slots?"

Maxine shrugged. "Eh. I don't think I want to gamble."

Barry visibly relaxed. "I'm glad. I don't really want to gamble either. But that's what the rest of the gang is doing this afternoon. What else is there to do here?"

"Tons. I want to see a show, though you don't have to go with me if you don't want to. And I want to see the Hoover Dam." She laughed and looked at him to watch his reaction to her next list item. "And I really want to go see a wedding officiated by an Elvis impersonator."

Barry laughed. "What?"

"I really do. I think it would be as good as any of the billed shows. I wonder if you can just go sit and watch."

"What do you hope to see?"

Maxine sat and threw her arm over the back of the couch. "No idea. I just want to find out."

Barry nodded. "Well," he said, "we can probably go after the game tomorrow."

Maxine sat forward and grabbed his hand in excitement. "Really?"

With a shrug, he turned his hand so that he could grip hers. Maxine realized they held hands and slowly took hers back. She put it on her lap and gripped it with her other hand. Barry didn't seem to notice as he stood and went to the kitchen. "Sure. Why not?"

"That's awesome. What about a show?"

He came out of the kitchen with a bottle of water. "I'd been kind of hoping that Elvis would make you forget the show." He softened that with a smile, which she returned in the humor that he intended. "I'm sure the other wives already have the tickets secured to a show. This is all of our first trip to a bowl game in Vegas. They usually have a whole schedule mapped out to the minute. Let's join them for lunch and see if there's anything you'd want to do with them." Maxine wondered if he realized that he included her in with the wives when he said, "other wives."

She enjoyed lunch with their group. After lunch, she and Barry separated from the couples, leaving them at the entrance of the casino while the two of them worked with the concierge and discovered a helicopter tour of the Hoover Dam. He pulled some strings and got them tickets on a flight that would leave from their hotel roof. They only had about twenty minutes before the flight departed, so they went straight from the lobby to the roof where they found the helicopter and pilot waiting for them.

Within ten minutes, the other passengers had arrived and they loaded into the helicopter and followed the pilot's instructions for fastening seat belts and putting on helmets that had built in speakers to provide a way for the pilot to give them the verbal tour.

They flew over the Grand Canyon and circled back to the Hoover Dam. Maxine sat by the window and Barry sat to her right. To get a better view, he angled his body so that he was pressed up against her back, looking out the window over her shoulder. It bothered her at first. She didn't like to feel trapped, especially by another person. So she leaned forward until her helmet hit the glass in front of her, trying to distance herself from him.

Some bump in the air, some air pocket or crosswind shook the aircraft making the other passengers gasp or exclaim. Barry's right arm came around Maxine's waist and stayed there even after the pilot smoothed them out. She immediately put both of her hands over his arm with the intent of prying it from her, but didn't. She stopped. It was time for this stupid fear of being touched by anyone—by men—to go away.

So the fingers that gripped his massive forearm

gradually relaxed. For the remainder of the three-hour flight, she slowly, inch by inch, relaxed against him, relinquishing the panic of being touched or held as she looked out the window first at the magnificence of God's creation as they flew down into the Grand Canyon, then at the brilliance of man's creation as they flew close to America's largest dam.

BARRY sat in the helicopter with his arm around Maxine, breathing in the scent of her hair, feeling the press of her warm, lithe body against his, and had to close his eyes to battle for focus.

To say that he had never acknowledged Maxine's attractiveness would quite simply be a lie. Even married, when he struggled with the pain of his wife's betrayal and wanting to keep everything right with God so that his prayers about his wife would be answered, he could not help but acknowledge Maxine's loveliness. Calling her beautiful would be an understatement. When she walked into a room, every man and many women would simply stop and look at her. Her physical beauty surpassed anything he could have ever imagined in a woman.

Except, beauty fades, and Barry knew it meant little. Once he learned how to redirect that initial punch of attraction every time he saw her, he almost got used to the way she looked. Then he got to know her spirit.

He had never met anyone so colorful in his life. She took life head-on, with a smile and a laugh. She took delight in little things like the wonderful taste of an appetizer at a social function, and took delight in fun things like getting tickets to a Celtics game. She was fun, and vivacious, and relished life. On top of that, her loyalty to those she loved knew no bounds. He'd watched her for three years with her sisters, with Derrick, with Tony, and stood amazed at the generous spirit she had for her family.

Getting to know her through sports, as platonic as it could possibly be, worked for him. She was just a "buddy" and he felt like he wasn't doing anything wrong—and nearly convinced himself of that. Sitting here, now, on this helicopter with his arms around her and her body pressed close against him, as he closed his eyes and fought for some measure of control against his attraction, he knew he'd been lying to himself the entire time.

Over the years, the shared football games and basketball conversations, and lately the workout sessions, had been nothing more than a way to spend time with her, however he could, in any socially acceptable way. He knew that should he ever desire to reconcile with God again, that would definitely be something he would have to face.

He wondered what to do about it. They had two more days, here. Should he pursue it? Was a quick bowl game trip to Las Vegas the right place for this? Would his pursuit cheapen what could be? He considered the line of men in Maxine's social life over the years and wondered.

A vibration in his pocket stopped his train of thought. He reluctantly relinquished his hold on her. When she shifted her body slightly away from his, he knew that the invite to touch had passed and that they would not return to their previous position. Then he looked out the window and saw the roof of the hotel approaching.

He fished his phone out of his pocket and saw the text message from Justin:

LAST MINUTE DINNER THEATER. LIMO IN 5 OR ELSE C U
AT BREAKFAST.

Their helicopter landed twenty minutes later, and they
unstrapped and handed the helmets back over to the pilot.
He showed his phone to Maxine. She looked at him, her
cheeks flushed and her eyes sparkling with the excitement
of the flight. "Wasn't that amazing?"

Barry tried to remember seeing anything out of the
window, but drew a blank. Instead, he remembered the feel
of her and the scent of her hair. "Absolutely. Definitely
worth the trip. I'd love to do it again."

She read the text message. "So it's just us for dinner,
then. Did you want to go anywhere in particular?"

With a shrug, he opened the door to the roof stairwell.
"The steak place here in the hotel works for me."

THEY headed straight to the restaurant without stopping
at their rooms first. They flashed their gold key cards and
found themselves seated almost instantly. While they
waited for their meals, Barry studied Maxine's face. She had
pulled out her phone, verified the local time in Boston, and
called to check on Robin. He watched her eyes in the glow
of the candlelight, watched them light up while she talked
with her sister about the baby and how Robin was feeling.
When she hung up her phone, she grinned at Barry.

"I don't think it will be much longer. Sarah's been
working the night shift lately, so she's been staying over
there while Tony works during the day."

Barry laughed. "I'm surprised Tony hasn't opened a

remote office out of his apartment."

"If there was room, I bet he would have by now."

"It's a good thing they haven't moved out to the coast, yet."

"He probably would have just hired a full time OB staff if they had," Maxine said, smiling as she put her napkin in her lap and leaned back in her chair to give the waiter space to set her salad in front of her.

Barry followed suit and took his spoon to his soup while they chatted about Tony and Robin. Their conversation moved from her family to football to working out to sports cars as they worked their way through soup and salad, thick T-bones, and a fruit and cheese plate.

As Barry signed the chit to have the meal billed to his room, Maxine suggested they walk the strip. "I know we saw it from the air this afternoon, but I'd love to see it up close at night."

"I think that's a great idea," Barry said. He helped her into her coat and slipped his on while they exited the hotel.

Maxine put her arms around herself. "Brr," she said. "I wouldn't have expected the desert to be this cold. I'm glad I thought to check the weather forecast before we left Boston."

Barry stepped closer intending to put his arm around her, hoping to help warm her, but she shifted away and pointed out some lighted sign. He watched her joy at all of the sights to see on their walk down the strip and enjoyed her much more than the man-made light show surrounding them.

Maxine surprised him when she took his hand. "Look!" She shouted. A woman in a wedding dress entered a building holding hands with a man in a tuxedo. Four girls in slinky red dresses and four men in tuxedos with matching red ties and cummerbunds followed. "Let's see if they're getting married," she said, pulling him forward.

She peered inside and laughed in delight. "Elvis is in there, all Blue Hawaii."

Barry looked over her head and grinned. "I can't see planning that."

She turned and looked up at him. He put a hand on either side of her head, boxing her in, and looked down at her. Her emerald eyes sparkled with joy and laughter, her cheeks and nose rosy with cold. "Planning what?" she asked with a smile.

"Planning to be joined together in holy matrimony by a 40-year-old man dressed like a dead rock star singing Blue Hawaii."

Maxine made a fist and playfully punched him in the stomach. "I think it would be fun as long as someone didn't try to take a pin and poke a hole in all the fun."

He slowly lowered his body so that he wasn't supported by his hands, but by his forearms, bringing him even closer to her. He could feel her body heat and only his knowledge of how she usually shied away from touch kept him from pressing all the way up against her. Instead, he stared down at her as the lights and the crowd and noise around him faded away.

Maxine stared up at him, and her smile slowly turned more serious as she looked away from his eyes and briefly to his mouth before looking back at his eyes. He desperately wanted to take that as an invitation to kiss her, but he had no desire to see her bolt. However, the temptation was too strong to ignore so he slowly, very slowly, just to give her time to get used to how close he was, to give him some signal that she would rather he not, he lowered his head until their breath mingled.

For the first time in her life, Maxine wanted—desperately wanted—to be kissed. The nerve endings in her lips came alive, aching, waiting, needing to feel Barry's pressed against hers. She held her breath, stared into his blue eyes, and noticed that they darkened when he watched the tip of her tongue dart out to lick her dry lips.

She wondered what to do from here. It seemed that if he wanted to kiss her, he would have already. A drive she didn't recognize compelled her to grab the lapels of his jacket and pull him closer. Just when she thought she would have to actually beg him to kiss her, he closed the distance and covered her mouth with his.

Maxine felt her breath shudder out of her body. No fear. She realized as her arm snaked around his neck and she raised herself up on her toes to get closer to him that she felt absolutely no fear.

How exhilarating!

He wrapped a strong arm around her waist and pulled her closer to him even as he stepped forward, pushing her further back against the window.

She wanted to feel him, touch him, caress him. A very base and visceral need rose up in her and made her head spin. Desperate to catch her breath, she ripped her mouth away and framed his face with her hands.

He pressed his forehead against hers and kept his eyes closed, breathing hard, gripping her hips with his hands. He smelled good. He felt good. She wanted to run her lips over his cheek, along his neck, feel his pulse under her lips.

He slowly raised his head and looked down at her while she leaned her head against the glass window behind her and solemnly returned his glance.

With achingly gentle movements, he brushed a strand of hair off of her face. Then he smiled, a smile that lit up his face and lightened his eyes. "Want to get married by an Elvis impersonator, Maxine?" he asked.

She somehow knew he was teasing, lightening the mood. But the answer popped out of her mouth as if from a wellspring deep inside of her. Before she knew what she was saying, the word was out.

"Yes."

CHAPTER ELEVEN

PRESENT DAY

As soon as **Maxine had** fallen asleep, Barry spent long minutes just staring at her, marveling at her beauty. He felt a thrill in every cell of his body at the sheer perfection, the indescribable loveliness of his beautiful bride. She presented such a tough exterior to the world, so confident, so self-assured. In the hours since the wedding ceremony, he had learned about a different person completely. In reality, she was so vulnerable and so fragile.

Despite the fact that she had visibly forced herself to relax each and every time he touched her, the fact was that she tensed up first and without fail, each and every time. Laying next to him, asleep, he reached out and tenderly ran his fingers through her raven tresses eliciting a contented moan from her in her dreams. There was no tension in her sleep, no fear, no unreasonable terror at his tender touch.

He lifted the covers, threw on his jeans, and slipped outside. He strolled over to the patio and opened the door.

The cold blast struck his bare chest and he thought better of it. He found her key, then, barefoot and shirtless, rushed to his room and threw on a cotton sweater. Looking at the time, he realized that the sun would soon rise over the desert.

Back in Maxine's room, Barry casually picked up the phone and dialed up room service. In a quiet voice, he ordered coffee, hot tea, and a continental breakfast and sides of breakfast steak and boiled eggs. He ordered pineapple juice, fresh cold milk, and four orders of yogurt. He asked that it be delivered in thirty minutes or so if possible.

Then he started to think. First, he reviewed the events of the previous evening. He had been engaged for less than two hours. During that time, he and Maxine got the paperwork handled and purchased the largest emerald encrusted diamond engagement ring this place had to offer. Then he had solemnly looked Elvis in the eye and answered, "I do."

Jacqueline had been dead and buried just over three weeks. Apparently, he chose to mourn his late wife by pursuing, marrying, and bedding the one woman whom he had found attractive since the very first time he had laid eyes on her. Any shred of self-respect he felt for himself after Jacqueline's betrayal vanished in a moment of self-loathing at his present low state.

The sick thing, the twisted thing, the awful thing that he could not have known until last night was that Maxine loved him. She loved him no matter how unworthy of accepting that love he felt. She loved him, she married him, and she surrendered to him. The look in her eyes when she said "I do," spoke volumes.

The terrible truth Barry wrestled with this morning, a truth that shook him to his core, was that he might not love Maxine in the same way. He felt like he had just stolen something he had no right to possess, like a low criminal. Like a deceitful thief. He felt dirty. He felt unworthy.

Room service quietly knocked and Barry bounded with surprising stealth and grace for a man of his bulk to catch the door before they knocked again. He handed the young man a huge tip, the crumpled cash from his right jeans pocket, and wheeled the cart inside himself. Peripherally, he heard the shower going in the next room. So, she was awake.

He poured himself a cup of hot tea and walked to the patio door. He held his cup in his right hand and leaned against the cool glass overlooking the rising sun, supporting his entire weight on his left hand.

He sipped the tea and contemplated how Maxine deserved so much better. She deserved so much more than he could offer. He would not run her home and introduce her to his family as the woman he had wedded and bedded in Las Vegas less than a month after his first wife died. He would not subject her to that kind of scrutiny. He would not subject himself to any backhanded whispered sneers. He refused to put them through that.

No. He would undo it. He would fix it. It was the least he could do for Maxine for the constant friendship and trust she had given him over the years. He resolved himself as the bedroom door opened behind him.

BARRY stood staring out through the patio door. He wore dark blue jeans and a cream colored sweater that stretched across his strong back. His feet were bare, and Maxine felt a little flutter of warmth at the intimacy of that. She thought back over the last several weeks, amazed at how the events transpired to bring them to this place, this here and now. Had it only been three weeks since Jacqueline's funeral? Since their shared dinner after fleeing from the church?

Barry turned as soon as she opened the door and their eyes met across the room. Maxine's smile froze at the stoic look on his face. "Hi." His voice sounded low, scratchy, thick. She wondered if he had slept at all.

"Hi." She smiled. She noticed the cup in his hand. "Is there coffee, too, or just tea?"

Using the cup, he gestured at the room service cart sitting next to the table and chairs. "I didn't know how to make the coffee, so I just ordered you some instead."

Warmth flooded her heart at his thoughtfulness. "Thank you." She crossed the room and poured herself a cup of coffee. Her hand shook a little bit. What did they do now? What did they talk about? How did she handle this first full day of being Mrs. Barry Anderson?

When she turned back around, she saw that he had silently moved and now stood next to the couch.

"Obviously, we need to talk."

She didn't like the sound of his voice. No warmth, nothing she had felt from him the night before existed in his tone. She gripped the cup so hard she was surprised it didn't shatter. "Yeah." Needing to ease her own tension, she teased, "Kind of a little late for that, isn't it?"

His bark of laughter signaled his agreement with her statement and she smiled a stiff smile as she crossed the room toward him. As soon as she sat on one end of the couch, with her back to the arm, he sat down, too, closer to the middle.

In a way, she was glad he didn't sit at the other end of the couch, thus leaving a huge expanse of leather between them. In a way, she wished he had, so maybe she wouldn't actually feel the warmth of his body and want to scoot closer to him. He set his tea on the coffee table and turned his body toward her. "I don't know what came over us last night—what came over me."

Maxine tilted her head and looked closely at his face. He had circles under his eyes. It didn't look like he'd slept at all. She put her cup down next to his and slid forward, fighting down years of survival instinct to take his hand. She cared about this man. She had cared about him for a long time. He was a dear friend, and considering the things that he had experienced over the years, she hated to think that she had added to any pain in his life.

"Shh," she said. Heart pounding in fear of being the first to move toward any kind of intimacy, she knelt next to him, one knee on the couch cushion while she planted her other foot on the ground to brace herself. Placing a hand on his cheek, she leaned forward and rested her forehead against his. "Last night was wonderful."

Barry groaned and gripped her hips with his hands. He closed his eyes and sighed. "Getting married wasn't the right thing to do."

"It's done, though."

When he opened his eyes, she leaned back away from the resignation she saw there. "I can undo it."

She raised an eyebrow. "Can you? It's legal, binding,

and consummated. What can you undo?"

He smiled for the first time since she came out of the bedroom. "I'm a lawyer, Maxi. I can undo it."

She wanted to scream, "No!" but instead started to shift back, to break the physical contact with him while she asked, "Do you really think we should?"

Before she could completely withdraw, he gripped her wrist to hold her still. "I value your friendship, Maxine. I've lost so much. I can't lose that, too."

Cupping his face with her hands, she gave him the gentlest whisper of kisses. "You haven't lost my friendship." She pushed away fully and straightened, pulling her wrist from his hand. She felt her pulse accelerate and her heart start to flutter. Panic made it hard to breathe, and she put a hand against her stomach. "What time do we need to leave for the game?"

Barry opened his mouth, then closed it again. He cocked his head and looked at her, then looked at his watch. "We have some time."

Maxine nodded. "Good." She rubbed her hands together, trying to stimulate some warmth. "Then let's eat, and I'll call one of the girls and see what everyone's plans are this morning." She froze when he reached out and gently took her left hand in his large grip. She looked down at him and saw him staring at her face. As soon as they made eye contact, he looked at her hand. "While you're out, I'll see about returning the ring."

How had she forgotten the ring? Wouldn't that have been the kicker? To go home with a wedding ring the size of Rhode Island on her finger? She felt a small tremble in her hands as she took the ring off and surrendered it to him. "Of course. I hope they'll take it back."

"I'll take care of it." His fingers closed around it and his hand formed into a fist. "Go ahead and make the phone call and I'll set out breakfast."

After breakfast, which ended up being the most tense, silent meal the two had ever shared, Barry went to his room. Maxine turned around in a circle in the middle of her huge suite, gripping the sides of her face, feeling as if the room would close in on her at any second. She wanted to scream and wail, but feared someone would hear, so she fell to her knees and sobbed, silently, heel of her hand pressed against her mouth to keep the sound down to low groans.

As soon as she felt like she could function, she rose to her feet and stumbled to her phone. Fingers quaking, she clumsily maneuvered the internet and worked the buttons until she found a flight out for Boston that morning. She called down to the front desk and requested a shuttle to McCarran, then very quickly packed.

She scanned the room for any rogue articles of clothing, and found Barry's shoes, socks, sweater, and jacket on the floor of the bedroom near the patio door. As much as she wished she could just sneak out without saying good-bye, she knew that was the wrong thing to do.

After washing her face and carefully applying makeup, Maxine took his folded clothes and left the sanctuary of her suite. She went to his door and lightly tapped.

He answered very quickly, opening the door as if expecting her. She noticed he'd showered and changed clothes.

"I, uh, didn't want to bother you," she started to say,

but he cut her off.

"You're not bothering me." He stood back and opened the door wider. "Come in."

No. No way. She couldn't go into his room. Chances are good she'd end up throwing herself at him, begging him to love her just a little bit, cherish her and protect her like Elvis had made him promise. Her heart stopped and she wondered where that thought had come from. "No thank you. I just wanted to bring you these things." She held out the neatly folded stack of clothes with his shoes carefully perched on top. "I decided to go on home. I'm not up for the game."

His eyes widened and he reflexively took the clothes from her. Before he could speak, Maxine pivoted and rushed back to her room.

"Maxi, wait!"

She turned as she unlocked her door and watched as he tossed the clothes into the room behind him before rushing toward her. "What, Barry?" Her voice sounded tired to her own ears.

"I'm going to get a flight out tonight, right after the game. I'll bring paperwork by tomorrow or the next day. Hopefully tomorrow since Friday's Christmas Eve. I'm not positive what hours the clerks at the courthouse are working Friday."

She almost asked him what he meant then realized he was talking about the annulment. For some reason, that made sadness overwhelm her again. But she knew it had to happen. "Sounds good," she said. "I'll be at Robin's. I just got a text from Sarah. Tony has some fire somewhere he has to handle out of town and won't be back until Friday.

So I'll just go straight there and stay through Christmas."

He nodded and she opened her door. He stood there, looking down at her. She waited several heartbeats before she spoke. "I had an amazing time, Barry. Thank you for inviting me."

Somberly, he nodded, his lips tight. "See you tomorrow, I guess."

She stepped into her room and shut the door in his face. The smile she'd forced faded away and her knees felt weak. Leaning against the door, she slid down until she sat with her back against the door and her face buried in her knees, silent sobs wracking her body.

CHAPTER TWELVE

Barry **brushed ice and** snow off his overcoat as he stepped into the lobby of Tony's apartment building. A security guard at the big circular desk looked up from his computer monitor and welcomed him by name. "Mr. Anderson, Mrs. V said to tell you that she and Miss Bartlett are running late, but to please go up and wait for them." He pushed a button on his console and an elevator door apart from the bank of elevators opened.

Barry nodded his thanks and shifted his briefcase to his other hand as he entered Tony's private elevator. It only went to the top floor, so the ride up twenty stories took no time.

He should have brought the annulment paperwork yesterday, but he got bogged down with work that accumulated during his brief absence. Since he couldn't ask his secretary or any of his paralegals to prepare the documents, he did it on his down time and didn't finish until late last night. Now here it was, not only Friday, but Christmas Eve. So even if she did sign tonight, they wouldn't be able to do anything with them until Monday.

What he ought to do, he thought, is just leave and make a lunch date with her for Monday, so that she didn't have to associate Christmas Eve with annulment paperwork. Still, getting it done as quickly as possible seemed better for all parties involved.

The elevator door slid open into Tony and Robin's apartment. He stepped out of the elevator into a small entryway. A coat stand beckoned. Out of habit, he removed and draped his coat on a spare hook. He set his briefcase on the small bench next to it and then walked fully into the apartment.

Stepping down a step into the living area, his feet sank into the plush carpet. The smell of gingerbread spice from the flickering candles on the fireplace mantle warmed him, and the glow of the huge Christmas tree standing next to the far window gave the room a loving, intimate feel. He had always felt as "at home" in Tony's apartment as he had in his own home, sometimes more-so. When Robin moved in after marrying Tony, that feeling had only become more intimate.

A large circular black leather couch surrounded the living area. Barry sat down and closed his eyes, weary to his bones. He hadn't slept much the last few nights. He scooted down and propped his feet on the coffee table, intending to doze until Maxine came back. Something pushed against his back and he shifted again, trying to get comfortable.

He winced and reached behind him, pulling a sketch pad out of the cushions. He glared at it, as if it were the cause of all of his problems, and started to toss it to the table but paused.

After some hesitation, he opened it, feeling a little like a kid sneaking a look at Christmas presents, or the pesky brother reading big sister's diary. Without permission, it would be wrong to look at this, but Maxine was the only artist in the house and the temptation overwhelmed him. So, with an ear tuned for the sound of the elevator's hum, he started flipping through the pages.

He had very little actual exposure to any of Maxine's work. He had only ever seen the pieces Tony owned. Only what he saw in the sketch pad stunned him. He didn't know it was possible to create the details he saw with a mere pencil. He didn't know that moods and entire depths of emotion could be portrayed in plain black and white. Reaching over to the lamp next to him, he flipped it on for better light by which to see.

The first sketch portrayed Robin, laughing and grinning, holding a pair of baby booties behind her back while Tony tucked a strand of hair behind her ear, looking at her with such an expression of love that the page nearly sizzled with it. Barry smiled, remembering that was how Robin had told him she was pregnant, by handing him a pair of baby booties. Another one showed Sarah in her nursing uniform, her curly hair barely contained by the clips that secured it back, her eyes serious behind her trim glasses.

He flipped the page and paused, staring at his own face drawn four different times on one page, showing different angles and expressions. She captured the details of his face so perfectly that it was like looking in a mirror. The next three pages were of him, lifting weights at the gym, sitting in that impossibly little metal chair at their breakfast cafe, standing by his Jeep with his skull cap pulled low over his ears while he drank a bottle of water after a morning run. He smiled and turned another page.

His stomach turned while he stared at the drawing. It was a woman, an older version of Robin, with haggard lines on her face and dead eyes. Her stringy, dirty hair crawled up in greasy strands out of a rubber band behind her neck. She sat on a worn couch wearing a T-shirt and jeans, staring down at the inside of her arm while a man with dark hair and hard, mean eyes filled a syringe from a dirty spoon with confidence born of experience. Glasses and a bottle of gin, a few beer cans, and cigarette butts littered the table in front of them.

Barry knew Maxine's childhood story. He had defended Robin's father a few years ago against murder charges. He knew enough of the story to know that the woman in the sketch represented their mother and her boyfriend, the man and woman whom Robin's father had slain.

The next few pages showed more of Robin, Tony, and Sarah. Robin in varying stages of her pregnancy, Tony in different poses, Sarah in various moods.

Then he saw himself again, more close-ups of his face, one of him gesturing at a football game on television.

Eagerly, he turned to the next page. Sick fear churned inside his gut before a slow rage overtook the feeling. A man loomed over a girl on a bed, one hand covered her mouth, the other pawed at the waistband of her pants. He leered down at her, his eyes insane, mean, unspeakably selfish. His unbuttoned shirt revealed a tattoo of an eagle on his chest. Barry didn't like recognizing it, but the girl beneath him was a very young Maxine. Hatred and tears filled her terrified eyes while she clawed at the hand covering her mouth. She had her knees bent as she struggled against her molester.

He didn't want to look at the picture anymore, so he turned the page and noticed the tremor in his hand. It was the last page in the book, and it was of him again, but not in this apartment like the others. This was in Vegas, in Maxine's bed, her head on his shoulder, his arms around her, her hair spread over them like a blanket.

He flipped back to the previous page, then forward again to the last one. So many questions answered from a simple pencil sketch. He had known Maxine's story. He had known that her drug addict mother had moved her and her three daughters from man to man, pimp to drug dealer. He had known that Robin and Maxine and Sarah's early years had been the building blocks of nightmares.

After serving fifteen years for dealing cocaine, Robin's biological father had walked out of prison and promptly murdered Robin's mother along with her current sleazy boyfriend. That double murder had sent Robin and Maxine into the system and young Sarah to her adoptive parents. He'd known that as soon as Robin turned eighteen, she got a job at Hank's Place and, with the help of her employer, obtained legal counsel and gained custody of Maxine. When Maxine was fifteen, they'd finally lived together as a family.

He had intellectually known all of that, but somehow had never applied it to Maxine; not to the Maxine he knew. She was so happy, so vivacious, so full of life that it never occurred to him to equate her with the girl who cowered in a closet while she listened to the gunshots that took her mother's life, to the young teen who clawed at the hands of the man with the eagle tattoo on his chest.

Not ready to face her right now, Barry shoved the

sketchbook back into the couch and sprang up. He hurried now, afraid that they'd step off the elevator any moment, worried that they'd cross paths in the lobby. He snatched up his coat and briefcase and left, pushing against the floor of the elevator with the bottom of his feet as if he could make it go faster. Thankful to find a lobby empty of anyone he knew, he mumbled some excuse to the guard and exited the warm building into the icy wet blast of the Boston Christmas Eve.

MAXINE laughed as she and Robin stepped off the elevator, bags in hand. "You shouldn't wait till Christmas Eve to go shopping, especially nine months pregnant," she said with a smile.

"I hate shopping." Robin set her many packages on the floor while she unbuttoned her coat and slipped it off her shoulders.

"Yes, I know, silly, but it still has to be done and waiting until Christmas Eve isn't going to make it any better."

"You're right. But it's done now."

"I just hope we can get them wrapped before Tony and Sarah get here."

Robin froze. Maxine had a moment of panic thinking she was about to say that the baby was coming. Instead, she put her hands to her cheeks and said, "Wrapping paper!"

Maxine hugged Robin, love flooding her heart. "I brought some. I know you, you see."

"Ugh! I can't wait to have this baby! I can't think when I'm pregnant."

They set up a wrapping assembly line in the dining room, working quickly while they chatted. "You haven't told me much about your trip," Robin said, folding the corners of a box that contained an engraved stethoscope for Sarah.

Maxine felt her fingertips get cold. She paused cutting the paper around a new scarf for Tony. What should she say? Should she say anything at all? "It was cool. We took a helicopter tour."

"Yeah," Robin said dryly. "You've said all that."

The scissors fell out of her hand and clamored onto the table. Tears welled up in Maxine's throat then, with a sob, poured out of her eyes. Robin immediately put down everything she was doing and wrapped Maxine into her arms, as she had when she was a little girl—when they were both little girls. "What's wrong?"

Maxine fought to control her voice long enough to blurt out, "Robin, I love Barry."

Robin had been rubbing her shoulder blades, but her hands froze. "What?"

Putting both heels of her hands against her eyes, attempting to stop the flow of tears, Maxine backed away. "I do. I love him. And I'm in love with him."

"Maxi." Robin said the word on a sigh and Maxine immediately felt defensive. She almost knew what her sister would say next. "You're in love all the time. Men come and go…"

The tears dried as a touch of anger wormed through. "Stop." Robin stopped with her mouth open, obviously unaccustomed to Maxine's anger. Maxine continued, "Stop talking. I have never come to you crying over any man. I'd appreciate it if you would respect my feelings."

"I…"

Maxine held up a hand. "No. I know your opinion about my relationship with him. I've listened to every word you've said. You don't approve. I get it. You think I will chew him up and spit him out. He's been hurt. Blah blah whoopity blah. The fact of the matter is that I am the one crying. I am the one hurt. And what you're not going to do is try to make me into some frigid, man-eating black widow who just leaves remnants of past relationships in her wake."

Robin reached out and touched her shoulder. "Maxi, I don't think that about you. I love you and admire your spirit and your nature. I've never thought that about you. But you have regularly professed love for one man or another since you were in high school."

Maxine took her sister's hand and looked her in the eye. "I've always hoped that the next guy, the next relationship, would make me forget. But they never have." More tears filled her eyes, spilled down her cheeks. "I kept thinking that this one could hold my hand and I wouldn't feel terrified that he'd pull me down, or that one with his arm around me in a movie wouldn't make me feel like I was drowning in fear."

Robin cried now. Few could relate the way she could. "I understand."

"But with Barry it's different. This weekend I realized how much I care for him. And I realized I am in love with him."

Robin paused and tilted her head. "But?"

With a sigh, Maxine squeezed Robin's hand and let it go. She picked up the scissors again and went back to cutting. "But—his wife has been dead for less than a month. But—he's twelve years older than me. But—he's your husband's best friend. But—he's undergoing a spiritual crisis right now."

Maxine heard Robin clear her throat. "Speaking of that," she said, picking up the tape again. "You haven't been to church since Jacqueline's funeral."

With a sigh, Maxine finished cutting the paper and started folding it around the box. "I know. That's what I mean. Now isn't good for Barry."

"So what will you do?" Robin held a piece of tape out on the tip of her finger.

Maxine took the offered tape. "I don't know what to do. I've never been in love with a man before. I guess give him some room."

"Why don't you pray about it?"

Her fingers paused on the package and she looked at her sister. "I know you get something out of that, but honestly, Robin, I never have. I don't understand how you do it. I don't know what to say or how to hear an answer."

Robin tilted her head and looked at her very seriously. "Do you believe God answers?"

"I don't know." She quit messing with the package and pulled a chair out to sit down, suddenly feeling very tired. "I don't know."

Robin pulled the chair next to her out and sat down, angling so that their knees touched. She reached out and took Maxine's hands. "Matthew seven promises us that

God will answer our prayers. What you need to do is relinquish that final hold you have on the control in your life to God, trust Him, and you will find an amazing whole new world out there with direction and purpose and security."

Maxine felt a longing in her heart, a physical tugging. Her breath caught so suddenly that she had to clear her throat. "I don't know how."

Robin smiled. "Let me pray for you. Just relax and close your eyes and let me pray." Robin bowed her head and after a moment, Maxine followed suit. Robin's voice very gently washed over her as she began praying. "God, thank You for my sister. Thank You for saving us, thank You for bringing us together all of those years ago. Thank You for Your son, Jesus."

Memories flooded Maxine's mind, of stench and drugs and screams and blood. She smelled gunpowder and felt hunger pains and fear. "Lord, I would like to pray for her right now. I'd like for You to guide her to You, to give to her what You have given to me; peace that passes all understanding, love beyond all measure, deep and abiding joy over anything else. Help her to trust You like she has never trusted another person. Teach her how to find in Your Word the direction she seeks, and answers to the questions that plague her."

The memories that assaulted Maxine faded into the background and a mantle fell over her, as if someone had laid a blanket over her shoulders. She felt her hands tremble in Robin's as a warmth flooded her body.

"If her love for Barry is what You would have, Lord, give her wisdom in how to handle the situation so that Barry returns to Your arms and they can worship You together. Thank You, God, for allowing us to come to You this way, for being our Father, for loving us so much. Thank You for the gift of your Son, and for our salvation. It is in Your Son's holy and precious name that I pray, Amen."

Sobs shook Maxine's shoulders as she fell out of her chair and onto her knees at her sister's feet. She lay her head in Robin's lap, against her sister's ample pregnant belly, and cried while Robin soothed her with hands running through her hair and her voice speaking calming, soothing words.

CHAPTER THIRTEEN

Sunday afternoon after Christmas, Maxine went back to her apartment to get ready for evening services at church. Weary, she got out of Derrick's primer gray Shelby Mustang and watched him squeal down her street. She had not come home in more than a week. First, on the Vegas trip with Barry, then spending the nights at Robin's house while Sarah worked the third shift and Tony worked out of town.

She spent Christmas Eve with Robin and Tony, Sarah, and Derrick and they all woke up Christmas morning to full stockings, compliments of Santa Tony, and a huge waffle breakfast, compliments of Chef Maxine.

Christmas evening, Derrick, Sarah, and Maxine went to the movies and back to Sarah's apartment for coffee and gingerbread cookies made by Sarah's adopted mom. By the time they finished their third round of Trivial Pursuit, during which Derrick and Sarah traded insults with alarming regularity, Maxine felt exhausted. Derrick offered to drive her home, but they quickly discovered that the rain which had started that evening had turned into an ice storm that trapped them. Sarah's roommate was stuck at the hospital working the third shift, so Maxine took her room. Derrick, who seemed uncharacteristically angry at the situation, took the couch.

All she wanted was her bathtub with the jets and whirlpools and some loud music drowning out any thoughts she might have the energy to think. As Maxine wearily climbed the steps to the entrance of her apartment, balancing boxes and bags of Christmas presents, an overnight bag slung over her shoulder, she saw a movement out of the corner of her eye. Startled, she turned and saw Barry walking toward her. He wore a heavy wool coat the color of burnt charcoal and a black ski cap pulled low over his ears. Her heart skipped a little beat at the sight of him. She hadn't seen him since the hallway of the hotel. "Barry. Hi."

He stopped at the base of her steps. From the middle step, she met him at eye level. "Where have you been?"

She frowned. "Been?"

"I've been trying to call you since last night."

"Oh. We got trapped by the ice."

"We?"

Maxine looked down the street where Derrick's car had disappeared and back to Barry's scowling face. "What's going on?"

"I'm a little curious about who just dropped you off."

Maxine felt her jaw clench in reaction to the supposition. "Oh. Well, that would be that 'none of your business' person." She whirled around and reached into her pocket to grab her keys to the outer door of her building when she heard the sound of the throttle of the engine of the Mustang pause behind her and Derrick's voice call out to her.

"Maxi!"

Closing her eyes and taking a deep breath, she turned and smiled. "Did I forget something?"

"You might need these," he said as he held her keys out through the open window. "They must have fallen out of your coat. I found them on the front seat." He looked at Barry. "Hey man. Check out the Christmas present from Tony!" He grinned as he revved the engine.

Barry nodded back. "He told me he was on the lookout for one but never came back with whether he'd found it or not. It sounds fantastic."

"Needs a paint job and a little bit of work. She'll be a beaut' when she's done."

"Oh, yeah."

Looking at Barry with her lips tight, Maxine shoved her boxes and bags toward him. With surprise on his face, he grabbed them to keep them from falling to the snowy ground while she carefully stepped down from the steps and walked to the curb. "Thank you for turning around. It would have been a cold afternoon waiting for someone to bring me keys."

Derrick laughed. "I bet. Merry Christmas again, and thanks for the jacket."

"Bye."

She turned around and glared again at Barry. "What were you asking again?"

"Nothing." He cleared his throat while she unlocked her door. "Always good to see Derrick None of My Business DiNunzio."

Maxine glared at him and fumbled with her keys with gloved hands. Barry said, "Hey, I'm sorry. I just…"

"Sorry? You just? What kind of girl do you think I am,

exactly?" She pushed open the door and started up the staircase to her apartment. Her voice echoed against the blank walls. "Never mind. You don't need to answer that." She stopped outside of her apartment door and turned to look at him. "I'm sorry. I shouldn't have gotten angry. I'm just worn out." She took the strap of her overnight bag from his shoulder. Setting the bag at her feet, she reached for the boxes he held. "I'll take these."

Barry shifted so that she couldn't take anything from him. "I'll carry them inside."

With a shrug, Maxine opened the door. "How was your Christmas?"

"Christmas?" Barry followed her into her apartment. She led the way to the living room, where she tossed her keys and purse on the black coffee table and gestured toward the tree. "You can set those things there, if you want. I'll sort through it all later." While he completed that small task, she noticed the light blinking on her answering machine. "Did you leave me a message?"

Barry turned and took his cap off as he did so. "No. I called your cell. Several times."

Snapping her fingers as if she just remembered something, she took her cell phone out of her purse. "I turned it off at the movies yesterday and forgot to turn it back on." As she pressed the button to power up the phone, she went to her desk and hit the "play" button on her answering machine.

"Maxine. Hi. This is Henry. From the office." Maxine shook her head. As if she wouldn't recognize or place the team member from a huge project she's been working on. "Listen, our meeting with Crow has been moved up to Monday morning. Vic is counting on you to make story boards. Just go with the last good idea we had. Thanks.

Nine a.m. Looking forward to it. Hope you have a good Christmas."

Maxine froze. The last good idea they had was to discard everything and start fresh Monday morning. She had missed a full week of work. She snatched the phone out of the cradle and checked recent calls. This message had been left Thursday evening—the day before Christmas Eve.

"Maxi..."

Remembering Barry, she slowly turned. "Barry, I can't talk right now."

She couldn't avoid doing the presentation. Crow Chicken was the biggest client to cross her firm's threshold ever. Daniel Crow had searched the city high and low for an agency that could present him with fresh new ideas, and he had chewed up and spit out nearly everyone on the block. Mitchell & Associates had an opportunity to step up to the big leagues, here. She didn't think Crow would accept the excuse of a junior associate who ran off to Vegas to watch a football game as a good enough excuse to postpone this meeting.

The only problem was she had nothing. Her mind drew a blank on any good idea she might have. Knowing how many firms he'd dismissed made any idea she could come up with in those terrifying first few minutes seem tired, used, unsellable. The right presentation would land her the much sought after partnership. The wrong one, well...

Her phone rang, startling her. Recognizing Sarah's number, she distractedly answered.

"Just checking to make sure you got home okay. Derrick drives like an idiot, and the roads are still so bad."

"I'm fine. Listen." Groaning out loud, she decided desperate times called for desperate measures. "Sarah, ' what's the first thing that comes to mind when you think of fried chicken?"

"The hapless genocidal slaughter of innocent hormone-fed fowl for the sake of human convenience and the almighty dollar. Oh! And greasy fried food clogging arteries and raising cholesterol, leading to high-blood pressure, Type II Diabetes, and heart failure. Why do you ask?"

Realizing the folly of asking her vegan sister's opinion on the matter, she snapped back. "Oh, give me a break. You couldn't help me out just a little here, could you?"

"Sorry, sis. Best I can give you. Want to talk about spinach?"

"Gee, thanks." She rubbed a sudden ache in the center of her forehead. "My entire career may be at stake, and now the only thing in my head is a gruesome picture of chickens running in terror from carnage while innocent diners drop dead from coronaries. Really appreciate it."

"Just keep thinking of it the next time you're trying to decide between the Caesar salad and the chicken salad. Then I'll know I've accomplished something."

Maxine blinked. "Sarah, you wouldn't pick the Caesar salad, either, because it has cheese in it, and, horror of horrors, dressing made from dairy products and salty little fish."

Sarah chuckled. "Well, for you, being that you are an unrepentant carnivore, we're taking it slow. Baby steps, hon. Baby steps."

Maxine rolled her eyes and ended the call abruptly. "Never mind. I've got to go. I love you." She turned to Barry, who was unbuttoning his coat. "What about you?"

"Me?"

"What's the first thing you think of when you hear the

words fried chicken?"

He responded without thinking. "Sunshine."

"Sunshine?" Her brow wrinkled in concentration. She still looked in his direction, but she didn't see him anymore. She saw sunshine. "Sunshine. Okay. What else?"

"Gingham checkered table cloth on lush green grass, blue skies, summertime, white dresses, potato salad." He shifted the coat from his shoulders and removed the envelope from the inner pocket.

The full power of her green eyes suddenly hit him once more, accompanied with a smile that warmed him more than that sunshine he'd just alluded to ever could. "Barry, you are wonderful. Absolutely wonderful."

She abruptly left the room, and he gave in to the impulse to follow her. "I think we need to talk, Maxine." He followed her through the apartment and through a door that led to her studio. He stopped suddenly, enveloped in a whole new world.

The studio was the size of an entire apartment. Bright light from the fluorescent lights she turned on lit the room with a white glow. Along one wall, supplies filled the shelves; paints and brushes and pencils and containers. A huge basket of clean rags sat on a shelf and a large basket of dirty rags overflowed below. One bookshelf held book after book after book of sketch pads. Against every wall, on every surface, she had stacked canvases; some empty, most completed.

Maxine went to a closet in the corner and opened it. Even more supplies lined the shelves in the closet. She drew out a stack of white drafting boards and shut the closet with her heel. "I know we need to talk, Barry. But I really need to work." She looked at him while she set the boards on her drafting table.

"Yes. But give me five minutes to show you this paperwork and we can meet for lunch tomorrow to go over it."

Maxine reached behind her head and started gathering up her long black tresses. Barry remembered the silky feel of her hair against his skin and suddenly and inexplicably missed it. "It will have to wait. I need to get this down before I lose it."

She grabbed a pencil from the holder in front of her and started sketching more quickly than he'd ever seen. It looked like her hand moved in double time.

Barry moved up behind her and watched a nearly identical scene to the one he had imagined unfold onto the blank space before her. A wrinkle of concentration appeared between her brow, and he found himself wanting to kiss it away. Within minutes she had the basic outline of people picnicking in a sunny field. The rough sketch looked perfect, and he watched as she set it aside and started working on a new scene on a fresh board.

"Snoop around all you want. I'll be done in a few minutes," Maxine said, her voice completely distracted, her mind elsewhere.

Curious, he moved toward a stack of canvases propped next to the window and began to inspect them. He started out just absently thumbing through the paintings, but ended up engrossed in them. They ranged in styles from abstract images, to portraits of photographic perfection, to landscapes. She had beautifully crafted each painting, filled them with detail, and imparted a range of strong emotions.

He moved to the shelf of sketch pads. Hundreds of them, he was sure it was hundreds, were stacked neatly and labeled with dates. Some ranged months at a time, some covered only a day. Deciding to fully accept her permission to snoop, Barry picked one out at random. The date on the spine went back five years, and he found sketch after sketch of Robin and Sarah. Another one chronicled Robin and Tony's wedding, detailing the elegance and grandness Tony had insisted upon. Book after book started giving Barry a view of her life from her eyes, something so few people could convey.

Three sketch pads were out of place under a box of paints. They were all over a decade old, and each had only one date on them. His hand trembled slightly as he opened the cover of the first one, instinctively suspecting the horror that would greet his eyes.

This drawing wasn't as—controlled—as the one he'd seen in Tony's apartment. The emotions of the artist poured out onto the page, making the lines almost jerky, the background details not as important. However, the details of the man were excruciatingly exact, down to a frayed buttonhole. The tattoo of the eagle on his chest was more exposed, and Barry saw that the tip of the wing headed toward the man's shoulder. His eyes moved lower on the page, but where Maxine should have been was just a shadow; no details at all.

He knelt on the floor next to the shelves and turned page after page as the image haunted him over and over again. Different rooms, different clothing, showing him that this wasn't a one time incident. On drawing after drawing, the girl remained shadowed.

"I used to have nightmares about it. I'd wake up and draw and draw until I couldn't even move my hand anymore." Her voice startled him. She stood directly behind him, her chin almost resting on his shoulder. "I burned most of the books, but eventually, I learned to keep them. I try to think of them as therapy. It was years before

I could put myself in the picture."

Barry cleared his throat. "Who is he?"

"His name's Monty Jordan." She settled onto the floor next to him. "He was a foster parent when I was fourteen." She drew her legs up and rested her chin on her knees.

"Fourteen?" His voice came out sounding like a harsh whisper, almost pulled from him.

Maxine nodded. "Robin and I went there together. That was our fourth home in less than two years. He wasn't entirely fond of someone with mixed blood living under his roof and had all sorts of ways to show me."

"What happened?"

She smiled, still remembering absolute shock entering those evil eyes. "Robin caught him in the act one day and stabbed him with his own knife." Maxine shuddered. "I was covered in his blood when the cops got there. The paramedics took me, too, because I was so bloody and hysterical they couldn't figure out if I was hurt or not. Thankfully, the doctors examined me thoroughly and found enough physical evidence on me to put Monty in prison for a while." She tore her gaze from his and looked at the floor in front of her. "The hard part was getting separated from Robin after that. They sent her to a home for girls, and kept me in the foster system. It was a terrifying year before she was able to get out and several more months before she could get me."

Barry swallowed. Rage and pain boiled inside his chest, choking him. "Maxi…"

She turned her head back around. "Hey, it's all a long time ago, now. I had an outlet for all of it. I never even dream about it anymore." She shook her head. "Well, sometimes I do. The other night I watched a bad scene in a movie at Robin's. So I did what I do. I drew it out, gave it its own life, and then let it die again."

"How can it be that easy?"

She laughed and turned to kneel, covering one of his hands with both of her own. "You think any of this was easy? This was twelve years ago. I still... a man trying to touch me—" She paused and looked down, a flush covering her cheekbones. "Barry, you're the first man who has ever even kissed me." She shifted until she faced him, both of them kneeling on the wooden floor, the sketchbook the only thing separating them. Without thinking twice, she took it from his hands and tossed it on the floor next to her. "You're the only man who has never once made me feel terrified."

"There's no way for this to work, Maxine," he said as her arms went around his neck. She felt his pulse beneath her touch, his heart pounded so fast and hard she could almost hear it. Despite his words, his hands skimmed up her sides and hauled her closer to him.

"Shut up, Barry." Her legs hooked around his waist, her arms locked behind his thick neck, and she dragged his mouth to hers. For a moment, he remained completely still, fighting it with all of his will. It was a worthless battle and, with a groan of surrender, he wrapped his arms fully around her in return and kissed her back.

Maxine felt everything become right and perfect in the world the second his arms went around her. She sighed and hummed, feeling her love for Barry flow through every nerve ending in her body, making her head reel and her fingertips ache to touch his skin.

The second his lips softened against hers and he deepened the kiss, she heard her phone ringing. Maxine didn't move, didn't make a move to stop, so Barry ignored it too. Until his phone rang. From his pocket, the tones of a special ring broke through the fog that enveloped them. He lifted his head and shifted her away from him. "That's Tony."

Maxine shook her head as if to clear it and jumped up. "My phone's ringing, too." She dashed out of the room while he took the call. "Hey, brother."

Without preamble, Tony said, "It's time. St. Mary's."

Knowing without asking for clarification, Barry stood. "I'm close by. See you there."

Maxine came rushing back into the room. "That was Sarah. Robin's in labor."

"I know. I'll drive. My Jeep will do better on these roads." He held out a hand and she placed her slim one in his. "Let's go have a baby," he said, leading her from the room.

CHAPTER FOURTEEN

After waiting with nothing to do with her hands for nearly an hour, Maxine begged Derrick to run to her apartment and retrieve her boards and colored pencils. If the baby came between now and eight, she'd have to go to the meeting. If not, someone from her office would need to have them, anyway. She might as well get them ready.

Normally, she'd have everything scanned into the computer for an electronic presentation. Due to the rescheduling, there was no time for that, so they'd go the old fashioned route and present with just her boards. The hard part, getting her ideas down, had been accomplished. Coloring in was mindless, but it kept her hands busy and at least part of her mind occupied.

She sat with Barry and Derrick in the private waiting room connected to the room Robin occupied. Occasionally, Tony came in for a break, and twice Sarah stepped in to give them a brief update, only to go back into the room almost immediately.

Eventually, activity increased through that door, and every so often the sound of Robin's voice reached them. Sometimes she cried. Sometimes she screamed. Maxine's fingers gripped the pencil tighter and tighter as the hours passed.

She sat on the vinyl couch, supporting a large board on her thighs with her feet propped on the table in front of her. She glanced out of the corner of her eye as Derrick sat on the cushion next to her. "We never talked about it this weekend. How's school going, Derrick?"

He ran a hand through his hair. "Half of it is a complete waste of time. The other half is only mostly a waste of time. I guess it was my mistake telling Tony I wanted to manage hotels. I should have picked something that didn't require a degree."

"Nah. He would have sent you anyway. Besides, college was fun." She threw down the yellow pencil and selected the shade of red she wanted to use to color in the gingham cloth on the emerald green grass. Emerald green was her trademark color. All of her ads had it in there somewhere. "Sometimes, I wish I wasn't in the nine-to-five world and I still had Art 101 at ten."

"Hmm. Well, I happen to know that most of what they are teaching is obsolete and I already have practical experience with the few things they teach that are useful. Usually, I feel decades older than the other kids. And, there's the fact that my idea of a good time isn't going to O'Malley's Pub and getting falling down drunk three nights a week. That's a bit of a problem."

She laughed. "Yeah? What is your idea of a good time, Derrick?"

He shrugged, a habit brought from his life on the streets that he never shed. "A quiet evening, an intelligent woman, good food, stringed instruments."

"Well, there's that fiddle some nights at O'Malley's."

His smile looked strained. "How can you sit there and color like that?"

With a smile, she colored in the blue eyes of the little girl happily munching on a chicken leg. "You nervous, Derrick?"

"Honestly? I'm very nervous."

A piercing scream came through the door and the pencil Maxine held snapped in two. With a sigh, she set the board on the floor by her feet. "Yeah, me too."

"Why don't you go in there, Maxi?" Barry asked from the chair across from the couch. For the last hour, he'd pretended to find a two year old parenting magazine highly engrossing, but had actually surreptitiously studied Maxine, noticing how she gradually paled as the minutes stretched into hours, watched the lines around her lips slowly tighten.

She shuddered and shook her head. "No way."

Another scream came, peppered with some rather ingenious colorful language. Maxine ran her hands through her hair. "Aren't there drugs or something they can give her?"

"She didn't want anything. She wanted to do this all natural." Barry stretched in the little chair and contemplated going for a cup of tea from the coffee shop across the street.

Maxine surged to her feet and paced the small room, avoiding looking through the small window of the door separating her and the rest of her family. "How can you be so calm and collected? Can't you hear that?"

"I have three sisters, Maxi, with seven kids between them." His eyes followed her pacing around the room. "You'll feel better if you would go in."

She stopped in her tracks. "Um, no I won't. Trust me."

Barry laughed. "Why?"

"Because there's pain in there. And blood. And probably needles. No way. I'm not going. I'll just wait here until they get everything cleaned up and I'll never know how the whole process happened." She visibly jumped with another scream.

He grinned. "You don't like blood?"

"What a stupid question. How can anyone actually like blood?"

"I'll have to remember to tone down some of my football stories."

She heard Tony's voice this time, but he wasn't speaking English. She whirled around and looked at Derrick. "What did he say?"

"Maxine, I don't speak Italian."

She snapped at him. "Isn't your last name DiNunzio? How can you not speak Italian?"

Derrick shrugged again. Maxine snarled. Barry's chuckle distracted her from her retort. She whirled toward him. If he did that one more time she was going to hit him over the head with something.

"You don't plan on having children, Maxi?" Barry watched as she turned her back on him and paced the length of the room at nearly a jog. At the wall she stopped, tense and drawn. When she came to rest, she resembled still photographs of athletes taken the very instant before they spring into a sprint or set the world record for the longest jump. Her body nearly vibrated with restrained energy. She spun around and paced back to the table.

Barry's question confronted her. At the notion of children, all of the thoughts she had ever had about children over the course of her life, including her own childhood experiences, tumbled through her head as she paced. Her face turned to study the sketches she had brought to life of imaginary families enjoying a summer picnic. She mentally overlaid their generic faces with her face, Barry's face, and the children became a blend of the two of them. His children. Her children. Their children. Children they would shelter and keep safe; children she could nurse, nurture, and feed; children he could teach, guide, and mentor. Children who would reach noble heights because, while they would understand the pain and horrors the world could bring to their doorstep, they would never personally experience it as long as blood beat through her veins.

Soundlessly, she studied Barry, and her possible future stretched out before her in the space of her glance. Then she remembered that Barry had some paperwork that would ensure none of those children would ever exist. Quietly, she said, "Maybe someday."

The moment broke when Robin's voice reached them again. Maxine began pacing again and offered, "But they have technology nowadays that makes all the pain just go away."

Twenty minutes later, the door opened and three sets of eyes flew to Sarah. The smile on her face helped them all relax just before she spoke. "We have a boy!" she said with a grin.

"A boy. Oh, how fun. Robin wanted a boy." Maxine rushed to her sister. "What about Robin?"

Sarah laughed. "She's wonderful. A little hoarse, but fine." She opened the door again and looked over her shoulder. "In a few minutes it will be safe for you to come in, Maxi. Just let me get some of this cleaned up."

Maxine looked through the window and caught a glimpse of the baby as another nurse handed him to Robin. She felt a familiar hand on her neck and suddenly felt exhausted. Without a second thought, she leaned against Barry's side and smiled.

THE second she had her apartment door open, Maxine started moving. She whipped her shirt over her head on the way to her room, stopping only long enough to kick off her shoes. "Can you get those boards into my car?" she asked as she opened the door to her bedroom.

Barry heard his wife's words, but Maxine might as well have spoken them in some foreign tongue. The majority of his awareness was still trying to permanently burn the glimpse he'd gotten of her smooth brown back and the curves he had observed as she undressed mid-stride into his memory. She had been so casual about disrobing in his presence. He felt his pulse beating heavy in his fingertips and lips as memories of their wedding night flooded his mind.

"Barry?"

He cleared his head and her words all suddenly became clear in his understanding. Fit those boards into her tiny little sports car? "I doubt it."

"Argh!" Thirty seconds later, she stuck her head out of the doorway. This time, he caught sight of lace nearly identical to the color of her skin. His mouth went dry. "I don't have time to take the train. Maybe I'll call a cab?"

He shrugged. "I don't know if I'd trust a cab on this ice."

He could hear muttered words as she went back into her room.

Distracted by the thought of her dressing in the other room, he picked up the telephone and dialed his office. His secretary picked up on the first ring. "I'll be coming in late this morning. Send flowers to Robin Viscolli at St. Mary's. She had a little boy early this morning."

"Aww. Do you have the stats?"

"What stats? She had a baby. She didn't win the World Series."

"The baby's stats. Height, weight, all of that."

"What does that matter? The baby's healthy and Robin's doing fine."

"For heaven's sake, Barry, we've been through this seven times with your sisters. This is important information."

He sighed and rubbed his eyes, dimly remembering other conversations like this one. "Call Tony's secretary. She'll probably know."

"Okay. Do you at least have a name?"

"Antonio Frances Viscolli, Junior."

"Aww. What are they going to call him?"

He saw the envelope with the annulment papers in it.

He reluctantly picked it up. "Am I supposed to know that, too?"

He heard a sigh in the receiver. "Never mind. I'll just call the Viscolli offices. What time can I expect you?"

He caught a whiff of perfume and glanced up as Maxine walked by him, wearing a bright yellow suit. The jacket fit snugly and the skirt barely brushed her knees, showing off her long legs. Her hands were up and behind her head while she whipped her hair around, twisting it into a fancy knot as easily as if she were putting it into a rubber band. As she turned her body to nudge the door to the dining room open with her hip, he noticed that she had hair pins clenched between her teeth.

Whether Elizabeth was still talking to him or not, he didn't know. "Listen, I'll be in later this morning, maybe. I'll call back later and let you know."

He hung up without waiting for confirmation and followed the trail of the spicy scent Maxine wore as if in a daze. He went through the dining room and into the kitchen, finding her biting into an apple.

"Did you call a cab?" she asked, catching a wandering drop of apple juice on her chin with her finger and gesturing at the phone in his hand.

The only thing he could think of was that she must be a witch who'd cast a spell on him. Otherwise, he wouldn't find a fully dressed woman eating an apple so completely tantalizing. "No. I'll just drive you."

Her expression didn't change as she eyed her husband's steady gaze. "What time is it?"

"Just after eight."

She nodded and brushed by him. "Okay. I can put

makeup on during the ride."

He caught her arm and whirled her around. "Just a second."

"Wha…" Before the word was completely out, his mouth covered hers, sealing the question. The apple fell to the floor with a thump while Maxine smiled and stepped further into the circle of his arms.

MAXINE stepped out of the elevator and carried the boards through the hallway, already five minutes late. She didn't run, though, because she had the presentation to give, and she didn't want to show up out of breath. Peter Mitchell was already going to be rather peeved that he didn't get the quick rundown she'd promised him on the phone that morning, and she didn't want to add sloppy presentation skills to the strikes against her.

Still, as she nudged the door to the conference room open with her hip, she smiled to herself. The extra fifteen minutes she'd spent at home with her husband was worth all that trouble and more.

"Good morning everyone," she said, getting herself completely into the room. She headed straight for the head of the table, where the empty tripod awaited her boards. She spoke as she checked their order and neatened up the stack. "I'm so sorry I'm late. My sister had a baby boy this morning, and I'm afraid I didn't anticipate the traffic from the hospital." She turned and felt her smile freeze. Ten sets of eyes faced her, ten stony expressions. The only slightly pleasant face in the room was Pete's, and she could see through the slick expression down to the annoyance.

Four of the men allegedly were on her team, but they were the ones who dumped the entire project in her lap right before Christmas. She knew half of the reason they were angry was because Pete probably spent a good portion of the morning gouging them for doing just that. The other half was due to her coming in late with the boards because it showed the clients who among them had actually done the work. She gave all of them her sweetest smile. Only one, Henry Monroe, shifted in guilt.

The clients took up the other side of the table. Though she smiled and met each of their eyes individually, she received nothing in return. She sighed inwardly. This team had ripped through ten different agencies in a quarter, and she could already see Mitchell and Associates being added to the rejection pile.

"Before you begin," came a voice from the foot of the table, "and since you weren't a part of the initial consultations we've had with your firm, I'd like to make it clear that if you have anything even remotely similar to the ads that have been run in recent history for my company, my time is valuable and I don't want it wasted."

She focused on the source of the voice and could immediately see how this company had risen through the ranks of national fast food chains established decades in advance to become one of the fastest growing franchises in America. Power practically emanated from him as he sat there, sitting completely still wearing a spotless silk business suit. He was also incredibly handsome, obviously Native American, probably full blood, with his black hair tied in a ponytail on the back of his neck, and eyes dark enough to be nearly black.

Maxine had Tony Viscolli in her life for over three

years. Dark, handsome men who radiated power no longer intimidated her. Rather, she found him endearing.

Added to that, she'd just spent fifteen minutes in Barry Anderson's arms, so she was completely unaffected by his otherwise devastating good looks. She was certain the ease with which she held herself as she responded surprised him. She knew that men in his position were used to some reverence from everyone. "You're right, Mr. Crow, I wasn't a part of the initial consultations. I apologize for going into this rather blindly, but I've seen the ads that have been produced for you in recent years, and to be honest, they did nothing to make me want to buy your chicken. Pop-culture hype may appeal to a younger audience, but it never appealed to me and I bet it didn't appeal to your primary demographic, your tried and true customer base, either."

Pete cleared his throat, and the other men shifted uncomfortably, but she ignored that when she saw the corner of Daniel Crow's mouth tilt up. That helped her relax almost completely. Not entirely. She still had to sell this. She cleared her throat.

"Again, I'll apologize ahead of time for the roughness of these boards. Half of them were done in the hospital waiting room, and part of them didn't get colored in so I'll ask you to use your imaginations."

She opened her mouth to speak, but was interrupted again by Mr. Crow. "And was the rest of this group at the hospital working on this with you?"

She flashed him a brilliant smile. "No, I'm afraid not."

Crow glanced at the men sitting across from him at the table. "So, they gave you conceptual ideas and let you run with them?"

Still smiling, Maxine said, "No, the ideas you will see are entirely mine."

He nodded. "Then," he turned to Pete, "why is this crack team sitting in here this morning, Peter? Trying to learn something?"

Pete began with, "Mr. Crow, I assure you that…"

Crow held up a forestalling hand. He turned back to Maxine and nodded, and she took that as his permission to continue. "When I think of fried chicken, I don't think of a wild character screaming all over the screen with loud music playing. I think of summer afternoons, the deep south, sunshine, picnics." She removed the cover board that contained the logos of both companies and started going through the concept. Her words helped enhance what her drawings conveyed; a nearly dreamlike sequence with hazy light and a summer field, gentle music playing, views of a happy family picnicking among the flowers, children playing, the sun shining down, laughter, all while they ate fried chicken from a Crow's Chicken box.

"No spoken words. No written words. Just the visual images. Then we'll fade into your logo at the end. It gives you instant cross-cultural appeal when we market overseas because nothing gets lost in translation. Also, it makes your brand completely unique. While every other ad your demographic will experience will be screaming, thumping, flashing, loud, rushed, explosive conflict—your ads will be that momentary quiet, that peace. That comfort consumers are desperately seeking. That's what we sell. Nostalgia. Mom, apple pie, and Crow's Chicken."

She risked a glance at her so-called team and caught

them glaring at her accusingly. She felt like sticking her tongue out at them. Pete looked from her to Daniel Crow, his head moving back and forth as if watching a tennis match. Crow's group gave absolutely nothing away. They stared at their leader with completely blank expressions. Maxine knew that Daniel Crow was the ultimate authority, probably the only authority, in this decision.

Crow sat staring at her, as if waiting for her to bring her attention back to him. The second she did, he nodded. "I like the concept." He pushed away from the table and stood. Almost comically, the rest of his crew stood with him. "I like it very much. I'll get back with you later today with my decision."

As soon as he was gone, she collapsed into the nearest chair. "I'm so glad that's over."

The head of the Crow account, and one of the partners, Victor Adams, turned on her the instant the door shut. "That was entirely uncalled for."

She sneered at him. "Oh? Well, Vic, the next time I'm given the task of single-handedly securing a national contract, are you saying I shouldn't try so hard?"

"That isn't what I'm talking about. I'm talking about making the rest of us look like cronies who did nothing more than show up this morning."

"I'm confused. Isn't that exactly what you did?"

"No. We spent hours on preliminary work."

She knew he was bloviating for Pete's benefit, but she refused to fall in line. "Last Friday, we all agreed that the preliminary work was no good, that we would go over other options in a meeting this morning for the presentation two days from now. *And*," she added emphatically, "I've been gone for a full week on vacation. What has the team accomplished in that week?"

He gestured at the last board, a rough sketch that had no color. "What we developed in prelim would have presented better than this. At least we would have come across as something other than some local, two-bit, fly-by-night company."

She rose to her feet. "Do I have to remind you that we're agency number eleven in ninety days, and he said he liked the idea. *My* idea."

His eyes skimmed her up and down. "I'm betting he just liked your skirt."

"That's quite enough, Vic," Pete said.

Maxine slapped her hands on the table and leaned forward into Vic's face. "You dumped this on me knowing I was out of town. You called my home and not my company provided cell, probably because you couldn't come up with anything on your own, and by giving it to me on my home answering machine you knew I wouldn't get the message until it was too late, probably hoping that the ultimate failure would be entirely mine. Well, Vic, looks like that backfired on you, because now the ultimate success is entirely mine, and you can eat your heart out."

She straightened and whirled toward Pete. "I have sick time and personal time up the whazoo. I'm taking the rest of the day off to go visit my new nephew."

He probably would have said something if she hadn't stormed out of the room. She was angry enough that it had been on the tip of her tongue to quit, which was why she was just going to leave and deal with it all tomorrow.

Her assistant jumped up from her cubicle as she

headed toward her office door. "Maxi!"

"Not now, Julie," she said, pushing the door open and slamming it shut behind her. She was halfway across her office before she saw Daniel Crow standing at her window. She froze, barely stifling a scream, and took a deep breath, desperately trying to get a handle on her temper.

He turned at the loud crack of the door slamming. His hands were in the pockets of his pants and he gave her a slight nod of his head. "We haven't been formally introduced," he said by way of an opening.

No longer feeling like she was going to scream, she extended her hand and stepped forward. "Maxine Bartlett." In her heels, she met him at eye level.

Instead of shaking her hand, he took it in both of his and held it. "Bartlett. A white name. So your mother was Native American?"

Using more force than should have been necessary, she reclaimed her hand. "No, actually my father. But I never knew him and don't know anything about it."

"So you know nothing of your heritage?"

"Not really. It's not something I've ever bothered to research."

His eyes were dark, searching. "And why is that?"

"Let's assume I'm as interested in my father as he was in me." She took a step back. "Did you have questions about the presentation?"

"You wear jewelry, but no wedding ring." His smile could barely be called a smile. "Can I assume this means you're not married?"

She sighed inwardly and took another step backward.

"You know what, Mr. Crow? I've been awake since yesterday morning, and I was just getting ready to leave for the day. Why don't we arrange a meeting later in the week so I can answer any questions about my proposal?"

"I'll take that as a no." He glanced at his watch. "My mind is made up about whether to give your agency a pass. My marketing team can take it from here. I came to your office to see if you would like to have dinner with me tonight."

Her morning was steadily going downhill. "And if your pass at me doesn't go your way, will my reply affect your decision to 'take a pass' on my agency?"

He cocked his head and almost smiled again. "What if I said yes?"

With a bright smile, she said, "Then I'd have to ask you to find yourself another rep, sir. The sooner, the better."

It surprised her when he threw back his head and laughed. "Now, I am very intrigued." He stepped forward and took her hand again. She bit back panic, her heart racing. As much as she pulled, he wouldn't release her. She started feeling trapped. "No," He asserted. "Your response will in no way affect my business decision." His smile disappeared and his eyes grew serious. As he spoke, her office door opened. "Now, will you have dinner with me, lovely Maxine Bartlett?"

Maxine stared into his rich black eyes, eyes that stared at her like a starless night. His face was youthful and ancient at once, a perfect symmetry carved from the brown earth with lips that could be cruel or let slip ancient wisdom. She felt her hand relax, no longer struggling to pull her fingers from his grasp and thought of all of the different ways she could sketch this face.

Why couldn't Barry look at her like that? Why couldn't he hold her hand like that? She remembered how he had snatched her up this morning, claiming her mouth with his, conquering her hurried rush with his slow desire. She remembered the feel of his iron muscles wrapping her up, covering her like a warm blanket, shutting out everything save his touch and his mouth.

"Miss Bartlett. How nice." Barry observed from behind her. Barry. Her husband. Maxine closed her eyes and groaned.

CHAPTER FIFTEEN

By the time she disengaged her hand from Daniel Crow's, Maxine realized that Barry had already vanished. Daniel Crow smirked and asked, "Boyfriend?"

Maxine, deflated, answered, "No." She wearily walked to her desk. She slipped her black wool coat on over her yellow suit, wrapped her white scarf around her neck, and picked up the purse and briefcase she'd haphazardly tossed on top of her desk when she rushed into the office less than an hour ago.

Hopefully, Crow followed up with a raised eyebrow and an inquiring, "No?"

Maxine shook her head, her eyes level with her client. "That was my husband." It didn't feel wrong to say the word out loud, as it related to Barry. It felt very right.

Crow had the dignity to look surprised. He actually took a step backward, perhaps considering Barry's hulking size. "Oh."

"Mr. Crow, it was nice to meet you. I look forward to

working with your team." She gestured toward the door. Maybe he didn't notice that she failed to offer her hand this time—maybe he did. She honestly didn't care.

"I'm sure we'll meet again. I'm sincerely sorry…" he gestured vaguely, "for my part in any misunderstanding with your husband. I'm happy to do whatever it takes to clear it up."

Maxine didn't reply, but she nodded her head and followed him out. She stopped at Julie's desk and, as soon as she was sure he was out of hearing, said, "Don't allow clients into my office without me. There is proprietary information on other firms in there."

"I know," the eclectic woman before her said. She wore earrings in the shape of New Year's party hats that moved and glittered. "He kind of strong armed his way inside. He's a little bit intimidating."

Maxine felt her lips thin. "Then you should have been standing in there with him until I arrived or else simply called security." She slipped her briefcase and purse straps over her shoulder and pulled black leather gloves out of her pocket. "I'm taking a personal day. No calls."

SINCE Barry brought her to the office, Maxine's car was still at her apartment. She took a cab to her church, the sprawling church in the very center of one of Boston's most troubled neighborhoods. The giant complex filled two city blocks with buildings and schools and chapels. The cab dropped her off in the main parking lot in front of the sanctuary building. As she stepped out of the taxi, she looked up at the huge steeple visible for blocks around. A weight settled over her heart, making her steps to the front door feel heavy laden.

The door opened without resistance, and she stepped into the huge entryway. It felt very quiet, very empty. She knew the staff was working, she saw their cars in the parking lot, but no one came to the vestibule to see why the door had opened and shut.

Why had she come here? "I don't know what to do," she whispered. In her mind, she heard the word as if it had been spoken out loud. Pray.

She pushed the coat from her shoulders as she crossed the large lobby. Her heels clicked on the marble tile, echoing in the surrounding space. Doors to her left and right led to stairwells that went up to the balcony levels or down to classrooms and offices. Huge sets of doors in front of her led to the sanctuary, and that is where she headed.

The warm scent of lemon oil welcomed her as she entered the giant room. She could see the gleam of the old wooden pews and guessed that they had recently been polished. She had thought she would slide into the first pew she came to, but instead felt compelled to keep walking all the way down to the front where the altar was strategically lined with boxes of tissues and evenly placed on the floor next to where people knelt in prayer.

As she stepped, she stripped off her gloves, scarf, and coat. She laid them in a pile on the front pew, then fell to her knees and bowed her head, resting her arms on the prayer bench. For the first time in her life, she prayed out loud. "God, please help me."

Her voice sounded odd to her own ears, but she kept

going, fervently appealing to God almighty to show her what to do. "Father, You know, even before I knew it, that I've loved Barry forever, even when I probably wasn't supposed to. You know that my heart is good where he is concerned. But I'm afraid that impulsiveness ruined what could be." She smiled. "I'd like to say that You led the two of us to get married, but I doubt either one of us were open to You at the time. But doesn't Your Word say that all things work together for good if I love You?" With tears choking her words, she said, "God I love You. I don't know that I knew before. I don't know if I was just going through the motions to please Robin or if I was really sincere, but right now I know I love You. I know I want to serve You. I know I want to live my life for You and give myself to You. And now I just need You to tell me what You want me to do."

For an hour she prayed on her knees. When her knees and back started to hurt, she shifted backward until she sat on the first pew, but she kept her head bowed and kept talking to God. Without actually ending the prayer, she eventually quit speaking and just sat there, letting her heart do the talking for her.

Eventually, she felt someone sit next to her. She raised her head and saw Abram Rabinovich, a very close friend of Tony's and a pastor at the church. Maxine had always liked him very much. He taught Old Testament classes at the school. As a former rabbi who had come to know Christ well into adulthood, he was very well versed in the Law of Moses.

"Want to talk about it?" he asked.

"I'm not sure," she said. Strangely, the surge of emotions she expected didn't happen. She felt wrung out, tired, but the weight on her heart had lifted sometime in the last hour and she felt lighter. "I think I just spent the last hour talking about it."

Abram chuckled. Maxine heard both compassion and wisdom in that soft laugh. He shifted in the pew until he could face her fully. "Excellent point."

"I'm just trying to figure out where to go from here."

"Did you find your answer?"

"How will I know?"

He put his hand out evenly and pursed his lips. "God speaks to us all in His own way, and to each of us as we need to hear His voice. But He does speak, Maxine. Sometimes, God says 'yes.' Sometimes, He says 'no.' Sometimes, it's 'wait.' If you don't know, then God hasn't answered yet. But He will, I promise you."

She could hear the assurance in his voice. He spoke of certainties. "What do I do now?"

Abram patted her on the shoulder before he stood. "Be still." He loosened his tie and looked up at the massive cross that towered behind the choir loft. "Christ Himself often sought solitude to talk to God and to listen to Him. Why don't you go somewhere quiet and just let Him speak to your heart?" He looked back at her and smiled. "And then do what He tells you, without question, and without hesitation. Stop trying to tell Him what to do. Put your life fully in His hands. Do it and know in your bones that He will work out the details."

He sat back down again. "When I came to know Christ, I was teaching in a Jewish Orthodox university, and quickly rising up through the ranks of rabbi. My entire family for thousands of years had worshipped Jehovah

God a certain way, and I had to turn my back on all that. Doing so made me an outcast, a leper so to speak. It wasn't easy, but it was God's will and when I surrendered to His will, God opened doors all around me. I got this wonderful job here, my beautiful Sofia has brought her brother and her parents to know the Messiah, and I was blessed to see my mother accept Christ before she passed. Now, my father is starting to speak to me again. Even if it is only to debate with me, still we are talking again. And there is love there."

He stood again. "God will make the way clear when the choices you make are in accordance with His will and His purpose, when you listen to His desires for your life." Slipping his hand into his pocket, he pulled out his phone and read a text message. "Now I must meet my beauteous Sofia for lunch. Would you care to join us, child? Sofia would be happy to see you."

"No. Thank you."

He pulled a business card out of his front pocket. "I am available any time you need to talk. Please call me, if you have questions or just need an ear or a prayer."

"Thank you." She took the card and clutched it in her hand. When she heard the last of his steps echo up the aisle and the large door gently close behind him, she stood and picked up her coat and her purse. Dizzy, she realized how exhausted and hungry she felt. Putting the business card in her wallet, she called for a cab and decided that a large pepperoni pizza was her first order of business, and her warm bed second.

UPON returning home from the church, Maxine ordered delivery pizza. While she ate, she called Robin, promising a visit in the morning. After eating pizza and changing into a comfortable pair of sweatpants and a sweatshirt, she had collapsed in exhaustion on her bed. At midnight, she woke up and ate more pizza, set up the coffee maker, and sorted through the mail that had piled up in her absence. Restless, she had gone back to bed and only slept a couple more hours.

She woke at four-thirty in the morning. She tossed and turned for a few minutes before finally getting up and out of the bed. She went to her kitchen and bypassed the coffee maker's timer, ordering it to deliver a pot right away. While she waited for the invigorating brew, she went back into her studio.

She stood in the very middle of her studio floor, barefoot, her body aching with fatigue and stress. Nothing felt right. Her apartment felt too empty, too lifeless. Her bedroom felt cold, barren. This home that she had poured so much energy into every decorating detail felt wrong. And in here, in this room where no one other than she had ever stood—no, wait. Barry came in here with her just two days ago, just the day before yesterday. She told him about Monty Jordan. Had it only been two days? How had so much gone on inside of her, outside of her, in such a small span of time?

She felt... ready. But ready for what? What was God telling her to do? When would He tell her to do it? Abram had advised that she be still and listen. With her hands on either side of her head, she spun in a circle in the middle of her studio floor and wondered, prayed, begged God to be clear when He gave her the answer because she needed to know what to do.

MAXINE hung up the phone for the dozenth time that morning. She rolled her head around, trying to ease the muscles in her neck. Two weeks had gone by since the acquisition of the Crow Chicken campaign. Two weeks of Crow cronies calling every five minutes with instruction, guidance, counsel, advice—constant interruptions about the final written proposal, statement of work, and detailed scope that they wanted by five o'clock today. If they would simply stop interrupting her…

A rat-tat-tat on her office door seconds before it opened interrupted even that thought. Peter Mitchell opened the door without waiting for her to answer the knock. "Got a minute?"

Maxine's eyes shifted to the clock sitting on the corner of her desk. Twelve forty-five. "Only if you have food."

Peter grinned and walked fully into the office, holding up a paper bag that bore the logo of her favorite sandwich shop. "Julie ordered for us."

She waved him forward as she shifted papers in order to clear a spot in front of her. "I think I love you."

"I'll be sure to inform my wife."

"She'd understand." Maxine greedily removed the white butcher paper that accommodated her favorite turkey Reuben on rye. Around a mouthful she asked, "What's up?"

"I just wanted to tell you that the preliminary work I've seen on the Crow scope is nothing less than exemplary."

Maxine lifted an eyebrow as she took another bite. Her teeth crunched through the toasted marble rye and crisp sour kraut. "You didn't bring me a sandwich to tell me I do good work. I've been trying to get a meeting with you for over a week and I feel like you've been dodging me. All of a sudden you're in my office with a bag of buttered rye in hand. What's up, really?"

Peter did not take a bite of his own sandwich. Instead, he stood and wandered to Maxine's project bulletin board and looked at the various computer printouts and sketches and proposals for actors from agents for the Crow ad. "I'm not entirely positive that a partnership is going to open up."

Maxine sighed and put her sandwich down. She gingerly brushed the crumbs off her fingertips and thought very, very carefully about the words on the tip of her tongue. With a silent appeal to God to keep from letting emotion override common sense, she finally responded. "I have worked hard for you for over four years. Most weeks, I work six or seven days, sometimes pushing seventy or eighty hours. I do it without complaint because that's what it takes. And I single-handedly brought in the biggest client you have ever had." She stood only because she towered over him and wanted to have that slight advantage. "Single-handedly, Peter. Given that context, I need you to explain why you aren't entirely sure about a partnership offer."

He put his hands in his pockets and turned to face her. "I just don't know if it is the right decision. The timing..."

"The right decision?" With a huff of breath, she closed her eyes and fought for control. She picked up her sandwich and threw it into the trash can. "Well, let me tell you something about timing. I have a meeting with Crow's people at five. They'll receive the written scope and go over it, I'm sure, with a fine toothed comb. I will give you one week of being completely available to them for questions and concerns, because I care about this company and the fact that we have this big contract. But I also have fifty-two days of accrued leave. Starting tomorrow, other than direct contact from anyone at Crow, I'm taking those fifty-two days. While I'm gone, why don't you consider the timing so you can be sure?" She leaned over the desk and picked up his sandwich and threw it into the trash can, too. "My lunch break is over. I have to finish what I'm doing to prepare for that meeting. Thank you for finally taking time to speak with me."

She dismissed him by sitting down and putting the earbuds of her MP3 player into her ears and cranking up Skillet singing about the monster in the closet. She turned to her computer and didn't watch her employer leave.

RATHER than battle the rush hour traffic that is nothing less than agonizing in downtown Boston on a Wednesday afternoon, Maxine chose to walk to Robin's apartment after work. Inside, she still seethed over the impromptu lunchtime meeting with Peter. While she honestly felt like she had handled it reasonably well, the end result was that she now had over two months in front of her and wasn't quite certain what to do with herself in all that time.

She spoke momentarily with the guard at the big circular desk, then took the private elevator to the top floor of the building. Without knocking, knowing the guard would have announced her arrival, she pushed open the outer door and entered Tony and Robin's apartment.

Smiling, Robin rushed to greet her. Robin reached her and hugged her. "I'm so happy to see you. What a surprise!"

Maxine noted Sarah sitting on the big circular leather couch cradling Antonio Frances Viscolli, Junior—already nicknamed TJ for Tony Junior—in her arms. Sarah looked up and grinned. "Are you here to cook us dinner?"

Maxine laughed and returned Robin's hug before she dashed to scoop the baby up from her little sister. "I can. What is mommy hungry for?"

With a smile, she handed Maxine a burp cloth. "I think that anything Aunt Maxi makes will be fantastic. I'm just not sure what's in there. I haven't been to the grocery in weeks."

"I'll dig around." Maxine put her lips on TJ's perfect little head and inhaled the fragrant baby smell. "I love him so much. How can I love him so much when I've only known him for two weeks?"

Sarah smiled. "I feel the same way. I feel like moving back in here. Maybe if I go to graduate school, Tony will let me have my old room back."

Robin snorted. "Talk to me at feeding time at three in the morning and see if you still want to live here." She looked at Maxine. "What's up, Maxi? Everything okay?"

TJ gave a little snort and started rooting at Maxine's neck. She handed him over to his mama and watched while her big sister settled into a chair and started nursing him. Maxine sat on the couch next to Sarah. "I, ah, need to talk to you two."

Sarah pushed her glasses up further on her nose and shifted until she faced Maxine and had her back to the arm of the couch. "What's wrong?"

Maxine ran her fingers over the naked ring finger of her left hand. She cleared her throat. "When I went to Vegas…" She paused and looked at Sarah then Robin then back to Sarah.

Sarah leaned forward and touched her hand. "Maxi?"

"Barry and I got married." She blurted it out then froze. Both sisters just stared at her for a moment, then simultaneously, the words sank in and their eyes widened. Sarah was the first to speak.

"You did what?"

"It was just this spontaneous thing." Maxine surged to her feet and paced around the circular room. "I didn't think about it. We have always been such good friends. I don't know. I'm pretty sure I've always loved him. Even when he was with her," she paused as memories of Barry's marriage to that awful woman played through her mind like a little movie. "And then we were at this wedding chapel watching this Elvis impersonator do a Blue Hawaii wedding and the next thing I know, I was saying, 'I do.'"

Another long silence stretched throughout the room. Maxine slowly walked back to the couch and sat down. This time, Robin spoke. "Well, that is some news."

"Indeed," Sarah said. "Vegas was before the new year. What about since you came home?"

Maxine shook her head. "I think he had divorce papers ready when I saw him the day TJ was born, but the baby coming and the big project at work has kept me distracted for the last two weeks." She let out another breath. "I also took a leave of absence from my job today."

Robin repeated, "Leave of absence?"

Maxine waved her hand. "Vacation, really. But I have months of vacation due so we'll call it a paid leave." She told them about the partnership and the work and the project. Oddly, she did not feel emotionally overwhelmed. She felt blank inside.

Sarah scooted over until she could put her arm around her older sister. "What now, honey?"

Maxine lowered her head. "I just don't know. I am just waiting for God to tell me what to do. The break from work felt like the right decision. I don't regret it. Now I just need to see what's next."

Robin shifted TJ to her shoulder and leaned forward to touch Maxine's knee. "We're here for you, whatever happens. And we'll be praying for you."

She leaned back and started burping TJ, but Sarah grabbed Maxine's hand and put another hand on Robin's thigh. "Let's pray right now." The three women bowed their heads and closed their eyes as Sarah prayed for Maxine.

CHAPTER SIXTEEN

Nearly a week later, Maxine sat at her drafting table in her studio, a blank sketch pad in front of her. For the first time in her life, she could not find the inspiration to draw out her feelings. For over a decade, she'd used her gift of art to purge the demons from her mind, a cleansing ritual that worked nearly every time. Now, though, the pencil lay still in her hand and the unblemished page stared back at her, a stark white, mocking blank space.

"Well, God," she muttered, "I'm here. And I'm trying to be still. But I honestly just don't know how." She grabbed her remote control and pushed the button for music. Instantly, the sound of the Newsboys filled her studio. The speakers lining the ceiling flooded the surround sound of a ticker tape parade falling like a million pieces. She had spent a good portion of the last week purging her secular music collection and trying on different bands and different sounds. She loved hard, thumping music, and found herself pleasantly surprised at the different Christian offerings.

A restless feeling had sent her into her studio this morning. This was day three that she had holed up in her apartment. By noon every day, after baking some amazing bread or dessert, or cooking some rich stew that she promptly froze because no one else was around to eat it, she wandered into her studio. Inspiration never came, though, so she found herself going through her paintings and drawings, cataloging them, remembering times she painted them, reminiscing over her life.

She knew one thing. She would not passively allow an annulment. She loved Barry, deeply, truly. She longed to be the wife he deserved, the wife he may not even know he desired. How to go about that, though?

Her mind wandered, and she thought of ways to communicate to him, writing him a letter, sending him an e-mail, showing up at his office. Nothing appealed to her, though. As she thought, her hand moved of its own accord and she very quickly recognized what she drew. Barry's house. She filled in the bricks, added the trim, drew his Jeep in the driveway. One word went through her mind as she worked. "Home."

THE next day, Maxine found herself back in the front pew where she had spent so many hours praying that day not too long ago. Today, she waited for her turn to join Robin and Tony on the chancel stage as they dedicated baby Tony to the Lord. She still found herself waiting for an answer from God about what she should do, but the more time she spent in solitude with Him on her knees in prayer, the more confident she felt that He would answer in His good time.

As pastor called the family, she and Sarah climbed the steps of the chancel stage. As she walked toward Robin and Tony, she was pleasantly surprised to see Derrick and Barry walking toward them from the other side of the chancel. Unlike Robin, Tony had no family. He treated Derrick and Barry like brothers as much as if they had been born to the same mother. The O'Farrell's, the youth minister of the church and his wife, also joined. They had fostered Tony through his early Christian life, rescuing him from the streets and providing a home for him.

Going through the dedication ceremony, Maxine could not help observing Barry. His face remained very stoic, and she silently prayed that God would take advantage of his presence for this ritual to convict him about his withdrawal from God's love. He seemed unaffected by any of it and refused even to meet her eyes. After the ceremony, after the family returned to their seats, she watched him leave the sanctuary. Unlike the day of his wife's funeral, she did not follow him. Instead, she listened to the sermon and felt a door in her heart open up. After the sermon, she found herself joining the wave of people going to the front of the church and fell to her knees before God and felt more doors open and His answer poured into her heart.

MAXINE rushed home from church, skipping the family lunch. She burst through the door of her apartment and tossed her purse and keys atop the desk next to her phone. Taking her Bible to the couch with her, she sat with her back against the arm and spoke to God. "I know what

I think You want, but since I'm a little unschooled at listening to Your voice, I sure would like some confirmation. I hope I'm not doing something wrong by asking. Thank you for answering my prayer. Now, just to be sure, please help me confirm. Thank you."

She closed her eyes and opened her Bible, then opened her eyes and read at the first passage she saw. She read of Ruth, who mustered up her own courage and went to Boaz. In that moment, Maxine knew that what she felt stirring in her heart had come directly from God.

SIX o'clock Monday morning, Maxine rang Barry's doorbell. She waited a few moments and rang it again. And again. Finally, he answered. He wore jogging shorts and a sleeveless shirt. His muscles bulged against his sweaty skin and she knew she'd interrupted his morning workout.

"Hi," she greeted with a smile.

"Maxi," he said with a surprised look on his face. He looked past her, to her car in the driveway next to his Jeep, then back at her. "What are you doing here?"

"Freezing, for one." She stepped forward and he stepped backward until she crossed the threshold and shut the door behind her. "That's better." She peeled her red knit cap off and shoved it in the pocket of her gray wool coat. Her gloves followed, then she unbuttoned her coat and slipped it off her shoulders. "Did I interrupt you?"

He looked down at his attire, then shrugged. "I was just finishing up." He turned and started walking away. "I'm not really set up for company right now, Maxi."

"I'm not exactly company, Barry."

He nodded with a half shrug. "Care for some tea?"

"I'd prefer coffee," she said, trailing behind him. She stepped into the large great room, with its huge stone fireplace and plush furniture. The stairwell leading upstairs flowed to her left, and the balcony above revealed three closed doors. Barry continued walking through the room and through a swinging door into the kitchen, and Maxine followed right behind him.

A breakfast nook overlooked a snowy backyard. Stone floors and three walls of windows made the room kind of chilly. The large granite island, the commercial sized gas stove, and the double ovens in the wall made Maxine want to get cooking.

Barry pulled a cup from the cupboard above and filled it with water hot from the kettle on the stove. "I don't have coffee," he said. "I have tea. If you want some I'll be glad to make you some."

Maxine waved her hand. "No thanks."

He added a tea bag to the cup and turned to face her fully. She slipped into a bar stool at the island and smiled at him. He stared at her for a moment, then said, "Why are you here, Maxi?"

"Well," she began, excitement bubbling through her chest until she feared it would spill out of her and make her unable to form coherent words. "I'm here because I'm your wife. And as your wife, I should be living with you."

He stared at her for five long seconds. Finally, he blinked and took a sip of tea. "Really?"

"Really."

"And what if I say I don't want you to live here?"

Maxine hopped off the bar stool and came around the

island until she stood in front of him. "I'd say that if you didn't want me here, or anywhere else for that matter, that you'd have moved heaven and earth to get those papers to me to sign. I'd say that I know how I feel."

She put one hand over his heart, the other hand on his shoulder. She watched his eyes flare at her touch and could see the physical restraint he had to exercise over himself. "I'd say that I love you as a wife should love her husband. That I've missed you like you wouldn't believe these last three weeks, and that I prayed and prayed for God to tell me what to do, and every indication of an answer pointed me to this house and me coming to you. This is where I belong, Barry. Here. With you."

He put his hands on her shoulders, but didn't pull her close. Instead, he kept her from stepping any closer. "We can't be together, Maxine." he said, but she cut him off.

"We're already together. We're married. You haven't changed that. I don't want to change it. I want to live as your wife."

"People will say…"

"People will always say, no matter what. Barry, listen to me." Despite his resistance, she stepped forward and wrapped her arms around his waist. She leaned forward until her head lay against his chest and she could hear his heart beat beneath her ear. "We are one. It's that simple."

He didn't wrap his arms around her. He didn't pull her closer. He didn't kiss her. He didn't sweep her away. All of those things she secretly wished he'd do. But he also didn't push her away, so she took that as a positive sign. She smiled as she stepped away from him. "I have movers coming this afternoon. They're bringing some things I want from my apartment. Obviously I don't need a lot of the furniture, but there are some pieces I plan to keep." He merely raised an eyebrow as he took another sip of his tea. "I'm going to need a key. If you don't have a spare, please let me borrow yours so I can get a copy made. I'll be here when you get home from work tonight, so you don't have to worry about that."

He stared at her for one heartbeat, then another, then pulled open a drawer. He rooted around until he found a key which he tossed on the counter. "That was Jacqueline's."

"Wonderful," Maxine said with a grin as she scooped up the key. "I assume that anything that was hers, I can dispose of?" She held up the key hanging from the bejeweled key chain. "Aside from this, of course."

He offered a stiff nod just as the cell phone on the counter started vibrating. Without speaking to her, he picked it up and pressed a series of buttons, read either a text or an e-mail, then put it back on the counter. "I need to run."

After he left the kitchen, Maxine clasped her hands together in glee and gave a little spin. Then she rushed out of the kitchen and back through the large front room. No sign of Barry led her to believe he'd gone upstairs to get ready for work. She rushed outside, careful not to slip on the patches of ice that lined the driveway, and retrieved a tote bag from the backseat of her car.

She brought it back to the kitchen and unpacked the coffee maker and bag of coffee. She found the appliance a temporary home near the sink and determined that the first order of business for the day would be to scrub the kitchen. She wanted to learn where everything was and rearrange as needed to accommodate her left handed cooking methods.

CHAPTER SEVENTEEN

Barry stood staring at his reflection until the hot water pouring out of the shower caused the mirror to fog up and obscure his view. Finally, he stripped and stepped under the hot spray and closed his eyes, letting the water beat down on his head.

When had he lost complete control of this situation with Maxine?

The crux of it was that he felt a small thrill at the thought of her living here, of her being here when he got home from work tonight. Another part of him could only see her fingers in the gentle embrace of that man in her office, and her face got replaced over and over again in his memory with the face of his dead adulterous wife.

Maxine was right, though. If he truly didn't want to be married to her anymore, he would have moved mountains to get those annulment papers signed and filed. So what had held him up? What kept him from doing it?

A skitter in his mind suggested that he pray about it, but he dismissed the thought. He prayed no more. Not since the answer to his prayer had been his wife's death had he gone to God about anything. He certainly wouldn't risk Maxine that way.

Robotically, he slapped shampoo onto his palm and scrubbed at his scalp, then went through the motions to finish showering. The e-mail he'd received from Tony took an hour away from his morning. He wondered if his best friend beckoning him to the top floor of the Viscolli hotel and to his corporate offices had to do with business or Maxine.

As he stepped out of the shower and dried off, Barry realized that he'd have to take this opportunity of an unplanned meeting to confess to Tony what he'd done. Maybe he wouldn't have to worry about how he'd handle coming home to Maxine. Maybe Tony would just kill him and all of his earthly problems would be over.

With a sigh, he moved into his bedroom and kicked a stack of dirty laundry farther into the corner and out of his path to the closet. He walked into the closet and moved toward the blue suits, mechanically matching shirt to tie to socks to belt to shoes. There would be no easy death to get him out of this. No. Tony would make him suffer.

He slipped a tie around his neck, tied his shoes, and headed back downstairs. No sign of Maxine in the living room meant that she either left—not likely—or was still in the kitchen. He pushed open the door with his shoulder while he tied his tie, and immediately smelled the rich brew of her coffee. For some reason, the smell soothed him. He found her at the kitchen table writing in a notebook, the snowy back yard at her back, a steaming cup of coffee at her elbow.

"I have a meeting with Tony in a few minutes," he said,

retrieving his phone and keys from the countertop.

Maxine smiled. "You might want to talk to him. About us, I mean."

Barry sighed. "Have you talked to Tony about this?"

She smiled and shrugged. "No, but Robin knows we're married, so count on Tony knowing it too."

"Great." The knot complete, he tightened his tie and buttoned his jacket. "That's just great."

"It all had to come out, eventually." She rose from the table and approached him. He simultaneously wanted to run away and pull her close to him. So he did neither. She put a hand on either shoulder and stood on tiptoes to kiss his cheek. "I'll see you tonight. Please give me a call and let me know what time to expect you so that I can plan dinner accordingly."

She turned her back on him and went back to her list. Barry stared at her for a few seconds before leaving the kitchen and wondering, again, how he'd lost control of this situation.

WAITING in Tony's outer office, Barry checked his watch a second time. So far, Tony had kept him cooling his heels for fifteen minutes. He could not remember the last time Tony had kept him waiting. Barry had a feeling that the meeting this morning was not going to be about zoning problems for a Christian school gymnasium project.

When the phone issued a soft electronic tone, Tony's secretary, Margaret, nodded at Barry. He picked up his briefcase and walked through the double doors behind her desk.

Typically, at seven-thirty in the morning, Tony would have a breakfast spread laid out on his conference table. It would include such Barry-friendly items as yogurt, fresh fruit, his favorite brand of tea, perfectly brewed. And, typically, Tony would meet him at the door with a handshake and a "bro-hug" and the two would make their way over to the table as they chitchatted about life since last they saw each other.

Not this morning, though. This morning Tony sat behind his monstrous desk, signing papers. He gestured toward the chairs adjacent to him, but did not speak, did not stand and offer his hand, and did not give any kind of verbal or nonverbal salutation.

As much as Barry knew this moment would eventually come, he would have much preferred it had been on his terms. He'd had time in the last few weeks to talk to Tony about it, so the fact that he was on Tony's playing field was his own fault, but that didn't make it any easier to bear. Since this would be a fight, though, he could certainly throw the first punch.

"Maxine moved in this morning." He set his briefcase down at his feet as he loosened his tie and kicked back informally in the chair. "She's at the house making lists as we speak."

Tony's hand stopped scribbling the pen. For a moment he sat completely frozen, then he tossed the pen aside and made eye contact with Barry. "We obviously have some catching up to do."

Barry shrugged. "I'd intended to save her the embarrassment and seek a silent annulment. Things just didn't happen that way."

"You shrug?" Tony leaned forward and pointed at Barry. "You mistreat my sister this way and then shrug at me? As if it were nothing?" Barry could barely understand Tony between the suddenly thick Italian accent and rich South Boston dialects. Tony's elocution abandoned him, and all of the years spent shedding the outward evidence of growing up on the streets vanished. In that glimpse Barry caught sight of a tough kid who would do whatever he needed to do in order to survive.

"Mistreat?" Despite knowing that on some level Tony's antagonism had some merit, Barry felt the anger bubble up inside of him. "I have not, nor would I ever, mistreat Maxi."

"You take her to Vegas on your little annual excursion, then you—"

Barry stood and slapped his hands on Tony's desk. "Then. I. Married. Her." He spoke each word as if it were a sentence of its own. "I didn't seduce her. I didn't take advantage of her. I asked her to marry me and she— willingly—said yes."

Tony picked up his previous train as if he'd never stopped speaking. "And then you discard her and leave her brokenhearted and lost for weeks."

Barry shook his head. "Is your problem with the getting married or the problem with the not intending to stay married?"

Tony leaned back in his chair and rubbed his face with his hands. Barry slowly resumed his seat. Tony sighed, reached forward, and spun the pen that sat on his desk. "Maxine has been in love with you forever. I doubt she has fully realized it yet, but it's what spurred her friendship with you; the late night Sunday football, the golf outings, the funeral getaway. I think those feelings for you are what kept her from really seeking out God. Because she knew that you were married and finding ways to spend time with you, however she could, was quite sinful. But now she's come to Him. She has dedicated her life to Him, and is carving out a relationship with Him and it's beautiful to see. Yet all of this..." Tony's voice softened. "All of this is at a time when you have apparently turned your back on Him."

Barry gave a small shake of his head, very confused about the conversation. "I'm not understanding what you're upset about."

"She isn't strong enough in her faith yet to carry you both. If you can't find a way back to God, you're going to do nothing but hurt her in the end."

Barry felt a tug on his heart at Tony's words. However, he pushed it aside and stood. "My relationship with God is my own business. Maxine's feelings for me are her business. My marriage to her is our business. I don't need your counsel or your concern."

Tony raised an eyebrow. "And what about your feelings for her?"

The tug on his heart became quite painful. "What do you mean?"

"I mean, how do you feel about her, Bartholomew? Do you like her? Do you get a kick out of hanging out with her? Or do you *love* her? Do you love her with every molecule in your body and every waking thought? Do you put her needs ahead of your own? Ask yourself, would you die for her?"

The verse from Ephesians raced into Barry's memory, commanding husbands to love their wives even as Christ loved the church. It was a commandment without compromise, that husbands must love their wives sacrificially and more than their very own flesh. Emotion welled in Barry's throat, effectively cutting off anything he might have wanted to say or even could have said. He felt rebuked and suddenly ashamed. Instead of answering any of his best friend's questions, he glared at Tony, pivoted on his heel, and left the room, slamming the office door behind him.

CHAPTER EIGHTEEN

Barry closed the file and moved it to the outbox on the corner of his desk. He turned to his laptop sitting on his credenza behind him and made a notation about a deposition on Monday next week, then wrote an instruction for Elizabeth on a sticky note. As he turned to stick it to the outside of the file, he saw Elizabeth standing in front of his desk. She normally knocked, and rarely interrupted his Monday post-lunch organizational time, so he frowned and slipped off his reading glasses.

"Yes, Elizabeth?"

Her lips thinned in apparent disapproval over something. "Is there something you'd like to tell me?"

With his focus on the file he'd just closed, he had absolutely no idea what she was talking about or why. "I don't think so."

"There's a woman," and she said the last two words as if they left a bad taste in her mouth, "on line four who claims that she is your wife."

Barry blinked and felt the tips of his ears grow hot. "Oh, yeah. That."

"Mmm hmm." She held up her fingers. "Line four."

She stood there, obviously intending to listen to the way he answered the phone. Barry cleared his throat and picked it up. "Maxi."

Elizabeth's eyes widened, then rolled up before she shook her head.

Maxine said, "Barry. Hi. I was just checking to see if you had any clear idea about what time you'll be home tonight."

He checked his watch. "Probably after six. Maybe pushing seven."

"Wonderful. Thank you so much. I'll see you then."

Barry carefully set the phone back in the cradle and looked at Elizabeth. She had her arms crossed and tapped a finger on her arm. "When did you get married?"

He sat his chair up and straightened an already perfectly straight stack of papers on his desk. "Yeah. About that."

While he searched for the words to say, she interrupted his thoughts. "I hate to say it, Mr. Anderson, but I mean, this seems kind of sudden. I hope that, you know, you know what you're doing. Because you've been in a pretty vulnerable spot. Trust me, I've been there. And I'd hate to think that you are being taken advantage of by someone."

Barry waved his hand in the air. "Stop. I appreciate your concern, but that's not your business."

Elizabeth froze mid-sentence. Without changing her facial expression, even a fraction, she nodded her head exactly once and punctuated the gesture by answering with, "You're right." She pivoted on a heel and left his office without another word.

With a sigh, Barry stared at the closed door for several minutes before he picked up another file and opened it. For a while, he stared blankly at the page in front of him, then forced himself to focus and work on the task at hand.

MAXINE stood on the balcony of the second floor and looked down at the two men carrying the boxes of stereo equipment. "Just there, by the hearth, is fine," she said.

As she turned to go back into the master bedroom, the room in which Jacqueline had obviously resided, her phone rang. Glancing at the caller ID as she hit the button to accept the call she said, "Hi Robin."

"Hi. Just seeing how it went this morning."

"About like I expected. He didn't resist."

"What do you think that means?"

She moved the phone away from her mouth and spoke to the two men working in the huge walk-in closet. "Just box everything up. I don't want any of it."

She turned her attention back to her sister. "I hope it means that he'll fall madly in love with me and we'll have a beautiful marriage. If that isn't what it means, I'll know that I tried, if nothing else."

She could hear Robin sigh. "I hope you're doing the right thing."

Maxine grabbed the roll of packing tape and sealed the box of jewelry she had packed before the movers came. "I am doing what God told me to do. The rest is up to Barry." She marked the box. "Listen, I have boxes of jewelry and furs - real furs. Any idea what I should do with them?"

"I don't know. Did she have family?"

Maxine smiled. "I knew you were my sister for a reason. Brilliant girl. I'll find out her parents' address and get them delivered."

"Glad I could help. I love you."

"I love you, too. I'll talk to you later."

The bedroom was about the size of Maxine's living room. A small sitting area with two winged-back chairs facing a small round table sat next to a fireplace. Maxine ran her fingers over the table and thought a marble chess set would look perfect there. She went to the nightstand where she'd set her notebook and made some notes about decorating the mantle. A noise in the doorway broke her concentration and she looked up.

"We have boxes of clothes, ma'am," the supervisor from the moving company said. "We just need you to tell us where to put them."

Maxine huffed out a breath. "As soon as they're done cleaning out this closet, I want you to put them in here."

"When we've finished that, I think that will be all, ma'am, unless you had something else."

She glanced at her watch. They'd made great time that morning. "That will be it for today. Thank you for doing such a great job on such a short notice."

BARRY stood in the living room of his home—their home—the residence once central to the worst marriage on planet earth. Now he apparently shared that exact same domicile with another woman. A new wife.

The room glistened, sparkled, and smelled good. A new table stood by a different lamp. The couch sported brighter pillows and colorful throws. The intense stereo system sat unboxed next to the entertainment center. From the kitchen, the smell of roasted meat and baking bread warmed him and tempted him.

He set his briefcase near the stairs and moved through the room, letting the sound of thumping music lead him to the kitchen. Maxine stood at the sink, washing a large pot. He noticed the coffee pot almost right away and smiled for the first time that day. The red cloth covering the table warmed the snowscape beyond the windowed walls. Candles stood unlit and serving dishes sat covered, waiting.

While he felt comfort, warmth, and appreciation, nothing else stirred. He had shut his emotions off for so many years, he didn't even know what he was capable of feeling, much less his actual emotions. He felt irreparably damaged inside and wondered if Jacqueline might have broken him. He couldn't understand what Maxine saw in him, or why she intended to pursue this. He could certainly imagine loving her, if he understood the word. He had some affection for her and he really enjoyed her company, so he was willing to see what ended up coming of it.

"Hi."

She spun around, soap suds flying from her hands. When she saw him, she smiled. "Hi. You startled me."

He gestured at the radio on the counter. "The volume must have muffled my arrival."

As she approached him, he steeled himself for her wrapping her arms around him and hugging him. He didn't return the gesture of affection. But he did put his hands on her shoulders and smile down at her. "Smells good."

"Do you want to eat now?"

"I'm good." He looked at his watch. "I'm a little later than I said."

She waved a hand at him dismissively. "The meal is one that isn't time reliant. Roast beef is easy to keep warm. Go ahead and wash up and have a seat. I'm afraid the dining room is kind of a staging area for my stuff right now, so we'll have to eat in the kitchen."

"I've been eating standing beside the sink for years. It'll be a treat to sit down for dinner."

They chatted comfortably while they ate the amazing meal Maxine set out. After dinner, they washed the dishes together, then went into the living room and enjoyed watching a basketball game. As the time passed, Barry grew more apprehensive about the coming end to the evening. Lending credence to his concerns, when the game ended Maxine rose and stood next to him, lightly placing a hand on his shoulder.

"I feel like there's a big wall between us right now," she said. He opened his mouth to speak, but really didn't know what he intended to say. He didn't have to worry about it for long, though, because she leaned her hip against the arm of the couch and leaned toward him, her arms slipping around his neck, her elbows resting on his shoulders. Were it not for the arm of the couch, she would be in his lap. "Shh. I know you feel all gallant and chivalrous. That's fine. I've moved into the master bedroom, because that's where we belong... together. But I also found your room, where you obviously lived before. I understand your hesitancy.

I'm okay with it. Just know that when you are ready, I love you, and I want you to join me in our room."

She framed his face with her hands. He closed his eyes and savored the feel for just a moment. Then he opened them again in time to see her lower her head and brush his lips with hers. "Good night, Barry, my amazing husband."

He watched her walk from the room, up the stairs, and listened for the sound of the master bedroom door shutting, a sound he had heard most of the nights during his married life with Jacqueline, but the sound never came. After about twenty minutes, he rose and went up the stairs himself. As he reached the top landing, he saw the door standing wide open. Invitingly open. For the second time that day, a verse ran through his mind. "Knock, and the door shall be opened unto you."

He put his hand on the doorknob to his room, but it took several long heartbeats before he turned the handle to let himself in, and it was much, much longer before sleep finally found him.

CHAPTER NINETEEN

Maxine drew in the warm spring air in one long, deep breath. Oh, how she loved springtime. While she couldn't possibly fool herself into thinking the warm weather that greeted her this first Saturday in March might stick around for even a few more weeks, she certainly intended to savor every single second of it while it lasted. The late morning sun warmed the skin of her arms beneath her short sleeved shirt. What a treat to wear a short sleeved shirt in March.

She carried a notebook filled with rough sketches. She used it to devise landscaping and planting ideas as she walked the perimeter of the property. As she plotted outdoor furniture, a patio kitchen with a grill, and dreamed of possibly inaugurating the first annual Anderson Fourth of July party, the back door opened and Barry joined her outside. With a grin, Maxine held out her arms and lifted her face. "Look!" she said, "The sun! It shines!"

Barry smiled in return. "About this time of year, I start doubting its return myself."

He wore khaki pants and a collared golf shirt that accentuated the shape of his broad chest. She gestured at the keys in his hand. "Do you have to work today?"

"I do, some, but I can do it from here." He rubbed the back of his neck. "I, ah, have a church budget committee meeting, though."

Maxine felt a little burst of excitement, but she tried not to show it. She had lived here for five weeks. For five weeks, she'd prayed alone before every meal. She'd come and gone to this church function or that church meeting alone. She'd hosted only one small Sunday School gathering. Barry knew everyone, seemed to enjoy the fellowship, but he didn't even talk about it afterward. He'd shown absolutely no interest in anything related to his walk with God or their church, so his announcement loomed tremendously in her heart.

"Oh?" She crossed the patio to him and slipped her arms around his waist. "I'm so happy you're getting back into it." She laid her head against his chest and breathed in the scent of his aftershave. Just as she started to pull away, his arms came around her. Another first.

Savoring that moment, she closed her eyes and just abided. She thought maybe she could stand like that all day. Smiling, she pulled her head back just enough to smile up at him. He used a hand to brush a wayward strand of hair from her forehead and, for a moment, Maxine was certain he was about to kiss her. Then the cell phone in his pocket vibrated and chirped.

A look of annoyance that mirrored how she felt flickered across his face. Maxine stepped back and let him dig the offending device out of his pocket and answer it in the middle of the fifth ring, seconds before the call would have forwarded to voice mail. She watched as he glanced at the caller id as he answered. "Good morning, mom."

Maxine stepped even farther back, smiling her understanding, and went back to her sketch pad. The first time she met Barry's mother and sisters had not gone well. Those women had come to the meeting hostile, having already made up their collective minds about the newest addition to the family long before anyone ever laid eyes on her.

Given their rather sudden nuptials, while considering how poorly his first wife had treated everyone, Maxine had known it wouldn't be easy to win over Barry's family, so she wasn't hurt or upset by the attitude. Instead, she made it her mission to have an intimate meeting with each of them. Lunch with his mother, brunch with a sister, shopping with another sister. Eventually, they each learned of her commitment to God, her long-standing friendship with and respect for Barry, and of her genuine empathy for Barry's previous relationship.

Asking Barry's accountant father to prepare her taxes also helped seal the deal on acceptance of Maxine into the fold. If they suspected that she might simply be interested in Barry's material wealth, then exposing her own surprisingly substantial personal portfolio in such a subtle way put an end to that notion rather quickly.

As the weeks went by, his family had warmed and opened up to her. She knew how much Barry loved his sisters and parents, and how important they were to him. Establishing relationships with them would make the rest of their life together much easier and happier.

Putting her mind back to her plans for the back yard, Maxine wandered away from her husband and inspected the fence line, thinking to herself that some flowering bushes in the far corner might look nice. As she scribbled in her notebook, Barry interrupted her.

"Mom said 'hi' and wanted me to remind you about dinner tonight?"

She slapped a hand to her forehead. "I'm glad she called. I forgot all about it. Honey?" She grinned. "We're supposed to have dinner with your parents tonight!"

"It's okay. I rescheduled. I told her I had other plans."

Frowning, Maxine looked up at him. "Other plans?"

He slipped an arm around her waist. "Yeah. I told her I had to take my beautiful bride out to dinner tonight."

Maxine's heart began to flutter. She felt emotion surge up and tighten her throat, threatening her eyes with tears. "I..." Nothing would come out.

Barry shushed her and gently put his hands in her hair. As his lips met hers, the tears spilled from her eyes and flowed freely down her cheeks. She stood on her tiptoes and slipped her arms around his neck. The kiss was beautiful, amazing, left her aching and wanting. She needed more of his taste on her lips, needed to step even closer to him.

Just as he angled her head to deepen the kiss, the cell phone in his hand vibrated against her skull. Barry pulled back and looked at it, scrolling through a message. He cleared his throat as he took a step backward. "Apparently, your sister needs some sunshine on her skin. Her husband is requesting a foursome of 9-holes followed by lunch at the club."

"What about TJ?"

"Aunt Sarah's baby-sitting but will join us there, with

him, at lunchtime."

Maxine glanced at her watch. "What about your committee meeting?"

"I can hit that first and catch up with you guys on the course." He pushed a series of buttons and slipped the phone into his pocket. "Do you want to do that or did you have other plans?"

As she shrugged, she smiled. "Sure. That would be fun. We should all enjoy this weather while we can before the dreary cold comes back next week." She shut her notebook and slipped the pen into the spiral top. "And dinner tonight?"

He put a hand on her shoulder and ran it up the side of her cheek, then gently squeezed the back of her neck. She leaned into his touch, enjoying it. "Dinner tonight will be a little more than lunch at the club. How does Benedicts sound?"

Maxine grinned. "Wonderful."

"Good." He fished some keys out of his pocket. "You have me blocked. Just take the Jeep. I'll load both sets of clubs before I go. I'll take your car and meet you all there."

"Oh, you'll just use any excuse to drive my sports car, won't you?"

He grinned, then kissed her good-bye. Another first. As soon as he was out of sight, as soon as she heard the sound of the powerful little engine in her car fade, Maxine spread her arms out and lifted her face to the sky, praising God for the miracles of this morning.

Then she checked her watch and rushed back into the house to change into clothes appropriate for a morning of golf at Tony's club.

Barry had loaded the golf clubs as promised and, twenty minutes after confirming the plans, Maxine backed the Jeep out of the garage. It felt strange driving the cumbersome vehicle compared to her slick little machine. It didn't respond to her the same way her car did, and she found herself stalling out at the first stop sign.

Annoyed, she paid closer attention to the clutch and less attention to the warm sunshine. At the exit gates of her housing complex, she came to a full stop. Sitting at the stop sign, she faced a six lane highway. Traffic, heavy for a Saturday morning, whizzed by with barely an interval. Her road sat halfway down a large hill, and every time she thought she had a break in traffic, another three or four cars crested the top of the hill and raced down toward her. Just when she decided to simply turn right and make a U-turn a little farther up, a break in the traffic magically appeared. With an audible, "Thank you," she went for it.

Maxine lifted her foot off the clutch and the Jeep bucked and groaned, jerked once, then stalled out dead in the middle of the road. "No!" Maxine managed to get out while she pushed the clutch back in and turned the ignition.

She had the engine started and had begun to ease up on the clutch and press the accelerator as far down as it would go when she heard the blaring of a horn and the screeching of tires. She whipped her head to the left a split second before her field of vision filled entirely with a chrome grill. The world suddenly shrunk down to a pinpoint perfectly surrounded by pure pain.

Then the pinpoint vanished.

CHAPTER TWENTY

Barry jotted some notes in the yellow legal pad in front of him but, honestly, he struggled to keep his thoughts on the proposed budget for the church's soup kitchen. His thoughts remained on his wife. His wife. Could it be that this was the first time he had thought of Maxine as his wife in his mind?

He looked forward to spending the day with her, and with their family. Even more so, he looked forward to spending the evening with her. He let his mind play out the scene of the two of them walking into the dining room of Benedicts. He savored the idea of walking into a crowded restaurant with the most beautiful woman in the world on his arm. He imagined slipping the emerald encrusted diamond ring back onto her finger—the very same ring he had kept in his pocket since the moment she handed it to him in the hotel room in Vegas. The very same ring he touched a hundred times a day, thinking of placing it on her finger, of kissing her and officially sealing their marriage, of their wedding night. The very same ring he had never returned to the casino shop, that he had never intended to return in the first place.

Perched next to the legal pad, his cell phone vibrated with an incoming call. He glanced at the display and, not recognizing the number, stabbed a button that sent the call to voice mail.

He tried to return his attention to the associate pastor who spoke at the head of the long conference table, but again, his mind wandered away from the rising cost of bread flour to emerald green eyes framed by long dark lashes surrounded by an impossibly lovely face.

Absently, he answered direct questions, but he glanced at his watch three times in five minutes, wishing that the meeting would just end so he could join everyone on the golf course. He grinned a little grin at the thought because, truth be known, he didn't even really like golf.

His phone vibrated again and he saw Tony's number flash across the screen. Barry knew that the meeting hadn't run late yet, and Tony knew he was at the church. He decided that whatever it was could wait. If he interrupted the meeting for a phone call, the meeting would only last that much longer.

Not two minutes later, the door to the conference room flew open, flung wide by Caroline O'Farrell, who nearly fell into the room, her hand over her chest, breathing hard. "Sorry... to... interrupt," she gasped between breaths. Her eyes found Barry. "Had to run here from the house."

Barry didn't know why, but flutters started low in his stomach and moved up to the back of his neck, tingling tenseness into the muscles there. The other men in the room sat silent, unmoving. It created a strange tableau, a portrait of tension and alert anticipation.

As Barry's phone vibrated again, Caroline nodded her head toward it. "Answer it, Barry," she whispered, as Barry scooped up the phone and hit the button to take the call.

"Barry…" Tony's tone sounded impatient, worried, and uncertain.

Barry felt his heart stop. The tone of voice spoke volumes. After all, he'd taken just this kind of call before. *Mr. Anderson, there's been an accident. Your wife sustained very serious injuries and was rushed here less than an hour ago.*

He knew. He could tell. Still, he had to be sure. His voice came out in a scratchy whisper. "What happened?"

"It's Maxine."

The world around him started to gray as panic flooded his veins and color abandoned his face. "Tony, tell me what happened."

"There's been an accident." Tony said, "She was driving your Jeep and…"

"Where is she now?" Barry interrupted.

CAROLINE'S husband, Peter, drove. Barry sat in the passenger's seat of Maxine's sports car and pushed against the floorboard with his feet, willing the car to go faster. Begging the car to go faster. Peter drove the little green bullet with absolute precision, darting in and out of traffic, cutting off this car or shooting past that car, going through a few lights that were more red than yellow. Barry didn't care. He just counted off blocks, then miles, then blocks again as they raced to the hospital nearest to his home. Their home. His and Maxine's home.

He saw Tony's car skewed carelessly across the line into the "No Parking" zone and knew he'd beat them here. Peter barely had the car stopped before Barry had the door open and his feet on the asphalt of the parking lot, running—driving toward the emergency room doors. He turned sideways to slide between them because they opened too slowly. He barely noticed how people leaped out of his way as he dashed into the waiting area.

He scanned faces in the waiting room, taking in Robin's tears, Tony's stoicism. Sarah, who looked shell-shocked but calm. He picked Sarah as he rushed forward. Sarah the nurse. Sarah who would understand.

"What have they told you?"

Sarah reached under her glasses and rubbed her eyes. "Nothing. Absolutely nothing."

"Will they let you go back and see her?"

She pressed her lips together and shook her head. "I've tried twice in the last ten minutes. They won't let me."

Barry ran a hand through his hair, not surprised to feel his fingers shaking. "What does that mean? That can't be good, can it?"

She gave half a shake of her head before she stopped herself. "We don't know that. Better if we just wait and see."

"Oh, dear God," Robin breathed

Barry whirled around to see what had made Robin gasp that little prayer. A trauma team had thrown the emergency room doors open as they rolled a gurney through in a real hurry. A nurse crouched atop the bed, straddling the patient, pressing up and down on her chest. Two nurses pushed the bed toward the elevator doors a third nurse held open. A female doctor at the side of the gurney squeezed a breathing bag every few seconds. Barry made out a strand of jet black hair against the bloodstained sheet seconds before the bed disappeared into the elevator.

CHAPTER TWENTY-ONE

The wait was interminable. Sarah continued to try to get information—any information at all—but all she could get out of anyone was that Maxine was still in surgery. They wouldn't even tell her what was being operated on, they just directed them all to a waiting room on the surgical floor. The family moved up there to hold their vigil.

Barry signed form after form for the hospital. A police officer came to speak to Barry, and the group learned what had happened. Maxine apparently stalled out in the middle of the road and was t-boned by a driver of an SUV. Forensics verified that the driver had only been doing the speed limit of 45 miles per hour. The impact turned the Jeep around until it faced oncoming traffic, where it was hit head-on by a midsized Honda. Both the driver of the SUV and the driver of the Honda were saved from serious injuries by their air bags and were able to leave the hospital with little more than stitches. Both drivers confirmed what the crash site investigators predicted. Maxine had simply stalled out in the middle of the road.

"I don't understand. Maxine could out-drive any Formula One racer. She's the best driver I know." Robin said. "How could she stall out?"

Barry sat in the vinyl chair with his elbows on his knees and stared at the tiny black specs in the white tile floor. "The clutch has been sticking lately. I noticed it last week. It hadn't gotten too bad yet, but I should have taken it in." Guilt clawed at his chest and tried to rip through his flesh.

Robin put a hand on his shoulder and squeezed, then shifted TJ from her breast to her shoulder. "There's no way you could have known."

He sighed and stared at the floor. "I should have taken it in."

The door flew open and Caroline O'Farrell hurried in, closing her cell phone. "I've updated the prayer chain." She looked at Robin. "If you're done nursing the lad, I'll take him home with me," she said. "I have three teenaged girls at home who can help me watch him."

Robin started to protest, "No, please don't worry about it."

Caroline put a hand over Robin's, stilling her patting on TJ's back. "You have to worry about the other men in your life right now. Let me take my first grandchild home with me. You can come nurse him in a few hours, or I'll bring him back here, whichever."

Tears spilled out of Robin's eyes and flooded her cheeks as she whispered, "Thank you."

Caroline gingerly took TJ from his mother's arms. "Come here sweet pumpkin. Come see your *Seanmháthair.*" She patted the baby's diapered bottom as she rounded up the diaper bag and stroller. In a few moments, she departed with TJ and all his gear.

Barry watched the door shut behind them and sank further into himself, feeling the dark fist of despair clutch at his chest with jagged claws. The spots on the floor shimmered and shifted until he closed his eyes so that he wouldn't have to use the energy it took to focus.

If only. If only he had moved her car out of his way and driven his Jeep. He had been fighting the temperamental clutch all week and wouldn't have stalled it in the middle of the intersection, which meant that two cars wouldn't have plowed into his wife. Then Maxine wouldn't be lying on a table while doctors tried desperately to repair her shattered body.

The tendrils of fear sank deeper, blackening his thoughts, banishing any hope. He just realized how much he loved Maxine—how much he wanted to give it his all, and he realized that she may never hear the words pass his lips.

The door opened again, but he was afraid to look up, afraid to see compassion in some doctor's eyes when he told them how they had done everything they could, but that her injuries were too severe. How despite their best efforts, Maxine had died.

He braced himself to simply hear the words, nearly the same words he had heard once before. Before, his feelings were so confused. When he heard them today, his world would crash down around him and life would lose meaning. He braced, except he didn't hear a stranger's voice. He heard Derrick's.

"I just got your message. Do we know anything?"

"Nothing yet," was Tony's reply. "We're still just waiting."

He felt the brush of clothing as Derrick took the seat next to his. "What happened?" He talked to Tony over Barry's hunched form.

Sarah answered him. Sarah, the calming force for all of them that day, set aside her animosity and spoke kindly to Derrick. "She stalled out in the middle of the road. The other driver said it looked like she'd just got the car restarted before he hit her."

Because, Barry silently added, her husband left her with a broken vehicle to drive. Because he couldn't be bothered with something as mundane as swinging by an auto mechanic when he obviously had more pressing business at hand.

He couldn't take it any more. Barry lunged to his feet and ripped the door open, never looking behind him. Scanning the halls for the exit sign, the need to escape flooded him, panicked him. Then immediately departed. He found he didn't even have the strength to go back into the room. Leaning against the wall, he raised both hands and pressed them against his eyelids. All around him, he heard the sounds of a hospital, and wanted to scream and find out how people could be going on with their lives as if nothing had changed. As if the world wasn't teetering on its axis, ready to collapse in on itself.

Barry lowered his hands when he felt Tony take up the wall space next to him. They didn't immediately speak, because no words needed saying, but Barry was surprised when he realized just how much he required the company of his friend.

"She loves me," he said at one point.

"I know." Tony shifted and crossed his ankles in front of him. "I think she always has."

"It just dawned on me what I might lose."

Tony sighed and rubbed the back of his neck. "Bear, if Maxi doesn't make it, she gets to go home. One day, you get to go home and you'll see her again. But we're going to count on her pulling through this."

Barry took Tony's rebuke to heart with a single solemn nod. "My head is spinning."

Tony stood straight. "You'll go insane pondering the 'might have beens.' I have to believe, and Robin has to believe—and you have to believe—that she'll pull through. We have to have faith. If not, whoever walks through the door next will find a group of raving lunatics."

Barry leaned his head back against the cold wall—Why were hospitals always so cold?—and pressed the heels of his hands to his eyes again. "I know. I know. You're right." Pushing away from the wall, he looked down the hall to the set of doors that led to the operating rooms. There was no movement that he could see.

The cry in his heart that he had ignored all of these months suddenly became audible to him. The unexpected death of his first wife sent him careening away from God. The impending loss of his current wife, this beloved woman, almost sent him to his knees. He turned his head and looked at his best friend, at his brother, as tears burned the back of his throat. "Will you do me a favor?" he asked, his voice hoarse with emotion.

"Of course, *mio fratello*."

"Will you pray with me?"

Tony faced Barry and placed both hands on his shoulders. "It would be my honor."

IT was the darkest part of the night, the part of the night that hangs on just before dawn takes over. Peter had come and gone with TJ, bringing the baby to be fed, comforting both infant and mother. Derrick vanished and shortly returned with food that no one ate and strong coffee that everyone made disappear. Sarah went back and forth pestering the staff, finally finding someone that would tell her only that they were still working on Maxine and offered vagaries about internal bleeding. Mostly, they all sat silently, each numb from the worry and the fear, no longer even interested in the pretense of conversation. At last, the doctor finally arrived.

"Brian?" Barry stood as the doctor strode into the waiting room, his voice echoing his surprise to recognize a longtime friend of his father's.

"Glad I was on call tonight, Barry," Dr. Brian McDonald replied, extending his hand.

Dr. McDonald looked as ragged as they all felt. Barry searched his face, trying to read his eyes, but found only weariness. The doctor gestured for Barry to retake his seat before he slowly lowered himself into the chair beside Barry, turning to face him fully.

"Your wife is in recovery, now," he said by way of a preamble. A collective breath was released, and they all tried to release some of the fear and brace for her condition. "She's very weak, and I'll honestly tell you that for the next several hours it's still going to be touch and go."

"How is she?" Robin asked in a rush.

The doctor pursed his lips and looked into every face. "Her condition is critical. I have to tell you it isn't good. The entire left side of her body was basically crushed, and we had to get her put back together. We salvaged her spleen and her liver and that is very, very good, believe me. It does a lot to increase her chances. We're trying to save her kidney, too, but we really need to watch it closely. We might have to go back and take it. The next few hours will tell. We're watching her fluids very closely. She's a fighter. She tried to leave us a couple of times, but hung on in the end."

"What…" Barry cleared his throat, but the doctor seemed to know what he was asking.

Brian ran a hand through his hair. "There was a lot of internal bleeding because one of her ribs punctured her lung."

Barry's stomach churned and Robin gasped, covering her mouth with her hand. The doctor continued. "It's repaired, and we replaced several liters of blood. Somehow, that was the worst of the internal damage. She's not out of the woods, but she's stable for now.

"Her left arm was broken in a couple of places. Her left hand and left leg got trapped when the door buckled in and… both were crushed. We called in an orthopedic surgeon who worked on her leg and hand. He's the best, and we were lucky he was in the hospital tonight. Without him, I'd have put her chances of ever walking again at zero. Even with him, we still debated the merits of radical amputation."

He put a hand up to forestall the protests and mitigate the indrawn breaths. "I'm just telling you it was considered. Instead, he did a superior job of reattachment and reconstruction. There's going to be more to do. It's going to take at least two more surgeries on her hand—probably more—and a lot of therapy. Still, and this is just a preliminary guess, but I think with some serious physical therapy, she has a chance of a meaningful recovery assuming she survives for the next few weeks."

Barry felt the room swirling around him, imagining it draining him into a dark abyss. "It's touch and go with her hand. If she doesn't sustain an infection, she should be able to keep it, but she'll probably never have full use again. The bones were badly crushed. We'll really have to just wait and see how she heals. You should know that radical amputation of some of the digits is still on the table, especially if she starts getting septic. The bottom line is that her internal organs are too damaged to fight off a serious infection."

He paused for a moment. Sarah nodded her understanding, silently communicating that she could answer any questions her family might have about what he had said so far. The doctor continued.

"You should know that she appears mentally altered."

Sarah interrupted for the first time, "What was her...?"

The doctor forestalled the entire question when he held up three fingers by way of answer. Sarah's entire body tensed.

"Best we can guess, her head hit the steering wheel. It hit something solid and unforgiving, for sure. There's no fracture but there is major blunt force trauma and there's some swelling of the brain. There's some bruising, but that should slowly go back to normal over the next few weeks. Neuro's keeping a close watch. We want to make sure she doesn't hemorrhage or have an aneurysm. There is likely going to be some immediate effects from the head injuries when she regains consciousness, but hopefully they'll diminish over time. Try not to be concerned if she acts confused or forgetful for now."

He pushed himself out of the chair. "She needs to heal, and she needs to be still. If she were conscious and in this much pain, there's a risk of shock. We're going to keep her in a medically induced coma for the next twelve hours at least, maybe for a few days while we watch all of her vitals. As soon as she's out of recovery, we'll move her down to intensive care. That's two floors down. Family can see her just one or two at a time, no longer than ten minutes every hour. You need to know that she's going to look pretty rough. Sarah can probably explain what all the tubes and hookups are there for. I'll be here…" He rubbed his eyes and looked at his watch. After grinning a private, ironic grin he continued,"… later this afternoon if you have any questions or problems. Does anyone have any questions before I go?"

Barry found a thread of propriety and stood with the doctor. He held out his hand to shake Brian's. "Thank you"

Brian released the handshake and put a hand on Barry's shoulder. "She's tough. You can tell." He pulled him in for a quick, familiar hug. "Call me at home if you need to. Margie and I will be praying for you both."

"Thank you."

As soon as the door closed behind him, Robin started

crying. Tony pulled her into his lap and tucked her head under his chin.

"It's silly to cry now," she said, brushing at the tears impatiently. "But all I can think about is her hand."

"Why?" Derrick asked.

Barry swallowed and forced words past a throat that hurt. "Because she's left-handed. A left handed artist with a crushed left hand."

He leaned his head back against the wall and closed his eyes, preparing his mind to wait another several hours before he could look in on her. He slid off the chair and turned so that his knees were on the ground. He clasped his hands, bowed his head, and began appealing to God with a desperate plea. He felt Tony kneel next to him on one side and Sarah kneel on the other.

BARRY had to stop for half a minute when he entered the room. He thought Sarah had prepared him for what Maxine would look like, but he wasn't prepared for the physical hurt that looking at her would cause. The bed seemed far too large for her thin frame, and tubes and lines ran from machines and bags, snaking under the blankets all around her. She lay completely still with her eyes taped closed.

A tube attached to a respirator was taped to her lips and presumably went all the way down her throat. A white bandage, that looked stark against the black of her hair, covered half of her forehead. Her left arm lay on top of the covers, a bandage covering the tips of her knuckles to the top of her shoulder. A chest tube went under the covers on the right side of her body, keeping her lung inflated. A monitor beeped the steady rhythm of her heart and the respirator made a rasping sound as it breathed air into her lungs.

Barry collapsed in the chair next to the bed and gingerly touched her right hand. His touch elicited no response. Not even the flicker of her eyelashes beneath the tape. He bowed his head, resting it on their joined hands. "I love you," he whispered. "Maxine, please stay with me."

THE only time he left her side was when the medical staffed forced the issue or one of the others came to visit. Sarah came before and after her shifts and Tony and Robin took turns with the baby and came in and out.

Once a day he left while Robin sat with her, to go to his house and shower and change clothes. He couldn't stand being away for long, and returned within the hour. They all took turns trying to persuade him to leave, to go home and sleep, but he wouldn't do it. Once he made it out to the parking deck before he turned around and went back inside. By Tuesday night, he felt tired enough that he thought he might sleep, so he stretched out on the master bed—the bed in which she slept but he had never shared with her—after his shower. Her scent overpowered him, seeped into his pores, tortured him until he knew he would find no rest.

And still there was no change.

Nurses removed the tape from her eyelids and they carefully cleaned her with cool, damp swabs. They tended to her, administering drugs, replacing full bags with empty bags and replacing empty bags with full bags depending upon protocol. Occasionally, Doctor McDonald would pop in and tell him how good her results were looking, or that he would be taking her out of the coma soon, or that he would continue to pray for healing. His grip on Barry's shoulder before departing always afforded Barry some comfort.

When they were alone, Barry talked to her, revealing everything inside him. He revealed regrets about the past and plans for their future. Peppered through it all, he lavished her with words of his love for her—the love he carried around inside for who knows how long, the love that had always been there. He prayed to God that he wasn't too late.

And still she didn't move. She didn't wake.

It terrified him.

On Wednesday, he reached his limit. He caught himself breathing in time with her ventilator, counting the breaths, and slowly let out a long breath, hoping it would relax him. He realized at that point how very close to the edge of collapse he was, but he didn't know what he could do about it.

He leaned forward, gripping her hand in one of his, laying his other one on the bed and resting his head on it. His hand swallowed hers like a whale swallows a shrimp. Confined to the sterile sheets of the hospital bed, she looked like a very small child resting next to a giant. He closed his eyes and willed her to wake up, willed her hand to squeeze his, willed her not to die. A wave of tiredness born of raw exhaustion and fear washed over him. Gripping her hand tightly, he let the wave take over and lull him into oblivion.

CHAPTER TWENTY-TWO

Maxine floated on a wave of nothingness, surrounded by a soothing, comforting void that cushioned her from something she didn't want to face. She remembered driving the Jeep, stalling out, then a very loud noise. She remembered every single vivid detail until the blackness took over after the impact. She couldn't remember exactly what happened next, but knew her last coherent thoughts had to do with fear and pain. So she enjoyed where she was, knowing on some instinctive level that when she finally woke, it would hurt more than she could imagine.

She had no sense of time. She could have existed in her void for five minutes or five years. Disjointed sentences from voices she recognized occasionally penetrated the darkness. She felt more aware when she heard them—aware of the weight that seemed to press down on the left side of her body, aware of a steady rhythmic beeping, aware of her hand being lifted or touched. She could hear the voices, but never comprehended the words. During those times, she felt comfort knowing that people she loved were nearby.

Eventually, she tired of the dark. She wanted her color back, her visible spectrum that gave the world its beauty. Somehow she knew that pain would exact a toll for the color, but she thought maybe she was ready, so she slowly pulled herself forward, toward the light, toward life.

Thirst was her first sensation. She felt thirstier than she had ever felt before. Thirst almost won out over the dull throb in her head, over the tight pain in her chest, over the weight on her left side. Almost, but not quite.

She wanted to move, to shift around a little and maybe help alleviate some of the discomfort, but found herself unable to do so. It was disconcerting to feel trapped, tied down, and she had to shake off the panic that lobbied to claw its way to the forefront of her thoughts. She pushed it firmly back because she sensed that panic would make it hurt worse.

She felt sort of light, as if ever since the impact that had crushed the Jeep, she'd accidentally tripped into an abyss. She felt as if she had simply fallen and fallen and fallen this entire time.

Suddenly, she realized that she had finally hit the solid ground at the bottom of that endless pit. She had come to earth and hit the ground with every single part of her body. Hard.

It all registered at once. She hurt. Lord in heaven, she hurt everywhere.

There was no more thought of shifting to ease discomfort. She didn't think she could move at all. The steady beeping noise she had been hearing suddenly sped up, went out of control, the weight of her own flesh felt like an elephant sitting on top of her, and something was choking her, blocking her throat making it so hard to breathe. She gagged, muscles tensing, and it felt as if her entire torso was on fire.

Her eyes flew open, and if she'd had the breath she would have screamed in agony. She tried to draw in another breath, but couldn't and tried to lift her hand to claw at her throat, but it wouldn't move. The dim light above her wavered as tears filled her eyes. Oddly, she wondered how she could make tears when her throat felt as dry as a desert.

Lights glared bright, searing her eyes. Then a face filled her vision, blocking out everything else. She didn't recognize the face, a black woman with kind eyes and pearl earrings. She tried to focus, but her eyes swam with tears.

"Maxine, it's good to see you back with us," the woman said. Her voice was rhythmic, soothing, and Maxine clung to that. "You have a tube in your throat that's been helping you breathe. That's part of the reason you're panicking. I need you to relax so I can remove it. Blink if you can understand me." Desperate to have the thing removed, she blinked rapidly, ignoring the shooting pain through her temples that simply blinking caused. "Okay. Take a deep breath, as deep and big as you can. When you exhale, I'll take the tube out. Here we go."

The second it cleared her throat, Maxine felt herself starting to calm. Then the woman was back. "I'm Dr. Roxanne O'Neill. I know you're hurting, and the nurse is bringing something in right now to ease your discomfort. Just lie back and relax. You've been on quite a journey."

"I don't…" Maxine uttered, barely a weak whisper. She

felt her hand being patted.

"I know. There's time for that later. Right now, just close your eyes."

"Thirsty," she said, complying.

The doctor chuckled. "I bet. When you wake up next time, we'll get you some ice chips."

Maxine heard some shuffling and something warm shot through her vein and up her arm. "Barry," she whispered. The warmth turned hot as it reached her chest. Oblivion beckoned from the next heartbeat.

Maxine heard a chuckle and some more shuffling. "Your husband's here, hon. He's right outside for now. He hasn't left your side this whole time. He'll be back the second we finish."

This whole time? How long had she been here? Where was Barry? Could he salvage the Jeep? Were his golf-clubs okay? Was the other driver okay? Why was she so cold? Were they keeping her in a freezer?

She let the darkness overtake her, seeking the bliss that shielded her from the pain.

MAXINE slowly opened her eyes. For the first time since the accident, she felt that the rational side of her brain had a little more control over the emotional. She didn't know how much time had transpired since the first time she woke up, but it was a haze of panic and pain, of different faces and different voices, all soothing and calm while they did whatever they did before giving her the escape of the drug. Sprinkled among all the fleeting memories was Barry. Sometimes someone else in her family, but always Barry. Someone was always there when she opened her eyes, always smiling down at her and holding her hand.

She was in a different room than she remembered. This one was brighter, more open, lacking the constant beep and surge of machines. The walls were wallpapered with a pink and green floral design on a cream background, creating a very calming pattern.

She smelled fresh flowers. Carefully, to test her ability to move at all, she turned her head, surprised that nothing screamed in protest. There was a large window looking out onto the lawn of the hospital, and on a table in front of the window—actually, on the table, under the table, and to the sides of the table—were baskets and vases and jars of flowers. Every type of flower she could think of was represented, along with stuffed animals, balloons, and potted plants. She tried to smile, but her dry lips cracked.

"We've eaten all the chocolate, of course." Robin appeared from behind her. The way she adjusted her shirt as she came into Maxine's line of sight told her that her sister had been breast feeding the infant who was now propped on a shoulder.

"Of course." Her voice sounded like nothing more than a harsh whisper. She tried to swallow, but her mouth felt like an arid desert complete with gritty hot sand.

"You couldn't have flowers when you were in ICU, and by the time they moved you, the florists had such a backlog of orders that they brought them in waves, new ones every few days."

"Who?" Maxine croaked out.

"I've saved the cards. Old clients, business whatever's with Tony, Barry's clients, church." Robin hooked her foot on a chair and pulled it close to the bed while she patted TJ's tiny back to coax him to burp. "It's good to see your eyes focused."

"How long?"

"Yesterday made two weeks." Robin grinned and leaned forward to grip her hand. "I'm so excited. So glad you're actually lucid. I'll have to call Tony in a sec so he can come home and see you. He left for Florida when we knew you were out of the woods. He was supposed to be back any day, but once he hears you're awake, he'll come home immediately, I'm sure."

Robin propped her legs on the bottom of the bed and laid the baby's head near her knees, forming a natural cradle out of her long legs. "Sarah gets off at three. She's on the morning shift and hates it, so she'll have plenty to complain to you about while she's here. She had her lunch break at ten, so you missed her by an hour. Barry had court, and Derrick and I had to practically hold him at gunpoint to go. But I'm certain he'll be here mere minutes after it's done."

Maxine lifted her right hand, surprised at the effort it took. She waved toward Robin. Her hand fell limply back onto the bed and she stared at Robin. "How are you?"

Robin's eyes welled with tears as she smiled. "I'm strung out, emotionally spent, and physically exhausted." She leaned forward and lowered her voice. "But, I'm still better off than you, and I've found the sure fire cure for losing all the weight you gain with pregnancy. Your timing is and always has been perfect."

"Don't make me laugh." It was easier this time to lift her hand. "It will hurt."

"I know. Of all of us to get hurt, you have, by far, the lowest pain threshold. I'm sorry."

"Hey," she croaked, "at least I won't be scared to give birth now."

For just a second, Robin's face clouded. Maxine suddenly wondered just how extensive her injuries might be, and for the first time felt real fear start to creep up on her. She closed her eyes for a moment, tired from the effort to speak. "What happened?"

There was a pause and she opened her eyes to meet Robin's. "You don't remember?"

"No, not that. I remember the accident. What happened to me? How bad is it?"

"Maxi, maybe you should wait for the doctor... or Sarah. I don't know all the details about healing and therapy and recovery time and stuff."

"Tell me."

Robin blew out a breath and leaned back in the chair. "Your leg is broken in several places. I guess the door crushed it. You need another surgery on it. And your left arm snapped in two when your hand got caught between the door and the steering wheel."

Maxine looked down and stared at her hand, completely engulfed in bandages and a soft cast. Robin touched her arm. "The surgeon who worked on your arm and leg says you can heal. He says there's a really good chance you can walk again, sooner than you think." She squeezed Maxine's hand harder. "There was a moment when they wondered if you would be able to keep your hand or leg at all, so that's amazing progress. God is so good."

Maxine tried to raise her left arm, but had no strength. "My hand?"

Robin's lips tightened and she gave a short shake of her head. "It isn't good. It was crushed. With extensive therapy, maybe you can draw again. Maybe. It will take time."

"How much time?" Maxine asked, trying to keep her voice calm and sound unconcerned.

"Maxi, I just don't know. Doc Rox, the orthopedic doctor, can give you better information. But you can get better. That's what matters. Who cares how long it takes?"

Maxine enveloped her fear of never crafting with a pencil again, never picking up a paintbrush again, and tucked it into a far corner of her mind. "My stomach hurts."

Robin took a deep breath. "A lot of your internal organs were bruised. You bled a lot into your abdomen. They tell me you're healing up well."

Maxine searched her sister's face. "What else?"

"A couple of broken ribs. They had to fix a hole in your lung." Her voice was mild, and Maxine wondered if she even knew about the tears streaming down her face. "And your head injury is over. The bruise is even nearly gone."

She let it all digest slowly, one thing at a time. "That all seems pretty workable."

Surprised, Robin looked at her before she nodded. "You're only saying that because you're on some pretty powerful drugs right now."

"Probably." She smiled and felt her lips crack. "Can you find out if I can drink something? My mouth is so dry!"

"I bet it feels like it was stuffed with cotton and blow-dried." She stood and shifted TJ to her shoulder and walked out of the room. The second she was gone, Maxine covered her eyes with her right hand, noticing how badly it shook. She squeezed her eyes shut and pushed back the tears, promising them they could come back out when she was alone. Robin put on a good front, but she looked as close as Maxine felt to a breakdown, and neither one of them needed that right now. Taking some very careful breaths, she realized it didn't hurt all that much, and slowly inhaled and exhaled until she had warded off the panic. She sniffed and wiped her right palm dry on the starchy cotton blanket.

"Okay, you can have ice chips. The nurse said that's all you get until the doctor says otherwise. But, she's on the phone with her now, so maybe she'll clear actual water or something." Robin scooped a piece of ice onto Maxine's tongue before she sat back down.

"Mmm," Maxine said, closing her eyes and enjoying the cool wet in her parched mouth. "No, this is fine. Manna."

"I'm going to try to get a message to Barry, but he's in court. His secretary will wait outside of the courtroom, I'm sure, and he'll get back here as soon as he can."

Maxine wanted to stay awake, but her eyelids grew heavy and she felt herself drift away.

CHAPTER TWENTY-THREE

Barry stole a glance at the watch he'd laid out on the table in front of him. Two minutes later than the last time he checked. Another hour and forty minutes until lunch. He didn't have the focus he needed to be in here today. His mind was across town, lying in a hospital bed for the fifteenth day in a row. Maxine was out of ICU, which left Barry with little to no excuses to keep from showing up for work. The world didn't stop just because his life had a massive and sudden trauma, followed by a spiritual awakening he could not even begin to explain.

One hour and thirty-eight minutes.

He wondered what the person on the witness stand was talking about. He looked down at his legal pad and realized that what was left of his rational brain was sending signals to the hand holding the pen and he was at least taking notes.

A prior downtown Boston restaurant manager threatened Mr. Tony Viscolli with a sexual harassment charge. Since the restaurant was owned and operated by

Viscolli Enterprises, she thought she could extort the millionaire. Barry was still baffled as to how the case made it all the way to court. He wondered how opposing counsel, her attorney, could show such poor judgement.

He refocused on the witness, caught up with his notes, and took his turn questioning the human resources director of Viscolli Enterprises. When he finished, he sat down and looked at his watch again. One hour, seven minutes.

AS the judge dismissed the court for lunch, he called counsel into his chambers to review the plaintiff's motion to suppress the video of the accuser in Tony's office, threatening him with a lawsuit if he didn't give her a raise. Barry pointed out the signs throughout the hotel where Tony had his corporate offices that clearly read security cameras were in use, and showed that such a sign hung in Tony's office. "This is a professional building, judge. It's ridiculous to suggest that there isn't any security."

The plaintiff's attorney tried to turn his nose down on Barry, but Barry had a good seven inches on him. "Your Honor, there was no reason for her to think that the office would be monitored during business hours. She had a reasonable expectation of privacy."

"There wasn't any sign that said that the monitoring only takes place during specific hours. No indication was given anywhere for that to be the case. Her assumption, in addition to being logically baseless, has no legal standing. Employees should have no reasonable expectation of privacy when standing in their employer's office."

The judge shifted some papers on his desk out of his

way as his clerk brought him a sandwich. "He's right. Motion to suppress denied. Go eat lunch. I'll see you back in the court room in," he looked at his watch, "forty-seven minutes."

Barry went through the maze of courtroom hallways and went out a back door that he knew sidled next door to a deli. He ordered a roast beef on whole wheat to go, then reached into his pocket for his phone to check messages.

It wasn't there.

He patted his jacket pockets, his briefcase, re-checked his pants pockets... nothing.

He must have left it sitting on the table in the courtroom. Mentally rushing the deli clerk, he had a $10 bill sitting on the counter before she even finished wrapping his lunch in the white paper. As soon as the sack was out of her hands, Barry grabbed it. "Keep the change," he said, rushing out of the deli.

He had to go back through the front doors of the courthouse to clear security. Thankfully, the abnormally short line moved rather quickly and in no time he found himself in the inner sanctum of the courthouse. He took stairs instead of elevators and shimmied past groups of colleagues lining the halls until he made it back to his courtroom. As he walked to the front of the room, he recognized the back of his secretary's head. Elizabeth turned as soon as she heard the sound of the double doors swishing shut behind him.

"There you are," she said, holding up his phone. "I've been trying to reach you for an hour."

"What happened? Is everything okay?" Barry rushed forward.

"Robin called." Barry's heart nearly stopped as fear gripped it. "Your wife is awake, cognizant, and asking for you."

The air escaped his lungs in a rush. For a moment he just looked at her, then he gathered her into his arms and gave her a quick hug. "Thank God," he said, setting Elizabeth down gently.

"Ann Morganson is coming to take over for you."

Barry grabbed his phone and started scrolling through texts. "Good. We resume in twenty-two minutes. She needs to be here by then."

"She's in the building, so that shouldn't be a problem. I've talked to her myself."

He saw the text from Robin, and another one from Sarah. "Good. Good. I'll just go then." Distracted, he left Elizabeth at the table, walking slowly while he scrolled through a text. "Tell her the motion to suppress the video was denied, and that it's a cakewalk from here. She can read my notes." He paused and turned back, holding out his briefcase. "They're in here."

Elizabeth took the briefcase from him and shooed him with her hand. "Go. We got it. See you whenever I see you next."

Phone in pocket, keys in hand, he rushed out of the room. Elation, relief, joy... intense emotions battled for priority in his heart as uncharacteristic tears threatened. Awake. Cognizant. Two weeks ago, there was some doubt either one would ever happen again. A week ago, there was hope that she would wake, but uncertainty as to what her mental status would be. Cognizant was good. Asking for him was far better.

He drove her little green sports car through the lunch traffic, trying not to break any traffic laws, trying not to endanger himself in the process. While he drove, he prayed. He prayed a prayer of thanksgiving, hope, thanksgiving, joy... not even making a lot of sense to himself, but he knew God understood what he was saying.

As he entered the hospital, he nodded a hello to the volunteer behind the big circular desk. He wondered what they thought of the family members that they saw every day, week after week. Did they wonder? Did they know? Did they figure out who was visiting whom?

In the elevator, he happily bypassed the intensive care unit and made his way up to her floor. Nervous little jolts started zipping through his system. Excitement urged his feet to move faster down the hall. The wave of relief rushing through his system left his knees feeling shaky.

"MAXINE, you need the medicine." Sarah stood next to the bed with her hands on her hips, still wearing her nursing uniform, and staring down at her sister like a mother reprimanding a child. Meanwhile, Maxine couldn't help feeling like one. A nurse standing next to her held the syringe and an alcohol pad.

"I don't want it. I'd rather have some aspirin or something."

"You're only saying that because the last shot hasn't completely worn off yet."

Her voice was no longer a weak whisper, but it was still very scratchy. "I don't care, Sarah. The stupid shot hurts worse than anything on my body right now. At least let me see if I can manage the pain without it."

Sarah glared at her until a look of understanding popped into her eyes. Then she stepped closer to the bed and leaned down. "Maxine, please don't be stupid. You aren't going to become a drug addict because you received managed pain medication in the hospital after being in a car accident that nearly ripped you in half."

The only thing that kept her from rolling her eyes was the fact that they ached. She had honestly not thought about the fact that their mother had been a habitual IV drug user in years. "I'm not worried about becoming a drug addict. The shot hurts. Instead of my IV, they put it in my hip and it burned and ached forever after. I'd rather just try this without it."

"In about forty-five minutes, I promise you will regret this."

"I'll decide then, in that case."

Sarah sighed. "Listen, Maxi. I know you. You can't handle a nick on your finger when you're peeling potatoes. There's a lot of pain being shielded from your senses right now. Why suffer when you don't have to?"

"Because I don't like pain. Right now, my hip hurts worse than my arm, chest, or leg."

Sarah sneered. "You're not making any sense at all."

Barry stood in the doorway, so shocked he couldn't move. Twenty-four hours ago, Maxine had either been incoherent and delirious or completely still and asleep. Now she was arguing with her sister as if the last two weeks hadn't happened. He'd known that Doctor Roxanne had intentionally kept her heavily medicated to keep her movements to a minimum as well as combat the pain and shock of the trauma, and he'd known that they intended to change the dosage today, but he'd had no idea of the result.

Guilt immediately flooded his system, pushing away the elation and the joy. The first day he didn't keep a diligent post by her bedside and she was cognizant enough to win an argument with Sarah. Even the preparations for the court hearing today had been done in the chair next to her bed.

He suddenly realized how selfish he was being. Instead of feeling angry that he hadn't been present when she woke up, he should feel overjoyed. So he grinned and stepped all the way into the room.

"Welcome back," he said, moving around Sarah and the nurse to the other side of her bed.

Maxine rolled her head on the pillow. "Barry. Thank God. Will you please tell Sarah to leave me alone?"

When she spotted him at the door, his eyes had been swirling with emotion; relief, joy, anger, too many to count, really. By the time he'd made it to her side, his expression looked pleasant, his eyes nearly blank. He lowered his head and gave her the gentlest of kisses, barely touching her lips. She wanted to ask him about it, but she still had the syringe to contend with.

"Why would I want Sarah to leave you alone?" he asked, lowering his bulk into a chair.

"Because she wants her friend to stick a needle into my rear end."

Sarah sighed dramatically. "Barry, she's never going to be able to handle it when the pain medication wears off entirely."

He shrugged. "Then wait it out. Tell her you told her

so when she admits she was wrong. I don't see the point in getting her riled up now." He shifted his eyes to Maxine. "Why don't you want it?"

"Because it hurts."

He stared at her blankly, then blinked. "That doesn't make sense."

"It does to me."

"That's because you've had a rather serious head injury. You're confused," Sarah said with her hands on her hips.

Maxine sneered. "This from the woman who denies herself the basic pleasure of ice cream because it has mammal's milk and bird eggs in it. Don't talk to me about confusion."

Sarah turned to the other nurse. "Forget it. If she asks for this in an hour, I'd find ten other patients to see to first if I were you."

The nurse chuckled and recapped the syringe. "Just buzz me if you need to, Mrs. Anderson."

"Thank you."

Sarah leaned over and kissed Maxine's cheek. "I'm glad you're alive. I'm glad you're back to being my annoying big sister. I'll see you in the morning."

"Okay." She let out a breath and closed her eyes for a moment. Arguing with Sarah was easy, but this time it took a lot out of her. Feeling like she'd recouped some of her strength, she turned her head toward Barry again. "Did you win today?"

His head was still reeling from seeing her so awake and... alive. "Win what?"

"Whatever you did in court."

"Oh." He shrugged. "Probably. They didn't have much of a case."

"What was it?"

He caught himself staring into her eyes, green pools that captured him and held him. Once dazed with drugs, her eyes now looked clear and sharp. "What was what?"

"The court thing."

"Sexual harassment."

The pull was immediately broken when she closed her eyes for a moment. He shook his head to clear it and rubbed his own eyes. He must be more exhausted than he realized. "Who were you harassing?"

"It wasn't me. It was Tony."

She smiled. "I'd laugh, but I'd end up needing that shot if I did."

He smiled. "I know. I think she thought we'd settle out of court instead of going all the way with it. But she rather irritated your brother-in-law with the whole thing, and he refused to settle anything."

Her eyes were closed and she grew quiet, so he settled back in his chair. The relief at seeing her like this lifted such a huge load, one he'd gotten used to carrying over the last two weeks. As soon as it was gone, he felt all the nervous energy he'd been riding on leave him behind. His eyes burned and his arms felt heavy.

Her voice startled him, and he realized he'd nearly dozed off. "I want to talk to you, but I'm so tired."

He gingerly lifted her hand and gave her the lightest of kisses on her knuckles. "Shush. Rest. We have later. We have the rest of our lives."

BY the end of the first week of consciousness, Maxine thought she was going to go out of her mind. She'd managed to avoid taking the shot for the pain, though there were two nights when she thought her resolve might vanish. It was silly, she knew, to manage the pain of a broken body to avoid the pain of the shot. Illogical, actually, but a phobia was a phobia. She couldn't grasp the concept of willingly subjecting herself to the shot regardless of the bliss it would have provided.

Robin came daily for short bursts of time because of the baby. Tony saw her twice in between court and traveling to one of his businesses in Utah, and Sarah stopped by for a few minutes before and after her shifts and on her lunches.

Every morning before work, Barry came to see her. Every evening, he would come in after work. Most nights he slept in the chair next to her bed, but occasionally he went home only to return within just a few hours. He would come in, brush a feather light kiss on her lips, then sit and talk. Many of their conversations were lighthearted, as if they were seated across the table from each other at dinner. Sometimes he prayed with her, sometimes he talked about work, sometimes he told her football stories, sometimes he talked about his family.

He was driving her up a wall.

If he touched her, he always seemed surprised. When he kissed her, it was so light she wondered if there was actual contact. He treated her emotionally, mentally, and physically as if she were made of glass, until she wanted to scream at him that she was still Maxine, broken bones or no broken bones. But while she couldn't remember the events leading up to the last week, her brokenness, her touch and go status, she knew that he could remember. He remembered vividly. Robin had finally broken down and told her what it was like. She guessed he just needed some adjusting time.

As frustrating as it was, she willed herself to wait until he figured out that he could at least give her a real kiss and she wouldn't shatter.

BARRY leaned back in his chair and closed his eyes. The state of weary had been a constant companion for weeks now, and he felt like he might be coming to the end of his rope. He needed to get some real rest soon. Except he didn't know how to turn it all off and rest.

He heard his office door open, but it took a moment for him to feel willing to open his eyes. Instead of Elizabeth, he saw his best friend.

"What's up, brother?" He asked as he straightened his chair and lowered his feet to the floor.

Tony smiled. "Robin said that they're releasing Maxi."

Barry felt a twinge in his heart. "To a nursing home."

The smile faded from Tony's face. Barry knew it had more to do with his tone rather than the information. His lips pursed and he offered, "I thought it was a long term care facility."

"It's a nursing home, Tony."

Tony held out an open hand and asked, "Problem?"

"Yeah. She needs to come home. She'll get better faster

at home."

"Okay." Tony sat back and Barry could see the wheels turning in his mind. "What will that take?"

With a gesture, Barry drew his attention to the stacks of folders and brochures that littered his desk. "Hospital bed, doors wide enough for a wheelchair, ramps, renovation on the bathroom to handle her needs, a physical therapist, some specialized equipment for therapy…"

"You have everything you need?"

Barry cocked his head and stared at his amazing, God given friend. He knew the question Tony was actually asking. Could he afford it? Did he need financial assistance or strings pulled? "I do. But I love you and appreciate you."

"Good. Let me know if that changes because I want to help any way I can. Your wife is my sister, after all."

"I know," Barry confirmed, nearly choked up on some unexpected emotion.

Tony cleared his throat. "I am here on a mission."

"Oh?"

"Yes. My wife sent me, so there is no arguing."

Despite it all, Barry laughed. "Okay."

"I am to take you to your favorite restaurant and buy you a thick steak. Then I am to take you to church tonight and attend the Wednesday night prayer meeting, where we'll pray over you. Then I am to take you home and watch whatever sporting event you pick from what you have saved in your recorder to watch until you want to go to bed. Then I'm to sit sentry in your home while you sleep tonight, knowing your sisters-in-law, your mother, and your sisters, will be with your wife."

That sounded... wonderful. "I..."

"No arguing." Tony stood. "Do you need to take any of that stuff with you?"

Barry shook his head. "I've called someone to handle the details for me."

"Good. Delegation. I do that all the time. In fact, Derrick is surprisingly good at project management. Maybe have your guy call him. He has spring break starting soon. He'll enjoy the project."

"Maybe I will." Barry stood and grabbed his jacket from the back of his chair. "Benedict's steaks?"

Tony pulled his keys from his pocket. "Wonderful choice."

Chapter Twenty-Four

Barry let himself into the house quietly, not wanting to disturb Maxine. He wasn't quite sure what his reasons were, but he wasn't sure of a lot of things about himself when it came to his wife.

His love for her was absolute, he knew that, but her feelings for him after the accident remained a mystery. Her spark was gone, which was understandable considering what she was going through. She found little joy in anything anymore, and the times she appeared to be enjoying herself seemed contrived. Toward him, she gradually became cool and detached, and the flicker of annoyance in her eyes as he bent to kiss her each night tore his heart a fraction at a time. Soon, she would be able to get up and walk away. Part of him wished she never could, and he hated himself for it.

He slipped his keys into his pocket and moved silently through the house. He'd converted the dining room to create a bedroom for her, and the glow of a full moon lighted the room through the thin curtains enough to see her perfectly.

Before the accident, she took over any bed, buried under covers, on her stomach, her head under the pillow. The hindrance of the cast on her leg had retrained her to lie perfectly still on her back. He wondered if she would ever get her vibrancy back, either asleep or awake.

Worried he would disturb her slumber, he stood in the doorway and looked in on her, but didn't enter the room. Instead, he moved silently through the house and up the stairs to his room. The master bedroom. Their room. He wondered if she would ever join him there, or if he was facing the end of their unconventional marriage. The last surgery on her leg was the last surgery the doctors would perform. They removed the cast tomorrow. Maybe another surgery would have to be performed on her hand, but that was inconsequential to the scheme of her freedom outside of this house. Their house. Their home.

Weary, he shed his clothes on his way to the shower. Every step toward healing was a step away from him, he feared. He didn't know how to bring it up to her.

"GIVE me two more, Maxine."

"You're out of your mind."

"Just two more and that will be it for the day."

Maxine closed her eyes and concentrated on lifting the weights. Her leg objected to the movement, tried to refuse to obey the command of her mind. After two more surgeries and three months of confinement in a hard cast, the muscles screamed in protest.

Sweat poured off her face, mixing with tears, but the weights lifted and fell again.

"Okay, once more."

She opened her eyes and glared at Muriel Harrison. For the first few days after her release from the hospital, Muriel had been her near constant companion, acting as nurse and physical therapist. Once the cast had come off her arm and her muscles started working again, she no longer spent the night, but came for several hours a day to torture Maxine. She stood tall for her lean frame, with dark straight hair she kept cut nearly to her chin, and light, light blue eyes. She'd been so kind and patient as a nurse, but the second Maxine's arm had been freed, she became a sadistic drill sergeant, pushing and pushing until Maxine knew she couldn't take anymore, then pushing her one more time.

"I hate you," she spat as her leg trembled from the force of the weights.

Muriel smiled and crossed her arms over her thin chest. "I know."

Maxine looked down at her leg as she lifted the weights and it became fully extended. Well, what was left of her leg, anyway. It was pale, skinny, and crisscrossed with scars from her surgeries. The scars would fade and the color would return to normal, but she didn't know if she had the strength any longer to build the muscle back up.

Slowly, she let the weights come back down, then leaned back against the seat of the machine and caught the towel Muriel tossed at her. She wiped her face and leg before she reached for the leg brace to strap it back on.

"You look tired, Maxi. Are you hurting too much at night? Do you need me to call your doctor to give you something to help you sleep?" Muriel moved to the weight bench across from her and gracefully sat down.

"No." She tossed the towel on the floor. "I'm just having nightmares."

Muriel's eyes were direct, unwavering. "Why don't you draw them out onto paper? It's good therapy."

Maxine stole a surreptitious glance at her mangled left hand and shrugged. "It'll pass."

The therapist stared for several more seconds before she nodded and stood. "Okay. You need a shower, I'll make us lunch, then I want to show you some exercises you need to do before bed every night."

Maxine nodded and inched forward on the seat while Muriel walked behind her. When she came back into view, Maxine's eyes widened. "Where's my chair?"

Muriel pushed a walker toward her. "No more wheelchair. It's time for you to be back on your feet."

She shook her head, as much to protest as to beat back the tension that mounted toward her neck. "No. I'm not ready."

"Maxine, your arm is strong, now. You need to start teaching your leg to work again."

She stared at the walker, her vision closing in until that was all she could see. "I could fall. You're not here all the time. I could fall and break my arm and I wouldn't be able to get back up again."

Muriel's expression never changed. "I'll go make lunch. If you want to eat, then I suggest you take a shower and walk into the kitchen."

Hot tears of rage quickly sprang to her eyes. "Why are

you doing this?"

Muriel smiled. "Because someone has to. Lunch in twenty minutes."

Maxine stared at the door, enraged that Muriel actually left, but not surprised. That was how she did things. A command, unrelenting, and then she'd leave, fully expecting Maxine to comply. Her eyes moved back to the walker.

She snarled at it. Then her stomach growled at her. Muriel would leave her there until the next full moon. Or until Barry came home, which would be hours yet. He would pick her up and carry her around if she asked.

Knowing that, she gripped the handles of the walker and pushed herself into a standing position. Barry would carry her around, coddle her, and then talk to her with that infuriatingly pleasant look on his face. Then he would tuck her into her bed downstairs, brush one of those whispers of a kiss on her forehead, and make his escape upstairs.

She'd get strong and walk again, if for no other reason than to follow him up and demand that he start acting like Barry again. A good rousing argument would be nice. A real kiss would be wonderful. Just seeing genuine emotion in his eyes would work for her.

Before she knew it, she had crossed half the room. It was slow, but the brace kept her leg from collapsing. It hurt a little. She knew enough about pain by now to know it was a good hurt—a muscles working kind of hurt. Her arms were strong, easily taking her weight while she compensated for the leg.

By the time she made it to the bathroom, she was a little tired, but energized at the same time. She'd just crossed the entire house, and it felt great. She sat on the lid of the toilet to get undressed, then used the bars that had been installed to help her maneuver into the tub. A chair had been installed inside the bathtub, and she smiled as she sat under the warm spray. Soon she would be able to stand under it.

Her workout clothes were gone and a towel and fresh clothes waited for her when she finished her shower. She was tired now, but it would do no good to call for Muriel. She'd said she would be in the kitchen, and that's where Maxine would find her, no doubt.

She slipped on a long, loose dress, her standard outfit since her release from the hospital, dried her hair with the towel, strapped the brace back on, and gripped the handle of the walker again. Her leg trembled a little, and acted like it wanted to cramp up, but she adjusted the way she put pressure on it and it felt better. Her left hand ached. As she walked into the kitchen, Muriel was setting plates on the table.

"Do you still think you're going to fall?"

"Not if I don't overdo it." She laughed as she lowered herself into a chair, sighing at sitting on something that wasn't her wheelchair. "And you were right, as always."

"Every patient thinks they're the only one who has ever been through it." She set glasses of tea in front of the plates before she sat down.

Maxine raised an eyebrow. "To us, we are."

Muriel paused before she nodded. "You're right. But I still have to push. Family won't."

Thoughts of Robin and Barry fluttered through her mind. "No, they wouldn't. I have the benefit of Sarah, though."

"Even Sarah wouldn't have left you alone with it. She would have hovered over you, worried you might fall. I knew you wouldn't."

"And if I had?"

Muriel snickered. "Then I would have been wrong. Very rare." She speared a piece of pasta from her salad with her fork. "I need a favor."

"Sure."

"My mother's birthday is next week. I was wondering…"

"You need some time off?"

She shook her head. "No. That wasn't what I was going to ask you. I was wondering if you would do a portrait of me. Not a painting, just a drawing."

Maxine's hand trembled and she set her fork down. "I'm sorry, but no."

"Why?"

"I'm not ready."

Muriel leaned forward. "Not ready for what?"

She hadn't voiced it, and her voice wanted to close in on the words. Tears quickly filled her eyes, and she bit her lip to fight them back. "Not ready to find out that I can't." Despite her efforts, the tears spilled over, rolled down her cheeks. "I'm afraid to try."

"You'll never know if you don't pick up a pencil and just draw."

She gripped her left hand with her right and held it up for Muriel to see the scars, the gouges of skin that used to be smooth. "Look at this. Nothing is like it was. My hand was literally put back together. I don't have the same grip. I won't have the same stamina…"

"I don't care. You'll try."

"I don't want to."

"I dare you."

Maxine snarled. "In three months you've never listened to me."

Muriel smiled. "I don't get paid to listen to you."

"I'm not ready," she whispered.

The doorbell rang, interrupting them. Muriel just raised her eyebrow when Maxine stared at her. "I don't live here," she said, making no move to get up.

Maxine grabbed her walker and glared at Muriel. "I swear I want to fire you," she said, moving as quickly as she could, balking at her slowness and weakness.

"You aren't the first and I doubt you'll be the last."

She slowly, frustratingly slowly, made her way to the front door. When she opened it, she was surprised to see her boss, Peter Mitchell, standing there with a large manila envelope in his hand.

"Peter," she said, a little breathless. "Come in. What's going on?"

"Hi Maxine," he said, shifting his eyes from her face to the walker. "I didn't expect you to answer the door. I was just going to leave this with you."

"What is it?" He held out the envelope and she automatically reached for it.

"Just your paperwork for termination. Retirement accounts and such."

"Termination?"

"We can't just have you hanging on. Work continues. We still need product. Your office, your secretary, your clients are all just hanging."

"We never discussed whether or not I would come back, and we never discussed the timing of anything," Maxine said. Her arm muscles were quivering, but she didn't want to show weakness so she kept standing.

"You said fifty days. It's been fifty plus three months. I think that has been enough time for you to consider whether you're willing to come back or not. From what I understand, you can't even grip a pencil anymore, much less do what we do. I cannot hold your position indefinitely."

Fear, failure, insecurity clawed at her throat. She wanted to walk away from Mitchell and Associates of her own accord, not because she got into a stupid wreck and couldn't perform anymore.

She would not cry in front of him. Exhaustion, muscle fatigue, emotions, fear—sadness choked her throat, but tears would not escape. "I'll look over these papers and let you know."

"The decision has all but been made."

Maxine opened the envelope and pulled the papers out. A quick glance confirmed her suspicions. "These say I'm leaving of my own accord. These say I'm quitting. Unless you come up with the gumption to fire me right now, then I will look over these papers and let you know what I decide."

Peter opened and closed his mouth, much like a fish trying to breathe the crisp air next to a mountain stream.

He finally nodded and stepped outside. "I'll give you to close of business tomorrow."

Maxine sneered. "Fine."

She slammed the door in his face, then, exhausted, lowered herself onto the little table in the foyer. When she looked up, Muriel was leaning against the wall, her arms crossed over her chest and grinning.

"Looks to me like you're ready for about anything," she said.

Maxine started crying, but it quickly turned to laughter that had tears falling out of her eyes and rolling down her cheeks. "You're right. Bring me my pad and a pencil."

BARRY rolled his head on his neck as he shut the door behind him. It was late, later than he'd anticipated. His meeting with the church board over zoning laws had gone much longer than he planned, which put him behind at the office and had him working too late. Of course, he had to admit to himself that a lot of the work he'd finished that night could have waited until morning, but it seemed easier coming home after Maxine went to bed.

He silently made his way through the house and, as he did every night for three months, stopped at Maxine's door. Clouds obscured the moon tonight, making it impossible to see any distinguishable shapes, but as he stood there and stared, he was certain that there was no form in her bed. Reaching behind him, he flicked on the hall light, bathing her room in a faint glow, and realized he was right. Her bed hadn't even been slept in. Her wheelchair sat in the corner, away from the bed.

He crossed the room, thinking maybe she had fallen and was on the other side of the bed, but found nothing.

Worried, closing in on panic, he pushed open the door to the kitchen. Could one of her sisters or one of his sisters taken her home with them? No. Someone would have called him. He stepped into the kitchen and spotted her.

She sat at the table with her back to him. Her left leg was kicked out to the side, covered with the brace that stopped at the hem of an oversized T-shirt. Her hair was piled on top of her head, tendrils escaping from the loose knot to tease the back of her neck. Whatever she was doing, she was engrossed in it, because she never looked up as he walked toward her.

He came around the table until he was facing her and realized what she was doing. "You're drawing," he said, frozen with surprise.

Her hand paused on the pencil and she glanced up at him through her bangs. There was no welcoming smile, no light in her eyes when she spotted him. "Yes. And walking."

"Walking?"

She went back to drawing. "Yep."

He opened his mouth to speak, but her pencil fell from her hand and she cried out, clutching her hand. He was at her side immediately. "What happened?"

"Cramp," she panted. He was close enough to see the sweat that formed on her brow.

Taking her hand in his, he started rubbing the muscles, coaxing them out of the claw position they'd taken in the spasm. "Maybe you're doing this too soon."

Her hand slowly relaxed and he watched her color

return. "I'm not doing anything too soon. I've just been at it on and off all evening. This used to happen even before it was held together with paper clips and sheet-metal screws."

The muscles under his finger were completely relaxed now, but he didn't stop in his ministrations. Instead, he rested his hips against the table as his hands slowly traveled up over her wrist, to her arm, lightly kneading the muscles, gently touching her smooth skin. She closed her eyes and sighed, leaning farther back in the chair.

This close he could see that all she wore was the T-shirt. The hem stopped somewhere at mid-thigh, and the entire length of her good leg was there to torment him. It made him wonder what was or wasn't under the shirt.

Feeling the slight tremor go through his own hands at the thought, he slowly released hers and straightened. "You should go to bed. You've done a lot today."

Her eyes flew open, the green sparking as they came to life. She kept her voice very calm. "Let me tell you something. Never in all the years I've been alive have I pined for my father or wished I had an older brother. I'm not looking for either one of them now."

He took a step back. "I don't know what you're talking about."

"Don't you?" She braced her hands on the table and pushed herself to a standing position, holding her hand up to ward him off as he started toward her. "I can do it. All by myself." She stood next to the table, facing him. "That's the first time that you've touched me for real since the day of the accident. You've been treating me like some porcelain doll, or your little sister or something, and, quite frankly, I'm sick of it."

"What was I supposed to do, maul you in the hospital bed?"

"You could have at least let me know you wanted to."

He stared at her, not seeing her standing there now, but seeing her as she had been that first day. "You were so hurt. You were so hurt and it was my fault."

Maxine blinked, trying to comprehend what he'd just said. "What?"

"If I had fixed my Jeep. If I had taken care of the clutch. If I…"

"Are you serious?" Using the table as a brace, she walked toward him. "You are serious. My heavens, Barry, you could go through dozens of scenarios of 'what if' and nothing would change. The first time I stalled out, I should have realized something was wrong. I'm of at least average intelligence myself, you know."

"You nearly died."

She finally reached him and put a hand on his chest. "But I didn't."

"And every time I come near you, it's like you're annoyed that I'm there."

"I have been annoyed." She let go of the table and put her other hand on his chest. She could feel his heart under her hand, felt it speed up. "I've been thoroughly annoyed with the fact that you don't want me anymore."

He tentatively cupped her cheek with his hand. "That's not it."

She turned her head and kissed his palm. "Prove it."

He slowly lowered his head and paused a breath away

from her lips. He stared into her eyes, watched the emerald pools flare and burn, and with a groan, closed the distance. She sighed and slipped her arms around his neck, opening her mouth under his. Six months of ignoring wants and desire flooded through him as he hooked his arm around her waist and pulled her closer to him.

She gripped his hair with her hands and completely gave herself to the kiss. When he tried to gentle it, she nipped his lips with her teeth and forced him back. She wasn't in the mood for gentle. She'd had months of gentle and tender. Now she needed to know her husband wanted her; that he needed her.

He lifted her in his arms and carried her out of the kitchen, passing her temporary bedroom, and strolled through the living room to the staircase, kissing her all the while.

"I missed you." Maxine's voice was muffled against his chest. She lay on top of him, her legs trapped between his. She didn't even know how long they had been lying there.

Barry didn't speak, but he let go of the hair he'd been playing with and wrapped his arms tightly around her and kissed the top of her head. She could hear his heart speed up.

She lifted her head and kissed his chin. "I have to move. This position is really uncomfortable."

He immediately rolled her over and propped himself up on his elbow, resting his head in his hand. She tried to read his expression, but his face remained solemn, his eyes guarded. He lifted a finger and traced the puckered scar that crossed her abdomen.

"That will fade," she whispered.

"Will it?" He ran his finger back up it, then traced the line of her face before he brushed some hair off her forehead. "Does it matter to you that much?"

"I don't have to look at it."

For a second his guard went down and she could see the anger flash in his eyes. It told her what she wanted to know, and she didn't even need to hear his next words. "Do you really think I'm that shallow?"

She shrugged. "People never know for sure what will bother them."

He put the tip of his finger back on the edge of the scar. "A doctor cut from here," he said, drawing his finger downwards, "to here. Then he repaired damaged organs and saved your life." Her eyes welled with tears, and he used the same finger to brush one away. "Did you believe that the evidence left behind as proof that I nearly lost you, as a reminder of the day I realized how much I loved you, how thankful I was to God for bringing us together, would turn me off for some reason?"

Her breath hitched and she realized that she didn't know what to say. "I… I…"

He cut her off as he cupped her cheek and closed his mouth over hers. The sweetness of it, the depth of the emotion that was conveyed through his lips made her throat tighten, made the tears in her eyes cascade down, soaking her hair and the pillow under her. He raised his head again and she was surprised to see the shine of tears in his eyes. His finger traced the scar on her forehead. "It's true. I sat in that chair next to your bed, and I held your hand and begged you not to die because I hadn't told you how much I love you. I told you over and over again, but you couldn't hear me and my biggest fear was that you were going to die never knowing."

Her heart started beating so fast it surprised her that it didn't beat right out of her chest and fly away on hummingbird wings. She wrapped her arms around his neck and hugged him tight. "I didn't think my feelings for you could ever get any stronger," she said, using his neck as leverage to raise herself up and kiss him. "I like being wrong."

He kept his weight off her, supporting himself on his elbows. "I am thankful for every breath you take. I want to spend the rest of my life never forgetting the blessings God has given us in our love. I want to serve Him with you. I want to make our lives—make His giving you back to me—I want all that for His glory."

Maxine scrubbed at the tears on her cheeks as she sat up, taking one of Barry's massive hands and sandwiching it between hers. She brought it to her lips and kissed the palm, then pressed it against her cheek.

Barry continued, "I want us to be man and wife, as God intended. I desperately want you to be the mother of my children," he said. "Your patience when you first moved in, the love you showed me, the depth of love that you gave me—I want you to teach that to me. I want to love you and honor you and worship God with you."

She was dizzy with joy and closed her eyes. "Thank you, God," she whispered.

She felt the bed shift and opened her eyes to see Barry digging through the pocket of his pants. He let them fall back to the floor, then turned back to her and opened his palm. In the center of his huge hand lay the platinum, diamond, and emerald ring he had first placed on her finger months before in a little chapel in front of an Elvis impersonator.

"My ring!" She said.

"I never could return it. I tried, but I didn't want to." Barry took her left hand and slipped the ring on her finger. "I should have known then that we were meant to be together."

Maxine cupped his cheek with her palm. "Forever," she said with a smile.

"And ever," he said, kissing her again.

THE END

TRANSLATION KEY

amico—friend, buddy

cara—dear (beloved, darling)

E' una tragedia—how tragic (it's a tragedy)

il mio amico—my friend

mio fratello—my brother

Seanmháthair—Irish for grandmother

Sei benvenuto—you're welcome

LUNCHEON MENU

S uggested luncheon menu for a group discussion about *Emerald Fire*.

Those who follow my Hallee the Homemaker website know that one thing I am passionate about in life is selecting, cooking, and savoring good whole real food. A special luncheon just goes hand in hand with hospitality and ministry.

For those planning a discussion group surrounding these books, I offer some humble suggestions to help your special luncheon talk come off as a success.

Quick as you like, you can whip up an appetizer, salad, entree and dessert that is sure to please and certain to enhance your discussion and time of friendship and fellowship.

The Appetizer:

Heathy Protein Packed Hummus

Barry's focus with food is good ingredients, high protein, careful sugars. This hummus is just what the lawyer ordered. Serve it with triangles of toasted whole wheat pita bread or as a dip with a vegetable tray.

INGREDIENTS

1 cup dried chickpeas (garbonzo beans) or

2 cups cooked chickpeas

juice of 2 lemons

2/3 cup Tahini Paste

2 garlic cloves

1 lemon

1/2 tsp salt (Kosher or sea salt is best)

2 tablespoons of extra virgin olive oil

1 tsp paprika

1 TBS fresh parsley

PREPARATION

If using dried chickpeas: Soak the chickpeas overnight —OR—cover with 2 inches of water and bring to a boil. Boil for 2 minutes, place the cover on the pan, and let sit for one hour.

Drain soaked chickpeas and cover with water. Bring to a boil. Reduce to a simmer. Cover the pot and cook for 1½ hours or until very tender.

Juice the lemon.

Chop the parsley.

⸙ ⅅIRECTIONS ⸙

Put chickpeas, tahini paste, lemon juice, garlic, and salt in food processor. Process until smooth. If it's too thick, you can add a little olive oil or water until it's the consistency you want. The result should be a smooth, slightly granular paste.

Put in serving dish. Mix the olive oil and the paprika. Drizzle over the top. Sprinkle with chopped parsley.

The Salad:

"Rabbit Food" Chopped Salad

What could be better than a one-bit appetizer that satisfies all of the tastebuds in your mouth. Here is a dish that is offered in Viscolli hotels worldwide.

⸙ ℐNGREDIENTS ⸙

1 cup feta cheese	$1/2$ cup extra virgin olive oil
3 TBS lemon juice	3 TBS water
3 TBS dill	3 small garlic cloves
3 Romaine Hearts	1 large cucumber
4 celery stalks	2 large carrots
1 large tomato	6 radishes
1 cup frozen peas	2 cans chick peas

fresh ground pepper to taste
salt to taste (Kosher or sea salt is best)

℘REPARATION

Grate the garlic clove

Chop the romaine.

Slice the cucumber, celery, carrots, tomato, radishes.

Rinse the peas.

Drain and rinse the chick peas.

ⅅIRECTIONS

Place the cheese, oil, lemon juice, water, dill, garlic, salt, and pepper in a food processor. Blend.

Mix all of the chopped vegetables. Toss with the dressing.

Serves 6.

The Entree:

Succulent Roast Beef

The first meal Maxine prepares Barry in their home is roast beef. This recipe doesn't use a lot of spices - it lets the meat and vegetables do all the talking.

ℐNGREDIENTS

1 3-pound Bottom Round Beef Roast
2 TBS flour
2 tsp salt (Kosher or sea salt works best)
1/2 tsp fresh ground pepper

1 TBS extra virgin olive oil
2 large onions
6 large carrots
2 lbs. small red potatoes
8 oz baby portabella mushrooms

℘REPARATION

Salt and pepper all sides of the roast. Rub with flour.

Preheat the oven to 350° F (180° C).

Quarter the onions

Peel & slice the carrots into 2-inch chunks

Wash the potatoes. Halve the larger ones, but the smaller ones you can keep whole.

Slice the mushrooms.

∂IRECTIONS

In a skillet large enough for the roast, heat the extra virgin olive oil. Place the roast in the oil and brown each side just until browned.

Remove and place in roasting pan. Add about 1/2 cup water.

Surround the roast with the vegetables, letting the onions touch the meat. Cover loosely with aluminum foil.

Bake at 350° F (180° C) for 2 1/2 to 3 hours. Remove from oven and let cool.

The Dessert:

Simple Fruit and Cheese Plate

Barry is very conscious about his diet. Instead of reaching for sugar as a dessert, he is prone to a simple fruit and cheese plate.

ℐNGREDIENTS

6 ounces Brie Cheese
6 ounces Stilton Cheese
6 ounces Gouda Cheese
1 large bunch purple grapes
1 lb. Ripe organic strawberries
4 Bartlett pears
Half of a ripe honeydew melon, sliced thin
Package of "Entertainment" Crackers (variety)

𝒫REPARATION

Slice the melon thin.

𝒟IRECTIONS

Artfully arrange the crackers, fruit, and cheese on different platters. Let guests mix and match to their individual tastes.

DISCUSSION QUESTIONS

Suggested group discussion questions about *Emerald Fire*.

When asking ourselves how important the truth is to our Creator, we can look to the reason Jesus said he was born. In the book of John 18:37, Jesus explains that for this reason He was born and for this reason He came into the world. The reason? To testify to the truth.

In bringing those He ministered to into an understanding of the truth, Our Lord used fiction in the form of parables to illustrate very real truths. In the same way, we can minister to one another by the use of fictional characters and situations to help us to reach logical, valid, cogent, and very sound conclusions about our real lives here on earth.

While the characters and situations in **The Jewel Series** are fictional, I pray that these extended parables can help readers come to a better understanding of truth.

Please prayerfully consider the questions that follow, consult scripture, and pray upon your conclusions. May the Lord of the universe richly bless you.

Maxine goes from a horrible foster home environment to one that is obviously very loving and Christ-centered.

1. Do you believe the church, as a whole, does enough to help the "widows and orphans?"

Barry suffered for many years with an unfaithful wife, determined that he could be holy enough for both of them and that one day she would come to God.

2. When should we, as Christians, give up on those we love. Should we ever?

Maxine disregards her sister's cautions about deepening her relationship with Barry because he was currently suffering a crisis of faith. Maxine disregards the conversation and jumps in with both feet.

3. Do you think we should avoid pursuing relationships with people who aren't spiritually steady?

4. 2 Corinthians 6:14 warns us not to become unequally yoked with non-believers, but Barry wasn't a non-believer. He was just struggling. When one person in the relationship is struggling with God, do you think it will typically have an adverse effect on the other person's relationship with God?

Maxine didn't feel the deep conviction Robin felt about God. She was just "doing church" to please the people in her life whom she loved.

5. Take some time to examine your heart. Are you on fire for God, or do you need an influx of the Holy Spirit?

Maxine moves in with Barry, determined to live with him and love him as a wife loves a husband.

6. What was your reaction when she did this?

7. Why do you think it took Maxine's accident to bring Barry back to God?

With more than half a million sales and more than 20 books in print, Hallee Bridgeman is a best-selling Christian author who writes romance and action-packed romantic suspense focusing on realistic characters who face real world problems. Her work has been described as everything from refreshingly realistic to heart-stopping exciting and edgy.

A prolific writer, when she's not penning novels, you will find her in the kitchen, which she considers the "heart of the home." Her passion for cooking spurred her to launch a whole food, real food "Parody" cookbook series. In addition to nutritious, Biblically grounded recipes, readers will find that each cookbook also confronts some controversial aspect of secular pop culture.

Hallee loves coffee, campy action movies, and regular date nights with her husband. Above all else, she loves God with all of her heart, soul, mind, and strength; has been redeemed by the blood of Christ; and relies on the presence of the Holy Spirit to guide her. She prays her work here on earth is a blessing to you and would love to hear from you.

You can reach Hallee via the CONTACT link on her website or send an email to hallee@halleebridgeman.com.

Newsletter Sign Up: tinyurl.com/HalleeNews/

Author Site: www.halleebridgeman.com

Facebook: www.facebook.com/pages/Hallee-Bridgeman/192799110825012

Twitter: twitter.com/halleeb

The Jewel Series
by Hallee Bridgeman

Book 1: *Sapphire Ice*, a novel

Book 2: *Greater Than Rubies*, a novella

Book 3: *Emerald Fire*, a novel

Book 4: *Topaz Heat*, a novel

Book 5: *Christmas Diamond*, a novella

Book 6: *Christmas Star Sapphire*, a novella

Available as eBook or paperback wherever fine books are sold.

EXCERPT: TOPAZ HEAT

SARAH stared dumbly at the dashboard of her car. Not knowing what else to do, she turned the key again. Nothing. None of the little warning lights on the dash even lit. She leaned forward and rested her head on the steering wheel. Not tonight. She didn't have it in her tonight. She hadn't been able to nap and instead decided to go visit her dad. The visit took a lot longer than she thought it might which is how she happened to have her car in the hospital parking garage. Then she'd gotten caught up in a difficult delivery and ended up working well past her eleven o'clock end of shift. At this point, she hadn't slept in more than a day.

Accepting that the car simply wasn't going to start, she determined that she'd have to walk. It would take longer to get seated on a train than it would to just walk to the apartment.

While she had worked the weather had turned and a light but very cold rain served as the harbinger of the harsh winter to come. With a sigh, she grabbed her purse and umbrella, deciding to leave everything else there, then locked the car. The apartment was just around the corner. Her feet ached, but walking would be better than waiting for a taxi in the light rain. By the time a taxi got there, she'd already be in a warm robe, sipping on a cup of tea.

On Friday nights, even this far into Saturday mornings, the downtown streets were far from quiet. The air felt a little cool, but the jacket of her nursing uniform shielded her arms, and after being in the controlled air of the hospital for nine hours it came as a welcome relief.

It never crossed her mind to worry about walking downtown after midnight. Of course, if she mentioned it to her mother, she'd hear every unpleasant possibility in a seemingly endless litany. She grinned as she rounded the corner. Her mother was a melodramatic worry-over-every-nuance kind of person. It helped when abstract details needed deliberation, but it grew tiresome when one was a daughter discussing a date or a social function. Thinking of the date as an ax-murderer could be hilarious in hindsight, but beforehand could put a damper on dinner plans.

Sarah reached the building and pushed into the lobby. She wanted to groan out loud when she recognized the guard working the security desk. Brian was nice, but extremely talkative. It was late, she was on the edge of exhaustion, and she just wasn't in the mood.

"Miss Sarah," he said with a surprised look on his face. "I didn't know you were expected tonight."

She didn't pause at the desk, but kept walking toward the elevator. She pulled her keys out of her pocket so she wouldn't have to wait on him to quit talking long enough to access the elevator for her. "Hi, Brian. Good to see you."

She slid the key into the lock and gave it half a turn. The doors immediately opened.

"Miss Sarah, wait!"

"No time, Brian. Sorry!" She hit the button and waved as the doors slid shut. She leaned against the side of the elevator as she felt the lift slide upward. Whew. Missed being trapped in a conversation for half an hour. Normally she didn't really mind, and she didn't want to be unkind, but fatigue weighed her down.

She was stepping down into the living room before she realized that something was wrong. The lights shouldn't be on full—they should be on dim. She froze at the bottom of the step. The television definitely shouldn't be blaring out an old black and white John Wayne movie. The clang of something hitting something metal in the kitchen made her heart pause, stop, then race.

Obviously, someone else was in the apartment.

FICTION BOOKS BY HALLEE

Find the latest information and connect with Hallee at her website: www.halleebridgeman.com

The Virtues and Valor series:

Book 1: Temperance's Trial
Book 2: Homeland's Hope
Book 3: Charity's Code
Book 4: A Parcel for Prudence
Book 5: Grace's Ground War
Book 6: Mission of Mercy
Book 7: Flight of Faith
Book 8: Valor's Vigil

The Song of Suspense Series:

Book 1: A Melody for James
Book 2: An Aria for Nick
Book 3: A Carol for Kent
Book 4: A Harmony for Steve

Standalone Suspense:

On The Ropes

PARODY COOKBOOKS BY HALLEE

Vol 1: Fifty Shades of Gravy, a Christian gets Saucy!
Vol 2: The Walking Bread, the Bread Will Rise
Vol 3: Iron Skillet Man, the Stark Truth about Pepper and Pots
Vol 4: Hallee Crockpotter & the Chamber of Sacred Ingredients

The Dixon Brothers Series COMING IN 2018

Find the latest information and connect with Hallee at her website: www.halleebridgeman.com

Courting Calla: Dixon Brothers book 1

Ian knows God has chosen Calla as the woman for him, but Calla is hiding something big. Can Calla trust Ian with her secret, or will she let it destroy any possible hope for a future they may have?

Valerie's Virdict: Dixon Brothers book 2

Since boyhood days, Brad has always carried a flame for Valerie. Her engagement to another man shattered his dreams. When she comes home, battered and bruised, recovering from a nearly fatal relationship, he prays God will use him to help her heal.

Alexandra's Appeal: Dixon Brothers book 3

Jon falls very quickly in love with Alex's zest for life and her perspective of the the world around her. He steps off of his path to be with her. When forces move against them and rip them apart, he wants to believe God will bring them back together, but it might take a miracle.

Daisy's Decision: Dixon Brothers book 4

Daisy has had a crush on Ken since high school, so going on just one date with him can't possibly hurt, can it? Even if she's just been painfully dumped by the man she planned to spend the rest of her life with, and whose unborn baby she carries? Just one date?

NEWSLETTER

Hallee News Letter

http://tinyurl.com/HalleeNews/

Sign up for Hallee's monthly newsletter! Every newsletter recipient is automatically entered into a monthly giveaway! The real prize is you will never miss updates about upcoming releases, book signings, appearances, or other events.

CPSIA information can be obtained
at www.ICGtesting.com
Printed in the USA
FSHW020811020220
66739FS